The Longing

WENDY LINDSTROM

Winner of the Romance Writers of America's
prestigious RITA Award

Books by Wendy Lindstrom

Shades of Honor
The Longing
Lips That Touch Mine
Kissing in the Dark
Sleigh of Hope
The Grayson Brothers boxed set

rustic studio
PUBLISHING

This novel is a work of fiction. Names, characters, places, and incidents are either products of the author's imagination or are used fictitiously. Any resemblance to actual events, locales, business establishments, or persons, living or dead, is entirely coincidental.

Originally published by St. Martin's Press
Copyright © 2003 Wendy Lindstrom.
Digital edition published by Wendy Lindstrom
Copyright © 2012 Wendy Lindstrom
Second edition published by Rustic Studio Publishing
Copyright © 2013 Wendy Lindstrom

ISBN: 1939263085
ISBN 13: 9781939263087

Cover design by Kim Killion of Hot DAMN! Designs

Publishers interested in foreign-language translation or other subsidiary rights should contact the author at www.wendylindstrom.com.

Chapter One

Fredonia, New York,
May 1871

Cold spring rain pounded across Kyle Grayson's broad back. He hunched his shoulders as lightning sliced a jagged white line across the sky. The desire to find cover for his skittish gelding warred with his need to reach Tom Drake's sawmill and discover why the man was betraying him.

Tom Drake had been friends with Kyle's father for years. Despite being competitors all their life, the men had respected each other, and when Kyle's father died five years ago, Tom had shown Kyle how to manage his father's sawmill business. Although Tom was twice Kyle's age and still a competitor, they had formed a deep, respectful friendship with each other. Now, for some unknown reason, Tom was changing, and Kyle's instincts warned him to beware.

It took him half an hour to ride to Tom's mill on Shumla Road, but the cold rain hadn't diluted his anger or washed away the ache of betrayal in his chest. Though the crew was gone and the saws were silent, Tom's mill was alive with the storm. Thunder rumbled to Kyle's left and streaks of blinding white light ripped open the sky with brilliant razor-like fingers. His gelding shied, but Kyle lifted his face to the wild, snapping air and inhaled the energy of the storm.

Beneath the anger, raw pain pulsed through his veins. He'd trusted Tom. Five years of friendly competition, of coexisting profitably in a plentiful lumber market, and their shared delight in going nose to nose on big orders like the railroad contract had garnered respect and admiration for each other as well as a deep bond of honor Kyle would have died to protect. But he no longer knew what to expect from a man he'd thought was his friend.

Faint light glimmered from Tom's office window just as Kyle had expected. Tom had taught him that any owner worth his sawdust maintained his books as meticulously as his saws. Kyle had followed Tom's example by reconciling his books and preparing his bids each evening before leaving his own mill. If not for the need to collect money from Tom, Kyle would be at his desk instead of leaving his work unfinished.

Dragging in a breath of moist air, Kyle tried to calm himself, to think clearly—and give Tom Drake the benefit of doubt, one last time.

He backhanded the rain from his eyes and entered the office where Jeb Kane, Tom's mill foreman, was leaning against a tall wooden file cabinet covered with a sundry of saw parts. Kyle had known Jeb nearly as long as he'd known Tom, and admired the man.

Tom glanced up in surprise before a smile of welcome filled his face. "What are you doing out in this storm?"

Kyle didn't return the smile.

Tom's expression flattened. "Has something happened?"

Kyle shook his head. "I just need to talk to you."

Tom pressed his fist to his heart. "From the look on your face, I thought someone had died. My heart's jumping like a bullfrog. What's so important that you would plow through this rain and scare ten years off my life?"

"I need the money for that section of pine you bought from me. It's been three months." Kyle hated confronting Tom, but being forthright and putting business first had helped him live through his father's death, the hard struggle of building a small lumber empire with his three brothers, and watching the woman he'd planned to marry take her vows with his eldest brother instead of himself. Despite the pain and setbacks, Kyle had survived. He'd been hardened by the experiences, but they had made him wiser. Dealing with his problems head-on had made him a successful and respected businessman. He wasn't about to start dancing around the truth at this point in his life. Not even for Tom Drake.

Tom sighed. "Jeb and I were just discussing that problem. My saw broke down again last week and it set me back a bit. Can you give me another couple of weeks?"

Even though Kyle suspected he was being railroaded, he couldn't force a negative response from his mouth. "I'll need it soon. I ordered another saw for my mill."

"I heard. I'm sorry about holding you up like this."

"Are you?"

Tom's brows furrowed. "What are you driving at, son?"

At one time being called *son* had made Kyle feel less alone, now it made him angry that Tom's greed was breaking that bond between them. "This is the third time you've put me off, Tom. I'm beginning to think you want to stop me from expanding my business."

Tom's chin jerked up as if Kyle had punched him. "Would you like me to forget you just said that?"

"I'd like you to be honest with me."

Tom's eyes darkened. "Have you ever known me to lie?"

"No," Kyle answered honestly. "Nor have I ever known you to renege on a deal. But you're holding me back and I want to know if it's intentional. Is my mill getting too big for your comfort?"

Tom's face flamed and he pointed at the door. "Go back outside and let the rain beat some sense into your head before I'm tempted to do it myself."

In a physical match Kyle could have taken both Tom and Jeb, who were at least twenty years his senior, but regardless how upset he felt about Tom's betrayal, Kyle could never harm either of the men he considered friends. "I want to know why you're playing this game with me."

Tom slammed his fist on his desk, his body visibly shaking. "This isn't a game, just an embarrassment I have to live with."

Jeb moved toward the desk. "Calm down, Tom. Doc Finlay warned you about getting upset."

Tom pointed a shaking finger at Kyle. "You listen to me, young man. Your father and I tangled over every stand of timber in this county for twenty years while we built our mills, but we never cheated each other. We played fair and never doubted each other's word no matter how tense the competition got between us. We even managed to become good friends through all of that." Tom grimaced and planted his fists on his desk. His arms shook and he gulped in deep breaths, but he continued in a harsh, strained voice. "When your pa died, I treated you like my own son and taught you how to survive in this business. How can you stand here and tell me I'm trying to cheat you?"

Shame filled Kyle. Tom *had* shown him how to keep his family sawmill from going under. While Radford had been too tormented by his war memories to stay and help Kyle with their family sawmill, Kyle had shouldered the responsibility of supporting his mother and two younger brothers. He'd managed it by working hard and running the mill with an iron fist. He'd survived because Tom had shown him how.

"Dammit, Kyle," Tom whispered, swaying over his desk. "I can't do this now. I'm not... feeling well."

Kyle and Jeb sprang forward together, but neither of them reached Tom before he collapsed on the floor with his fists pressed to his chest. They knelt beside him, but when Kyle felt Tom's heaving chest, panic filled his own. "Take my horse and go for the doctor!" Kyle commanded, so used to being in charge that he issued the order without a second thought. "Hurry!"

Jeb jerked to his feet and raced out the door, leaving Kyle with his own heart thundering.

Tom's gaze locked on Kyle. "I... helped you."

"I know. I'm sorry I pushed you about the money, Tom. I shouldn't have doubted you." Kyle stared at his friend, feeling helpless in the face of Tom's struggle. "You could have used your experience against me all those years ago, Tom," he said, using his voice to keep his friend conscious and focused on something other than his pain. "Instead, you made me a good businessman. You challenged me to educate myself and compete with you man to man. I've always meant to repay you for that. I've just never known how."

Tom gritted his teeth and panted. Sweat beaded his forehead. "Take care of Victoria... and Amelia."

"Of course. Until you're on your feet again."

Tom's face grew pale, but his gaze stayed locked on Kyle. "My daughter..."

"Amelia is fine," Kyle assured him, knowing the pretty schoolmarm would be safely tucked in her room behind the little white schoolhouse in Laona at this time of the evening.

"She needs a... husband."

"She needs you, Tom. So does your wife. Jeb will be back with the doctor soon. Just stay calm until they get here."

"M-marry her."

What? Kyle was definitely attracted to Tom's daughter, and would never forget the kiss he had stolen from Amelia at her father's lumberyard years earlier, but he had suffered enough heartache for a lifetime and had no interest in pursuing marriage. Not even with a gorgeous woman like Amelia Drake. Bachelorhood suited him perfectly.

Tom gripped Kyle's forearm. "Keep him away from her."

"Who?"

Tom shuddered.

Kyle gripped his arm. "Keep who away?"

Tom gasped. "Tell them... I love them and I... I did my best." A hard shudder passed through his body and he arched against the dirty pine planks of his office floor. He dug his fingers into Kyle's forearm. "Please, son. Promise me."

Guilt swamped Kyle. Despite Tom's recent behavior, Kyle owed this man more than harsh words and hurtful accusations. "Of course I'll take care of your wife and daughter," he said, trying to ease the anxiety in Tom's eyes. "I promise. Now stop worrying. It's not helping you right now."

Pain streaked across Tom's face and a dazed expression filled his eyes.

Kyle's stomach clenched and his throat filled with denial as he realized he was watching his friend's life slipping away. "Tom!"

Slowly, the deep lines in Tom's face eased as his tense body relaxed on the pine floorboards.

Kyle grabbed the man's limp shoulders and shook him, trying to jar him back to consciousness. "Tom!" he shouted. Another fierce shake loosened Tom's jaw, but no air passed his blue lips.

"Breathe dammit!"

Kyle shouted the order a second time, loud enough to rattle the windows, but Tom Drake couldn't breathe. He was dead.

Chapter Two

Amelia Drake propped her forehead in her hand and listened to the rain pummel the windows. It echoed across her empty schoolroom in Laona as she read a page in her teaching handbook—for the fourth time. To her increasing irritation, the words remained a jumble of nothingness. Between the noise of the storm and her wandering thoughts, she couldn't concentrate on her work for a minute.

The desk was distracting her again. Amelia slapped the book closed and shoved away from the massive pile of oak huddled in front of her like a mountain of secrets. She squeezed her eyes closed, but her imagination soared and fanned her private fantasies until her insides melted with longing. She craved the wild, reckless passion that had caused Miss Denby, the former schoolteacher, to toss away her teaching career and make love to a poor furniture maker on her own desk—the very desk Amelia was forced to work at each day.

There would never be a Gordon Prues coming to rescue Amelia from the life of sameness and solitude she'd been living since replacing Miss Denby. Amelia would continue to spend her hours with her students, and when they went home to their families each evening, she would stay behind in a cold, empty schoolhouse feeling her youth ebbing away. To know she would never experience anything as grand or exciting as Miss Denby's passionate affair tore a vicious wound in Amelia's soul.

Her own reckless actions had condemned her to this life of spinsterhood.

She should have said no when Richard Cameron had pushed her to make love with him.

A violent crack of thunder shook the building and lightning illuminated the damp, musty-smelling room. She crossed to the window and rested her arms on the sill, gazing up at the angry evening sky, wishing she dared to step outside and feel the rain sting her skin, to feel free and alive for a few stolen minutes. But Philmore Bentley, president of the school board, and his nosy wife, Eva, lived next door. If they saw her outside after dark, she would be severely reprimanded.

Life as a teacher was painfully restrictive, but it was a virtuous, respectful position that she had needed after her disastrous affair with Richard. For four years she had been trying to live within the board's strict dictates, but her true nature bubbled and spit behind her facade like a volcano on the brink of erupting.

Thunder rolled overhead and the front door creaked open. She shook her head and turned away from the window. Closing the door was a lesson she'd failed to teach any of her students. With a resigned sigh, she headed toward the front of the building to close it.

The shadowy outline of a man suddenly filled the doorway.

Amelia stopped mid-step.

Runnels of rain slid off the wide shoulders of the man's coat. He pushed the door closed against the wind, trapping her inside with him.

She stumbled backward, wondering if she could make it to the door of her apartment and lock it before he could grab her.

As if the man sensed her panic, he lifted the dripping hat off his head to reveal a handsome, familiar face. Stunned by Kyle Grayson's formidable presence in her humble schoolroom, Amelia couldn't fathom what would bring him here, in the pouring rain no less.

"You'll need your wrap," he said. "Ray Hawkins is coming with a carriage to take you to your parents' house. Your father collapsed with chest pains an hour ago."

Fear slammed through her chest so violently she couldn't breathe.

"I'm sorry," Kyle said softly, his voice filled with grief. "The doctor didn't arrive in time."

Her body turned hot and her ears rang, but the cry echoing in her mind never left her gaping mouth. Backing away from Kyle and the horror of his words, Amelia shook her head. It couldn't be true. Not *her* father. He'd started the fire in the schoolroom for her just this morning. He'd laughed and kissed her cheek before leaving to start his day at the mill. Just like he did every Thursday morning.

"Jeb and Doc Finlay took him home to your mother," Kyle said, his eyes dark, his expression filled with regret. "They're sending Ray down with the carriage for you. I told them I'd ride ahead and make sure you'd be ready."

Her father? He couldn't be... he just... no!

"I'll stay with you until Ray gets here."

Amelia shook her head. An unstoppable cry squeezed from her throat and tears blurred her vision.

Kyle's lips compressed and his nostrils flared, but his hard, unblinking gaze confirmed the truth.

"No... Oh, Kyle..." Amelia clapped her hands to her mouth as tears streamed over her fingers.

He caught her as she stumbled into his chest.

Sobbing, she shoved against him, trying to push him out the door. "Take me home."

"Wait for the carriage. It's storming."

Was he insane? What did she care about a carriage when her father... when he... oh, dear... her mother needed her! And her father... her poor father...

She tore herself from his arms and bolted outside. Rain slapped her face and wind ripped her hair from its prim chignon, but she barely felt it as she ran to Kyle's horse.

As she struggled to put her foot in the high stirrup, she heard the door to the schoolhouse slam shut. An instant later Kyle wrapped his strong hands around her waist. She gripped the saddle horn and hopped on one foot, frantically trying to hook her raised foot in the stirrup, but instead of lifting her onto the saddle, he tugged her back.

"Buck's too skittish right now."

She struggled against Kyle's grip. "Release me!"

He held firm.

With an angry screech, she turned and slapped his wet face. The impact snapped his head back and stung her palm, but his look of shock didn't stop her from reaching for the saddle horn again. She was going home, and she wasn't waiting for a carriage.

The horse reared and danced away from her, but Amelia charged forward to grab the slippery stirrup. Her feet tangled in the hem of her muddy, wet dress and she stumbled into Buck's side.

"Get back!" Kyle's voice cracked like the loud burst of thunder as he dragged her away from the rearing horse. "Ray will be here soon. Get your wrap and wait inside."

She refused to wait for a carriage or let Kyle take her back into the building. She faced him and struck his granite chest with her fists. Then she screamed with all the panic she felt bursting inside her. Even in the pouring rain and booming thunder, her neighbors would have heard the earsplitting scream. They would come outside and distract Kyle. Then she would take his horse and race for home.

He caught her chin and forced her to look at him. "It'll ruin you if you're found out here with me."

"My father's dead, Kyle! Do you think I care?" She opened her mouth, intending to scream until he released her, but Kyle hooked an arm around her waist and crushed her against him. He cupped the back of her head and pulled her open mouth against his thick-muscled shoulder.

Bound hard by his arms and partially sheltered from the rain, Amelia felt she'd been pulled beneath the protective limbs of a giant tree. Her heart and mind hung suspended in a weird silence that amplified Kyle's hard breathing and the sound of rain splattering against her skull.

The crack of a gunshot ripped through the night and jerked Amelia back to the present, to death, and the searing pain that shredded her heart.

Kyle's hand shot out and snagged the reins of Buck's bridle before the gelding could bolt.

"Unhand her this instant!"

They both jerked their heads toward Philmore Bentley who was marching across his soggy yard with a rifle in his hands. Eva Bentley, the strictest board member and town gossip, stood on her porch squinting in their direction.

Kyle urged Amelia away from him and the deadly end of Philmore's gun, but she clung to his hand. "Help me, Kyle. I need to get home."

Philmore cocked his gun. "I warned you to get away from her."

"Phil!" Kyle yelled through the rain. "It's Kyle Grayson."

Kyle pulled off his hat and faced Phil and his nosy wife.

Amelia yanked his sleeve. "Put me on your horse!"

"What's going on over there?" Phil demanded, as he lowered the nose of his gun toward the grass.

Amelia could feel a scream of hysteria rising in her throat and knew if it left her mouth, she'd scream until they hauled her off to the asylum. "Now, Kyle. Please."

"There's been an accident and I'm taking Miss Drake to her parents' house." He turned to Amelia and girded her waist with his fingers. "Put your hands on my shoulders and jump when I tell you to."

"That young lady needs a chaperone with her!" Mrs. Bentley yelled, charging off her front porch, her intent to stop them obvious in the militant thrust of her jaw.

"Jump!" Kyle whispered.

The instant Amelia bent her knees and pushed, she was airborne. The horse shifted as she hit the saddle, but Kyle held her steady.

"Hook your knee over the horn and hang on. I'm coming up behind you."

She'd barely managed to do so before she felt the sideways shift of the saddle as Kyle stepped into the stirrup and swung himself up behind her.

"You stop right there, Mr. Grayson!" Mrs. Bentley stood below them with her fists planted on her plump hips. The rain plastered her hair to her head and her chest heaved from splashing across the school yard.

"Beg pardon, Mrs. Bentley, but I've brought Miss Drake distressing news of her father's death and I need to get her home immediately."

"Oh, good heavens," she said, her expression shifting from outrage to a mixture of shock and sympathy. "I'm so sorry, dear. Phil will get the carriage and we'll take you home right away."

Not about to wait for Phil or explain that a carriage was already on the way, Amelia kicked the gelding's broad side and the horse lunged forward. Kyle's arm clutched her waist, but she had to grab the horse's coarse mane to keep herself seated.

"You're going to kill us," Kyle said, but he lifted Amelia off the saddle, settled himself behind her then let her bottom slip back into the cradle of his thighs. He pulled her against his chest then folded the sides of his jacket around her shivering body. "Hold on," he said then kicked his horse into a full gallop out Liberty Street.

Amelia didn't know if Kyle meant she should hold on to his coat or the horse, but the feel of his strong arm around her made her head reel. She felt trapped yet oddly protected by the warmth of his hard body. Still, his arms didn't keep her from falling apart. She wept hard as they raced past Kyle's sawmill in Laona and turned onto the road leading to Jamestown. Thankfully they would only travel a little over a mile to Shumla Road. Her teeth chattered and her shoulders quaked despite the warm nest Kyle provided with his body.

"We'll be there soon," he said near her ear as the rain and tears stung her eyes.

"What happened?" she asked between sobs. "Were you with Papa?"

"Yes."

Although Kyle had to raise his voice to be heard, his grief was apparent. She felt the tightening of his arm around her waist and wished she could bury her face in his shoulder and escape the pain that lacerated her heart. Instead she let the rain slash her cheeks and mingle with her grief as she clung to the thundering beast beneath her.

As he turned onto Shumla Road, Kyle flung up his arm to flag her father's head sawyer who was driving the oncoming carriage. "Ray!" Kyle yelled. "I've got Miss Drake with me!"

Ray Hawkins pulled the carriage to the edge of the road and Kyle slowed his horse. Amelia crushed Kyle's hand around the reins. "Don't stop. It'll take forever in the carriage."

He hesitated then waved Ray back in the direction from which he'd come. "I'll take her the rest of the way," he yelled then nudged his horse back into a gallop and left the carriage behind.

"Papa started the fire for me this morning." She needed to tell Kyle that her father had been perfectly alive that morning and none of this made any sense. "His chest hurt, but he thought he was getting a cold."

"I'm sorry. I didn't know."

She heard the apology in Kyle's voice and knew he was hurting, too. Her father had spoken of Kyle with pride on many occasions. Now her beloved father would never speak again. His arms wouldn't hug her anymore and keep her from feeling alone in the world. She would never hear his laugh or watch him slap his thigh when something struck his funny bone. He wouldn't knock on her door and break the monotony of her silent evenings by sitting at her too small table drinking her awful coffee.

Stinging rain streamed across her face and neck, but she couldn't close her mouth against the sobs erupting from her throat.

Kyle's arm tightened around her shuddering waist. "Your father said to tell you that he loves you. He wanted you to know that."

Her throat ached and she choked on her tears. How like her father to spend the last minutes of his life thinking about her. He'd continually pushed her to find a man who would make her happy, even though he knew no decent man would want a soiled bride. Amelia had reminded him each week that she wasn't allowed to marry while under contract as a teacher, and that her father's love was enough for her. Despite her chronic loneliness, it really *had* been. She'd adored him.

Feeling her composure eroding in the rain, she sought something solid to hold on to. She found Kyle's hand at her waist and laced her fingers with his, praying his warm grip, and the lights in the distance, would help her face what was waiting for her.

Chapter Three

The rain had stopped during the night, but the day dawned as gray and dismal as Kyle's mood. Regrets consumed him while he sweated through a long, grueling afternoon at the mill. He'd wanted to clear his conscience last night and tell Amelia the truth surrounding her father's collapse, to express his regret and apologize, but it would have increased her distress. So Kyle had given Amelia over to Jeb's keeping, offered his condolences to her mother, and escaped into the blowing rain before Amelia could take his hand again.

Seeing her look at him as if he were a hero for whisking her through the storm to her father's side had twisted Kyle's gut. He wasn't a hero. He was an idiot!

With an oath, he slammed his hand maul against the grapple hooks that bound a drag of maple logs. If Tom hadn't changed so much, it would have never crossed Kyle's mind to doubt him. But Tom had stopped swapping business news with Kyle and the other mill owners then he'd started cutting his prices and hoarding jobs. What else was Kyle to think? Even though Tom was an admirable man, his erratic behavior had shaken Kyle's faith and planted doubts in his mind. He had been justified in confronting Tom.

"Come on, dammit!" Kyle whacked at the metal links then gave them a yank. Breathing in the scent of wood and earth, he struggled to pry the metal clasps loose, but couldn't dislodge their grip in the bark.

Whether or not he'd been justified in confronting Tom, Kyle regretted it more than any mistake he'd ever made—and he'd made some blunders in his life.

More irritated with himself than the stubborn hooks, Kyle raised his arm and channeled his anger through the hammer. Iron struck iron and sparks flew. The hammer ricocheted off the hooks and drove straight into his shin.

Kyle heaved the hand maul across the yard.

"Red rip roarin' bastard!" He clamped his hands over his throbbing shin and plopped down on the rough bark of the maple tree that he'd been unchaining. "Good for nothing piece of rubbish! Stubborn hunk o'junk hell-minded hammer."

He rocked upon the tree trunk in excruciating pain while he tried to think of other appropriate expletives to curse the wretched thing. His head reeled and his stomach heaved. Feeling his shin swelling beneath his hand made him grit his teeth. He didn't need this on top of everything else! He rocked in pain for several minutes, and then with a final oath he launched himself off the maple log and limped across the field toward home.

Until today his house had seemed conveniently close, but the ache in his leg and the humid air made the few hundred yards seem like miles. Knowing he had to attend Tom Drake's funeral and face Amelia within the hour merely added to his misery.

As soon as he'd washed, shaved, and clothed himself in a suit, Kyle retraced his limping steps across the field to the barn. It was set well away from the mill in consideration of the horses, but close enough to house his bay-colored gelding and the heavy-muscled Percherons that moved the timber.

"What happened to you?" Duke asked from the open doorway.

As Kyle spun to face his younger brother, pain ripped through his shin and his leg gave out. He crashed into a stall and grabbed the half-wall to stop his downward plunge. "Dammit, Duke! One of these days I'm going to bust your head for sneaking up on me."

"That's how I catch the bad guys." Duke folded his arms across his thick chest, his biceps straining the sleeves of his full dress shirt that was devoid of his sheriff's badge. "I saw you limping in here and thought I'd better see how seriously you were wounded."

Kyle's lips twisted with disgust. "I hit my shin with that rotten hammer again. It feels like it shattered my leg."

"Do you think it's serious?"

Kyle grimaced as he flexed his foot. "Feels like it, but probably not."

"I've got the carriage. How about a lift to the funeral?"

"I doubt I could make it otherwise." Kyle hooked a hand over his brother's shoulder and limped from the barn. He glanced up at the dreary sky and sighed. "This is one rotten day."

"Any day you bury a friend is a bad day," Duke said, his voice somber. "I still can't believe Tom's dead."

Neither could Kyle.

Duke tried to assist him into the carriage, but Kyle smacked his hands away. "I can manage without your coddling."

"All right, hardhead." Duke climbed in and waited. "I pity the woman who ends up with you and your lovely disposition."

"At least she won't be coddled to death." Kyle heaved himself aboard. "How do you manage to stay alive? You're too softhearted to be a sheriff."

Duke slapped the reins and set the carriage in motion. "Just because I wear a badge doesn't mean I can't talk nice to a woman and give her a little affection now and then."

"Am I supposed to be gleaning some mystical wisdom from those words?" Kyle suspected Duke was alluding to his past blindness with Evelyn and he didn't want to talk about it.

"Sweet-talking a woman and coddling her is common sense."

"It's nonsense and a waste of time."

"Well, you can't treat them like one of our crew," Duke said. "You can't just snap out orders and expect them to jump for you."

Duke shook his head. "Women want affection, Kyle. They want to talk."

"Well, I don't, so save your philosophizing for someone who needs it."

Duke shook his head and chuckled, but he kept silent while Kyle spent the balance of the trip thinking about sweet-talking a woman like Amelia Drake.

⚜

A wave of grief washed over Amelia and she placed her palm on her father's chest. He'd given her all she desired, encouraged her education, and taught her to speak her mind with conviction. Every day he had been a shining example of integrity and honor. Instead of condemning her for making mistakes, he'd stood by her through one of the most humiliating times of her life. Now he was gone.

The only man who'd ever loved her was lying in a casket, dressed in a Sunday suit, his hair slicked back with pomade oil. This was not the man she had called father for nearly twenty-one years. She wanted to remember him standing beside a pile of hewn maple trees directing the transfer of logs to the sawing tables, his graying hair ruffled by the breeze and his shirt sleeves rolled to his forearms.

She adjusted the lapel on his coat then pressed a kiss to his forehead. "I'll miss you so."

"So will I," her mother said, startling Amelia as she came up to the casket and ran her hand over her husband's chest. Her gaze swept the ornate house, her green eyes dull, her lovely oval face strained with grief. "It's unbearable here without him."

Worse than unbearable. Amelia's heart ached so deeply it pained her to breathe. She clasped her mother's cold hands. "Papa would tell us to be strong and to look for the blessings in each day. We have to try to do that for him."

"Your father would also tell you to find yourself a man who deserves you."

Amelia would have married years ago, but Richard hadn't wanted her. "I don't need a husband, Mama. I have you."

Disappointment filled her mother's eyes. "Don't you ever want to marry?"

Yes, Amelia's soul whispered, but she shook her head, knowing she never would. "I'm proud of being a teacher."

"I know, honey, but you're missing something very special. Marriage to the right man is heaven." Her gaze shifted to the coffin. "Living without your father is going to be... so empty and unbearable."

Amelia's eyes welled up at the pain in her mother's bereft expression, but she had no words that would offer comfort for the depth of grief she and her mother shared.

"The mill would make a nice dowry," her mother said, straightening her shoulders as if gathering her strength. "There are plenty of men who would covet a good business and a beautiful bride. Find a husband while you're young and beautiful."

"How, Mama? I'm barely able to walk to town without an escort from the school board," Amelia said, pushing the words from her aching throat. "I'm sorry if it disappoints you, but I'm going to remain a teacher for the rest of my life."

"Then I'm going to have to sell the mill."

"What?" Amelia's heart jolted. "Why? Jeb and Ray can run it for us."

Her mother shook her head. "We have no ties to your father's crew. They could leave us tomorrow. If I can't make the mortgage payments, we'll lose the mill and the house. I can't risk our only security."

"But I remember everything I learned during the summers I spent with Papa. I can help Jeb."

"You would lose your teaching position the instant the board got wind of you being at the mill."

"Well, we can't just sell something Papa spent his whole life building!" For Amelia, losing the mill would be like losing her father a second time. She couldn't bear it.

"Then use it as a dowry," her mother said. "Find a man you can depend on, one who's smart enough to make the business thrive without sacrificing his life or your marriage to do so."

Amelia would gladly marry to save her father's mill, but there weren't any men in her life. Not one.

"Your father loved that place, honey, but look what it did to him." Tears filled her mother's eyes and her forehead creased. "He spent his whole life trying to keep that mill alive and now you and I are alone and we have to sell it off anyhow."

Amelia's heart broke and she put her arms around her mother. She would give anything to ease her mother's grief, but there was nothing she could do. If it were possible, she would run the mill herself. She had spent each summer there until she was sixteen years old, trailing her father's footsteps. She'd been daddy's girl and her father had humored her desire to be at his side. She'd begged his crew to teach her the business, but her father had refused, claiming it unsuitable work for a young lady. It hadn't stopped Amelia from observing and watching, and by her sixteenth summer she'd weaseled her way into helping him with his office work.

Her seventeenth summer she'd spent with Richard Cameron.

Her parents had been delighted to see her interest finally turn toward courting, but the romance that had given them such high hopes had ended after a few short weeks. Only her father had known why Richard had stopped calling.

Her mother cupped Amelia's cheek in her palm, her eyes filled with apology. "I'm sorry, but unless you marry a man who can provide for us, we have no other options."

Amelia bit her lip and nodded. Her mother was right. Unless Amelia could find a husband, she and her mother would have to depend on themselves. Knowing her options for marriage were nonexistent terrified her.

As soon as her mother left the room, Amelia spun toward the coffin, toward the security of her father. She took his unresponsive fingers in her hand and held on for life. "You're the only one I've ever been able to count on, Papa. How will we live without you?" She clutched his fingers to her chest, her heart cramped with pain. "I can't bear to lose you, or the mill, Papa, but I don't know what to do."

―◁― ▷―

The moment Kyle laid eyes on Amelia, guilt consumed him. She stood in her parents' ornate parlor beside her father's casket, a fragile ivory princess with eyes so large and sad that Kyle forgot he was standing in the crush of mourning friends and family members who had gathered for the evening funeral.

He didn't move or beckon Amelia in any way, but the instant she saw him, she left her mother's side and crossed to where he stood. Kyle's mind was so cluttered with apologies and self-recriminations, he couldn't utter a word of greeting.

She scanned his face then lowered her lashes and touched her fingertip to the red scabs crossing the back of his hand. "I'm sorry for this," she said, her voice soft and hoarse as her trembling fingers glided over his knuckles. She tipped her face toward his. "I want to thank you for everything you did last night."

Looking into her sad brown eyes and feeling the coolness of her hand covering his own made him want to bolt for the door. Silky skin and private conversation made for a lethal combination that Kyle wanted no part of, especially when Amelia's expression was so open and vulnerable. He was a fool for a woman in distress. He'd been the same way with Richard's stepmother, Catherine, who was watching them from across the room where she stood with her youngest sister, Lucinda.

Amelia laced her fingers in front of her slender, black-clad hips, the gesture capturing Kyle's full attention. She had long legs, he thought as his eyes scanned down the length of her skirt then back up over the slight curve of her hips. Dull black fabric encased her small waist and rounded nicely over her breasts.

"Mama and I would like you to be a pallbearer for Papa."

Kyle's stomach lurched and his knees turned liquid. He gripped the thick banister behind him to keep from sinking to the parquet floor. He couldn't remember a time he felt more sick at heart. Unable to form a sensible reply, he simply stared at her.

"Papa thought the world of you."

He had told Tom he was sorry, that he shouldn't have doubted him, but for all Kyle knew, Tom Drake had died hating him.

Kyle groped for words, the pain of losing his own father piercing him anew as he glanced at Tom's inert form shrouded in a coffin across the room. "I'm sorry." He wanted to say more, to tell her that her father had taught him as much about the lumber business as his own father had, that he was sorry he'd confronted Tom with his suspicions and upset him, but the constriction in Kyle's chest left his voice too rough for talking.

"If you're trying to say you'd rather not do this, I understand." Amelia averted her face, but Kyle heard the sorrow in her voice and it sliced through his defenses.

"I assumed you'd have enough offers from his friends and crew."

"I would rather have you do it." Tears glittered in her eyes as she looked up at him. "It would mean so much."

His resistance melted. "Are you sure"

"I'm certain." She took his hand and clasped it between her own. "Thank you for giving me someone to depend on," she whispered. "You have no idea what that means to me right now."

Pounding heat rushed through his head and neck until his collar felt like a noose that was slowly strangling him. His gaze ricocheted through the parlor in search of an exit, or an excuse that would extricate him from Amelia's presence. But all he saw was surprise in Catherine's eyes. Eva and Philmore Bentley stood a few feet away wearing appalled expressions. He'd obviously offended their sense of decency last night when he tossed Amelia on his horse and galloped out of the schoolyard, but they appeared outraged now by Amelia's overt display of gratitude.

As if she sensed their stares, Amelia released his hand and angled her back to them, making it look as if she were simply turning to head in the other direction. "I need to talk to you alone," she said quietly then lifted her skirt a modest half inch and made her way back to her mother's side.

Kyle didn't want to be alone with Amelia, especially now that she was touching him and looking at him with her expression all soft and needy. He didn't want to be needed. Needy women were dangerous. So were the intense stares of Eva and Philmore Bentley who looked as though they were expecting a marriage announcement from him and Amelia after the funeral.

He nodded to the older couple and gave Catherine a discreet glance of acknowledgment, but it was Jeb Kane who caught and held his attention.

The mill foreman crossed the room and met Kyle at the foot of the magnificent cherry staircase that rose in a slow arc to the second floor. Expecting a glare filled with animosity, Kyle was surprised that the foreman's eyes held only sorrow and sympathy. "Sad day," Jeb said, shaking Kyle's hand.

"And one filled with regret, Jeb. Believe me, I had no idea Tom had been so ill."

Jeb nodded as if acknowledging the sincerity in Kyle's statement. "Tom kept his troubles to himself."

"As I should have done. If you haven't already told Victoria and Amelia what happened, I intend to, at a more appropriate time, of course."

"Why add to their distress?"

"That's the last thing I want to do, but you were there last night, Jeb. You know I upset Tom with my suspicions. How can I not tell them that I caused his collapse?"

"It upset Tom that you thought he was trying to hold you back. That man loved you and your accusation hurt him."

Hearing it put so baldly drove a stake of shame straight through Kyle's heart. More than anything, he wished he could roll back time. He would swallow the suspicion of Tom's betrayal and accept Tom's word without question.

There was nothing he could say now that would change what had happened, no apologies to Jeb or Amelia or Tom's wife that would undo the damage. The only honorable thing to do was fulfill the vow he had made to Tom. He would do whatever it took to support Amelia and Victoria.

Jeb stretched his neck as if seeking a respite from his tight collar. "You're an ambitious man, Kyle, but a good one just the same. Tom knew it. And I know it. You hurt Tom's pride, but you didn't kill him. Tom may have been upset, but it was because he felt he let you down. He wouldn't have wanted things left this way. Don't crucify yourself over something you can't change."

Regardless of Jeb's words, Kyle knew he would never forgive himself. He'd sensed something bothering Tom for a long time; whatever it was, it had destroyed a good man. And Kyle had unwittingly sent that man to his grave.

"Come on," Jeb said, turning toward the pastor who was waiting beside the coffin. "It's time to carry Tom out."

After minutes of maneuvering through doorways, Kyle, Jeb, and six other men moved the coffin outside into the evening air. Then they made the long trek across a field to a tiny family cemetery surrounded by lilac trees bursting with fragrant purple blossoms. The throbbing pain in Kyle's shin made him clench his teeth, but it was nothing compared to the ache in his heart as he carried Tom Drake to his grave.

Kyle managed the walk and the struggle of lowering the casket to its final resting place, but as they concluded the ceremony and returned to the house, he stayed to the back of the crowd to hide his increasing limp. After endless minutes of standing in the parlor, he was light-headed and nauseated by the hot pain burning up his leg. He braced his hand on the back of a chair, but discovered too late that he'd caught his fingers in the back of a woman's hair.

He glanced down as Amelia stood up. She grabbed at the back of her chignon that was now falling free of its pins. She turned and stared at Kyle, her eyebrows raised in surprise.

For the first time all day, he saw her face bloom with color. His own face heated. "Sorry, Miss Drake. I meant to rest my leg a moment and didn't realize the chair was occupied."

"What's wrong with your leg?" she asked, gathering two thick strands that had fallen free then tucking them into the mass of hair she was holding behind her head.

"He hit it with a maul this afternoon," Duke offered.

Boyd turned from his discussion with Radford and Evelyn. "Was that the same one you hit last week?"

Kyle scowled at his younger brothers, praying the conversation their mother was having with Agatha Brown and Victoria Drake on the other side of the parlor would keep her occupied. If she knew he'd hurt himself, she'd pester him to death until she made certain it wasn't a serious injury.

"Maybe Doc Finlay should look at it," Amelia suggested.

"It's nothing. Really," Kyle said when she cast a doubtful glance at his leg.

She plucked the pins from her hair then gathered it quickly and twisted it up again. She was efficient and made quick work of it, but not before Kyle admired the multitude of colors that shifted through that long mass of chestnut hair. Then he remembered how gorgeous it had looked last night slicked back from her face and dripping with rain.

"Excuse me," she said, turning away. As she wove her way through the crowd, Kyle watched the sway of her skirt and cursed himself for doing so.

Boyd whacked Kyle on the shoulder. "That is one beautiful and eligible lady who is definitely interested in you. Do yourself a favor and don't be an ass this time."

Kyle caught the uneasy look that passed between Radford and Evelyn, but he knew Boyd wasn't trying to be cruel. He was offering sensible advice, but Kyle didn't want it. Women were poison and he had no desire to have his heart ripped out again. The only safe woman was Catherine. She didn't want a commitment or a man who would demand her heart. She wanted a friend and occasional intimacy, and that suited Kyle's life perfectly.

To his embarrassment, Amelia came back with Doc Finlay. "Let's have a look at that leg," the doctor said, directing Kyle to the chair Amelia had just vacated.

Knowing he would cause more of a scene by balking, Kyle sat and pulled his pants leg to his knee.

Doc Finlay squatted and inspected Kyle's purple-streaked, swollen leg.

Amelia looked on with a concerned expression that grew more queasy by the minute.

Focusing his gaze on the doctor's balding head, Kyle sat in stony silence as the doctor probed the area along his shinbone that was turning the color of eggplant. Pain raced clear to his thigh, but Kyle clamped his teeth together, refusing to let anyone know how much it hurt.

"The gash will heal without stitches. Other than a lot of swelling, I can't see any damage that won't mend in a few weeks." The doctor pulled the pants leg over Kyle's injury then stood. "You might have a fragment of bone floating around your shin for the rest of your life that could cause some discomfort from time to time, but you'll survive."

Amelia's face paled and her eyelids fluttered. The next thing Kyle knew she was falling forward into his arms.

The instant he realized he was holding her again with her bottom in his lap, he panicked. He looked for an empty chair or couch to deposit her on, but the house was packed with people. His heart pounded, whether from his quick reactions or simply panic at having Amelia in his arms again, he wasn't certain, but he was desperate to get rid of her. Everyone crowded in to see what was happening, the Bentleys standing front and center, his own mother's expression filled with concern as she guided Victoria Drake directly toward them.

Catherine turned away.

"Sit still so I can see what I'm doing," the doctor demanded.

With his heart hammering, Kyle sat with Amelia Drake passed out in his lap, her head lolling upon his shoulder while the doctor dug in his bag for smelling salts. The seconds seemed like hours as the heat of her limp body burned into his. Her slim derrière rested on the most inappropriate part of Kyle's anatomy, but he couldn't readjust her without knowing smirks from his brothers and those who had gathered around him.

So Kyle sat there not trusting himself to breathe. Touching Amelia was like rubbing a sore muscle; a perverse, intimately entwined feeling of pain and pleasure that his aching body craved.

Chapter Four

The first thing Amelia saw when she opened her eyes was Kyle Grayson's handsome face staring down at her. Frown lines sat above a fine straight nose. His lips were full and fit his face nicely. Anything less than a strong jaw would have ruined his looks, and his eyes nearly matched the rich brown of his hair.

Intriguing angles and contours tempted her to touch him. She glided her fingertips over the stern line of his mouth and over his cheek. The feel of firm skin beneath her palm and a pair of startled eyes staring down at her jerked her back to reality as abruptly as if he'd pinched her.

With an embarrassed gasp, she attempted to vault from the chair, but several pairs of hands kept her still, Kyle's arms anchored around her waist.

"Wait a minute, missy." Doc Finlay put a hand to her forehead. "You sit right there until I tell you otherwise."

Amelia glanced at the faces gathered around her, saw Eva Bentley's censuring look, and wanted to crawl behind the nearest piece of furniture. Kyle's brothers watched with a mixture of concern and a flicker of amusement. Her mother looked frantic with worry.

The pounding in her chest left her short of breath and she feared she was going to faint again. Despite her efforts to remain upright, she trembled and sagged against Kyle's chest. She turned her face toward the crook of his neck. "Get me out of here," she whispered. "Please."

"What did you say, honey?" her mother asked.

Mortified that her guests might have heard her, Amelia clutched Kyle's hand.

"She needs some fresh air," he said.

Amelia felt herself being gathered against Kyle's body and propelled upward as he gained his feet. He stood with her draped over his hard arms in the middle of the parlor with everyone staring at them. His formidable expression revealed none of the trembling in his body or the pounding of his chest against Amelia's side. "Excuse us," he said then limped across the parlor, through the foyer, and out the front entrance without a single word of explanation.

An airy grunt came from his throat as he carried Amelia down the steps.

She glanced up in alarm. "Your leg!"

"Is killing me."

"Then why on earth are you carrying me? Put me down." She tensed in his arms, but instead of a grimace of pain, Kyle gave her a sad smile that made her world tilt.

"I'll make it a bit farther, Miss Drake."

She tried to ignore the bunching and shifting of his shoulder muscles as he carried her toward a wrought-iron bench beneath a maple tree, but it was impossible to ignore a man like Kyle Grayson. At sixteen years old, she'd had the same problem whenever Kyle visited her father's sawmill. Despite being tense and too serious, he had been incredibly handsome and so mysteriously aloof that Amelia couldn't resist watching him. In her father's presence, she would share polite conversation with Kyle, but the minute her father was out of earshot, she had openly flirted. The more Kyle ignored her, the more desperately she'd craved a response. Finally, one spring evening Kyle pulled her behind a stack of lumber and kissed her. He gave her no warning and it wasn't in the least romantic, but it was the most thrilling, earth-shaking experience Amelia had ever had in her life.

While she'd still been reeling from the momentous impact of her first kiss, Kyle warned her to quit playing with him then stormed across the mill to finish his business with her father. Amelia had stood in ankle-deep sawdust with her heart pounding and her fists clenched, cursing him even as she prayed he would come back and kiss her again.

But he hadn't come back to her, nor had he shown any interest in doing so the rest of that summer or during his many subsequent visits to her father's lumberyard. She hadn't forgotten Kyle or his incredible kiss, but she'd eventually turned her attention to Richard, who had flattered her sore ego.

From beneath her lashes, Amelia peeked at Kyle's handsome face only inches from her own. He was still arrogant and aloof and too handsome for his own good, but she would gladly overlook all of that if he would kiss her again and make the world disappear like he had that day five years ago. She would give anything to escape the agonizing heartache tearing her apart right now.

Kyle lowered her onto the bench then collapsed beside her. Air hissed between his clenched teeth as he eased his throbbing leg out in front of him.

"A cold compress might help relieve the swelling."

"I'll be all right," he said, wishing she'd stop being so concerned about him. Every time she looked at him with those sad brown eyes it gouged his conscience. As soon as he caught his breath, he was making a straight line toward the carriage.

"Thank you for taking me out of there."

He nodded, relieved to escape the house as well.

"Did you see Eva's livid expression? The school board members are furious with me."

Kyle had been more concerned about the look in Catherine's eyes. He couldn't tell if it had been surprise or pain in her expression, but he would have preferred to spare her either.

"I'll probably lose my position," Amelia said. "I'm expected to protect my reputation at all times. In all circumstances."

"That's absurd." Kyle stared at her. "You were out of your mind with grief."

"The school board doesn't see it that way." She lowered her lashes and smoothed the pad of her thumb across her palm. "My curfew is dusk unless I'm with my mother or father, or at a function approved by the board. I can't wear bright colors. No consorting with men outside immediate family, even in emergencies. I'm not allowed to marry while under contract." She paused for a breath and met his eyes. "I think you understand where this is leading."

"Why do you agree to live like this?" he asked, feeling as if he were watching a favorite pet struggling against its leash. He could never live his life under such restrictions.

"I'm a teacher. It's expected of me."

"What does being a teacher have to do with the color of your dress?"

"I don't know," she said softly. "I think the board is afraid of making the same mistake that they made with Miss Denby. I can't blame them for being cautious."

"Climbing onto a horse because you needed help is a far cry from climbing onto a desk because you... well, the point is, we've done nothing wrong. They shouldn't punish you because of another woman's misconduct. You were upset last night. It was desperation that drove you to ride with me. That's all."

"I know, but my desperation could cost me my position."

Kyle pinched the bridge of his nose, wishing his leg would stop throbbing. "I'll make Phil understand that nothing improper happened," he said, lowering his hand. "If you or your mother need anything, though, I'd appreciate it if you'd let me know."

"Thank you." She inhaled as if trying to decide how to voice the question he saw in her eyes then she released her breath in a rush. "Was my father aware of what was happening to him when he collapsed?"

Unprepared for her direct question, Kyle remained silent. Though he wanted to tell Amelia about that night and clear his conscience, Jeb was right, now wasn't the time. She had enough worry without him adding burdens to her narrow shoulders.

"Did Papa say anything? Other than *he loves me?*"

He sure did. But no matter what Kyle owed Tom, wedding his daughter was out of the question. Tying himself to a woman who needed him but didn't want him was a recipe for disaster. Kyle had made that painful mistake once and had learned his lesson. Evelyn had needed him but she hadn't loved him.

He glanced at Amelia and wondered if there was a special man in her life who might step forward and offer to keep and protect her now that her father was gone, but he knew he couldn't pry into her personal life. Still, Tom had warned Kyle to keep someone away from her. Perhaps it was a man whom Tom didn't approve of, a man Amelia was seeing in secret.

"Your father asked me to look after you and your mother," Kyle said, searching for a way to broach the subject without offending her.

"Are you saying Papa knew he was dying?" she asked, her voice filled with pain.

The silence lengthened as Kyle tried to decide if it would cause her more heartache to know that her father had been aware of his impending death and appeared resigned to it, or if it would be kinder to tell her that he had been oblivious.

Her fingers curled lightly over his forearm. "Please. I need to know."

Kyle couldn't look at her knowing he'd been the one to cause the pain in her eyes. "Your father seemed more concerned about you and your mother than himself."

"He would."

Her quiet assurance fueled Kyle's self-condemnation. Tom Drake had been a man of integrity. If Kyle had reminded himself of that before he went storming into Tom's office, maybe he wouldn't be trying to avoid Amelia's tortured eyes and the feeling that he was being crushed by his own guilt.

Maybe he should just tell her everything. Just blurt it out and let her hate him. He could live with that. He deserved it. But she didn't deserve more heartache when she was suffering so much already.

"We're not your obligation, Kyle." Their eyes met. "Not that I don't appreciate your promise to Papa, or his concern for us. We'll be all right." She tried to smile, but it didn't reach her eyes.

Worry and fear lines etched her face and Kyle knew Amelia and her mother wouldn't be all right at all. The urge to smooth away her frown caught him by surprise. Maybe it was the pain in her eyes, or the tiny line marring her forehead, that melted him, but whatever it was, it weakened his resistance, which scared him. Before he was stupid enough to lift his hand, he linked his fingers together and braced his elbows on his knees. He wouldn't look at her. He would keep his promise to Tom, but he wouldn't let this urge to protect Amelia go any farther than financial support. She would have to find comfort from someone else.

"I wanted to talk with you privately," Amelia said, breaking into Kyle's thoughts, "because I'm hoping you can tell me what Papa's mill is worth."

Kyle's protective instincts snapped to attention and he sat upright, his chest filling with fresh air. Amelia could only be asking for one reason. As if Tom Drake had climbed up out of his grave and kicked Kyle in the shin to get his attention, Kyle suddenly knew he'd found the perfect way to give Amelia and her mother security.

By buying Drake's mill, Kyle could fulfill his promise to Tom, as well as make Grayson lumber the largest sawmill business in the county, which had been a dream of his for several years. Despite the poor timing of the huge financial undertaking it made sense to Kyle.

He would discuss the investment with his brothers before making an offer, but he knew they would ultimately leave the burden of this decision on his shoulders.

"To me, your father's lumberyard is worth more than anyone else will pay you."

Amelia's mouth dropped open.

"I assume you're asking because your mother intends to sell it," he said, beginning the process of assuming ownership of Drakes' Sawmill. "I'll need to discuss this with my brothers first, but Jeb can confirm the worthiness of our offer."

Something in her expression shifted and her eyes sparked with life, as if a lantern had been lit in a dark house. She met his eyes with a boldness that unnerved Kyle. "Mama's hoping I'll use Papa's mill as a dowry."

Kyle's heart jolted and he lunged to his feet. The pain in his leg, and the shock of Amelia's comment, made him grab for the back of the bench to steady himself. He'd made a private vow the night Evelyn broke their engagement that he would never ask another woman for a promise she might not keep. Never would he put himself through that nightmare again. He was content to pour his heart into his sawmill. He could depend on his business.

"Sorry, Miss Drake, but I'm not interested in acquiring a wife."

A bright flush spread across her cheeks and her shoulders stiffened as she stood to face him. "I wasn't attempting to gauge your level of interest."

She wasn't? Then why had she mentioned using the mill as a dowry?

"If you want to buy the mill, you'll have to approach my mother with your offer."

Kyle reached out to stop her from leaving, to tell her he hadn't meant to insult her, but she yanked her arm free and left him standing beside the bench feeling like an egotistical fool.

Chapter Five

Although the board members expressed sincere sympathy over the loss of Amelia's father, they filled her ears with a lengthy diatribe about the necessity and importance of proper conduct. They roundly chastised her for putting her reputation, and theirs, at risk. But after reviewing the rules of her contract and the circumstances of her misconduct with painstaking thoroughness, they allowed her to return to her position.

Instead of feeling relieved, Amelia was weary. She barely had the energy to visit her mother each evening, and for almost two weeks she spent her time huddled alone in her apartment, hating her life, missing her father with a desperation that frightened her, and cursing Kyle Grayson for buying the mill.

He'd delivered a bank draft to her mother that morning and the amount of his offer was blatantly commensurate with his aversion to marriage. Kyle had made it very clear he wasn't interested in Amelia or her indirect proposal. Why she had even mentioned her mother's idea about using the mill as a dowry Amelia couldn't say, but she wished she had never opened her mouth. Kyle's horrified expression had been a painful blow to her dignity.

Mortified that she might cross paths with him, Amelia glanced over her shoulder several times during her mile walk to town. It was the only bit of freedom the board allowed her. She dreaded meeting anyone, hearing sympathetic comments from neighbors and friends about her father's passing, or facing the stares of curious gossips. She didn't want to display her heartache for anyone, sympathetic or otherwise. She wanted to stay home and lick her wounds in private, but she had promised her mother she would take Kyle's draft and pay off the mortgage on the house. So Amelia swallowed her apprehension and entered the bank.

The unexpected sight of Richard Cameron strolling through the lobby leached every ounce of strength from her body. Her parasol clattered to the floor and her heart jerked so hard she clapped a hand over the cramp in her chest.

Richard swept up her parasol and smiled. "A pleasure to see you again, Miss Drake."

"What are you doing here?" she asked in breathless shock.

"I'm a partner in the bank now."

If the muscles in her legs hadn't gone lax, she would have rushed back outside, but it was all she could do to remain standing while several patrons, including two school board members, Clara and Art Bortwick, turned to see what the commotion was about. That Richard was here, now, while her reputation was already under so much speculation was too much to bear.

"You're white as wool, Miss Drake." He pointed toward a corner office with the tip of her parasol. "Come sit down a moment."

"I'll wait for a teller."

"Nonsense." He caught her elbow and tugged her forward. "I'm honored to help a friend."

To deny him would cause a scene she couldn't afford, so Amelia followed him into his office. He gave the door a nudge to close it, but she caught the edge of it to keep it open a few inches.

He glanced at her with a question in his eyes, but she ignored him. The Bortwicks were watching her through the six-inch opening in the doorway. They would flay her alive if she spent time alone with a man, especially if she was flaunting her breach of propriety in a public facility.

Richard gave her the parasol. "I'm sincerely sorry about your father. I just returned from Philadelphia and heard the news this morning. If there is anything I can do to help you and your mother, I would consider it a privilege to do so."

Amelia clutched her parasol and wondered how long her heart could endure the thunderous beating. So many years she'd dreamed of this moment, of Richard dashing back into town to beg her forgiveness and rescue her from going mad in her self-induced solitary confinement. But her girlhood lover wasn't on his knees begging her for anything. He was standing with his hip cocked, as arrogant and self-assured as ever.

She inched closer to the door. "Why are you in the banking business? I thought you had a law practice in Philadelphia."

"I didn't care for the legal profession." Richard nodded toward the empty chair. "Sit down. I won't bite."

Yes he would. If he was inclined, Richard would nibble and tease and seduce her until he ripped out another chunk of her heart. No matter how much she'd once adored him, or how intimately he was looking at her now, she refused to succumb to his charm. She wasn't the same naive girl who had melted the minute he smiled at her. She was just a little off balance and breathless from the shock of seeing him here. That's all.

Richard accepted the draft she handed him then sat in his oversized chair. He looked at the note and his eyebrows shot up. "Did the Graysons owe your father money?"

"They bought Papa's mill."

Richard's face turned ashen and he gaped at her. "Are they insane?"

"I beg your pardon?" she asked, offended.

"I... I'm sorry." Richard looked at the draft and shook his head. "I'm just shocked that Kyle would make an investment like this. Pardon my candor, but your father's mill is in terrible financial shape."

"It is?"

He glanced up in surprise. "You don't know about this?"

Amelia's stomach did a slow, sickening roll and she shook her head.

His expression filled with sympathy and he stood up. "I'm terribly sorry, but your father's finances aren't in the best of shape. I would have broken this more gently had I known you weren't aware of it."

"There must be a mistake. My father was a smart businessman."

He sighed and picked up a folder from his desk. "There are several outstanding mortgages tied to his business. His personal account is empty, so those liens will remain against the mill." He held out a thick folder. "Our bank files are confidential, but you're welcome to look through your father's accounts if you feel the need."

Amelia took the folder and flipped through the papers, her eyes seeking confirmation of the truth while her heart prayed Richard was mistaken. Slowly, as she scanned her father's records, her body grew weak and she sagged against his desk. From what she could understand of the documents, her father appeared to be broke. All her mother could depend on was Amelia's pathetic monthly teacher's salary that simply couldn't support them. They had nothing left but a house that her mother would lose if Kyle tried to back out of buying the mill, which he would certainly do the minute he learned about the liens.

Amelia's hands shook as she handed the folder back to Richard. "What am I going to do?"

"I don't know, but I'm willing to help you figure out a solution to the problem."

That he was sincere was apparent, but Amelia couldn't think past the disaster crashing upon her. "How on earth can I manage all of this on a teacher's salary?"

Richard dropped the folder on the desk then bracketed her shoulders with his warm palms. "I know things ended badly with us, but I would like to see you again. Let me help you. I'll come by this evening and we'll resolve this together."

Torn between kicking him for breaking her heart, and falling into his arms to weep out her problems, Amelia willed herself not to move, not to make a spectacle of herself again. Long ago she'd promised herself she would never again beg a man for anything, but she hadn't known how tempting it would be in a crisis.

She eyed Richard, wanting to believe he was sincere, but afraid to trust him. For three tense seconds their gazes locked then he smiled that half-smile that had cost Amelia her virginity. "I've missed you."

Oh, dear.

"I can help you, Amelia," he said, using her given name in that same seductive tone of voice he'd used to steal her virginity. "And you can help me."

Her stomach dropped and she held her breath. Maybe she wasn't seventeen years old, but Richard had the power to make her feel that way—naive and desperate.

"We're both lonely." He touched a finger to her cheek. "Don't deny it. I know how you've been living. I'm alone, too. Let's become companions."

"Companions?" She glanced toward the door and saw the Bortwicks pretending to be reviewing a paper with the loan officer, but she knew they were purposely observing everything that was happening between her and Richard. She moved back a step. "Have you forgotten that you walked out on me when I could have been in trouble? That was inconsiderate and cowardly. How do you expect me to be your companion when I despise you?"

His laugh echoed through the office and Amelia cringed. She knew the Bortwicks would be glaring at her by now, but she didn't have the courage to turn around and confirm her fear.

"We had something special once, didn't we?"

"Apparently not."

"I wasn't ready to marry."

"You should have told me that before you ruined me."

"I didn't ruin you. Forget the past, Amelia. I have. And I've forgiven you."

"For what?" she blurted, too incensed to control the increasing level of her voice. "For giving you the only thing that was ever truly mine? For letting you destroy my life?"

Richard glanced toward the lobby and nudged the door closed in the face of the Bortwicks' shocked stares. Amelia lunged for the brass handle, but he caught her elbow and swung her into his arms. "We both got hurt. Why not forget it and start over?"

She stared at him, wanting to believe that he was sincere, that the spark in his eye was love instead of lust.

"We were young, Amelia. I needed to go back to college. I told you from the beginning that I was going back to school."

He had, but she had believed their romance would change his mind. She'd thought he would stay and take a job at her father's lumberyard or go into the banking business with his own father. She'd thought they would marry and begin a family, but she'd been wrong. Richard had no interest in working a sawmill or riding on his father's success. He'd craved the big city and the sort of life she knew nothing about. Why he'd come back now she didn't know, but she was certain it wasn't for her.

She glanced at the folder on his desk and realized she was caught up in salving old wounds instead of trying to prevent the present financial disaster facing herself and her mother. Suddenly exhausted, she leaned against the desk and looked Richard in the eye. "Our past is inconsequential at this point. My mother is destitute and I have no idea how I'm going to support her."

"My offer of help was sincere." Richard cupped her jaw. "I want you," he said quietly. "Don't look so shocked. We're adults, Amelia.

I can see that we're both bored out of our minds. You need money. I want a companion. If you're willing, we can have a private, intimate relationship and offer each other something that no one else needs to know about."

Although they were behind closed doors, her jaw dropped at his audacity.

He took advantage of her shock and kissed her.

The heat of his mouth, the sweep of his tongue, jolted her. Her mouth remembered his as if only yesterday they were lovers, but her heart remembered Richard's betrayal and she pushed him away.

"I meant that as a compliment," he said. "A private relationship could serve both of us."

"Does that private relationship include marriage, Richard?"

"No."

"How chivalrous of you." She tried to push past him, but he caught her arms and held her immobile.

"This isn't an issue of integrity, nor does it have anything to do with our past. It's about need and desire. Plain and simple. We're two adults who need each other, and you know it."

Amelia stared at him, wondering how on earth she could be tempted by his outrageous proposition when he was so obviously a rat and when it went against every fiber of what she considered honest and decent. Maybe it was only desperation she felt. Maybe her fear over her father's dire financial situation was tempting her to accept Richard's offer. Or maybe it was a more pathetic reason. Maybe it was simply because she was dying inside and was hungry for any scrap of human affection tossed her way.

Chapter Six

Kyle gripped Tom Drake's business register in his hands, unable to believe he'd just made the biggest mistake of his life.

Tom Drake was broke.

Everything of value at Tom's mill had been mortgaged to the bank: the buildings, the timber, even the horses. Not only was Kyle out the money Tom owed him for the timber he'd bought, but Kyle had just used every cent in his and his brothers' joint business account to purchase a mill teetering on the edge of bankruptcy. He may as well have thrown their money into the boiler stove.

A sickening rush of heat filled Kyle's chest as he flattened his sweaty palms on Tom's desktop and looked up at his brothers. None of them could take on this avalanche of debt. It would bury their sawmill and jeopardize the livelihood of each one of them.

Panic pushed its way up his throat and one thought kept circling Kyle's mind. Did Amelia know about her father's debt? And if she did, why hadn't she told him?

He glanced down at the slanted writing in Tom's journal knowing that the need to ease his guilt and fulfill his promise to Tom had driven him to act in haste. He shouldn't have let his sympathy for Amelia overshadow his instincts. He shouldn't have put so much faith in Tom and believed him incapable of getting himself into a financial crisis. He should have researched his investment before giving Victoria a bank draft. He should have looked beyond Amelia's melancholy eyes and found out more about her father's business.

Boyd paced the floor and eyed Kyle with disgust. "You said this would be a good investment, but this lumberyard is a disaster!"

Judging by Radford's and Duke's matching expressions they had discovered the same horrid mess in the folders they'd been leafing through. Radford pushed the drawer closed with his elbow. "What could have caused Tom to get himself into this kind of trouble?" he asked, his voice filled with concern rather than the condemnation reflected in Boyd's comments.

Kyle had no idea. In a million years, he wouldn't have believed Tom would ever be desperate enough to mortgage his mill. That's what Kyle got for trusting someone. He should have learned his lesson when his own brother betrayed him.

Boyd scoffed in disgust. "You should have *known* what type of investment you were making, Kyle. You've drilled that lesson into my head every day for the last five years. All you've been harping about lately is that a tavern is a bad investment." Boyd stopped in front of the desk and shoved his dark hair off his forehead, his gaze boring into Kyle's. "At least the alehouse I want to buy has the potential for making a profit. This pathetic deal you made is going to ruin us."

Boyd spoke the truth, but all Kyle could think about was how he would tell Amelia about her father's debt. Or how he would manage to control his anger if she'd known about it and let him walk into a deal with the potential to destroy him.

Unable to look at his brothers, he fixed his gaze outside the window. If Amelia had given him the mill free of charge, he still doubted his ability to turn it around.

"How deep are we in?" Duke asked, leaning against the knotty-pine wall slats, casually folding his arms over his chest as though unconcerned over the potential downfall of their business.

Kyle stood up, needing to be at eye level with his brothers when he told them he'd just tied their mill to a sinking stone in an ocean of debt. "I invested everything in our account."

Boyd's expression flattened and he stared at Kyle. "What do you mean everything?" His jaw muscles flexed. "Be specific."

"I used all of our money, Boyd. Every cent."

"You'd better mean less my twenty-five percent because I told you I want out."

Getting pressured by Boyd while he was trying to think his way through the catastrophe snapped Kyle's patience. "Well, I'm sorry, but you're in this with the rest of us."

Boyd flung his arm out to encompass Duke and Radford. "The four of us own the mill. Who gave you the right to make decisions for us?"

White-hot anger surged through Kyle. He clenched his fists around Tom's register. "You gave me permission! Each time you left the burden of making a decision on my shoulders. A burden I didn't want that I've carried alone for five years. Every time we had a problem, you and Duke left me to handle it. As for Radford," Kyle said, glancing at his older brother, "he was too busy with his own burdens to worry about ours."

"I worried," Radford said, though his voice held no malice.

Kyle tossed the register on the desk, regretting his outburst. For years Radford had been tormented by his nightmares of the war. His inability to control his violent outbursts not only shamed him but nearly destroyed their family. Radford had gone through hell trying to work through his trauma, and Kyle was glad to see his brother learning to escape his memories and be happy again. "That wasn't meant as an insult, Radford."

"You two have already covered this ground," Boyd said, forcing their attention back to the problem at hand. "Give me my cut of the mill and you're free to do whatever you want with this calamity."

"I'm not mortgaging our mill to finance a stench-filled tavern so you can drink yourself into oblivion each night."

"Well, I'm not going to be imprisoned by your ambition, Kyle!"

"Then act like a man and use your head for once. You have as much responsibility to our mill as the rest of us. It's time you realize that and stop drowning your brain in ale every night. You're turning into a drunk."

Boyd dove forward, his fist arcing toward Kyle's face.

Duke and Radford snagged his arms and hauled him back.

Boyd yanked his arms free, but they kept him reined. "Kyle had no right to do this. He knew I wanted out. He tied up our money on purpose."

He spoke the truth, but Kyle refused to let his brother drink away the tiny inheritance he'd patiently nursed into a respectable amount of money.

"I made an investment I thought to be sound," Kyle said, hoping he could batter his point through Boyd's anger. "If you'll settle down and give me some time to think, I might find a way to make this work."

"Why waste the time? Just tell Miss Drake the deal's off."

Kyle looked at Radford and Duke and knew they agreed with Boyd. It would be the easiest way to solve their problem. And if she'd duped him, turnabout was fair play. Still, the thought of dumping the burden back in her lap only fed Kyle's guilt. Whether she'd intentionally misled him about the debt or not, he'd promised to take care of her and Victoria. Since they would never accept his charity, buying Tom's lumberyard was the only way to fulfill his commitment to Tom. Still, he had his brothers' welfare to think about.

Boyd jerked against his brothers' hands. "Let go."

"All right, but quit acting like an ass."

"An ass?" Boyd pulled free and glared at Duke. "Am I wrong because I want to make my own choices and live my own life instead of walking in the shadows of you three? I'm tired of being known as the sheriff's brother, or the brother of the most respected businessman in town, or worse yet, the brother of a war hero," he said, flinging his hand out toward Radford, whose expression registered surprise then insult. "If all I can amount to is a drunk then I'm going to own the tavern and be the best drunk in town."

Duke lifted a brow. "It's been a long time since I've thrashed you. If you embarrass Mom with your carousing and drinking, I'll make it a priority to do so."

A fire flared in Boyd's eyes as he sized up Duke's thick arms then he tossed his head back with a laugh, acting like his usual mischievous self. "That would be quite a row, now wouldn't it?"

"It'd be a dumb move on your part, but go ahead if you like."

Kyle slammed his fist on the desk. "Use your fat heads for something more than punching bags, will you? We've got a problem to solve."

"We?" Boyd turned to Kyle. "You made the problem. You solve it." He pulled open the door then turned back. "One month, Kyle. I want my money in four weeks. Not a day more."

Kyle ground his teeth as the door slammed. "What do you two want to do?" he asked, knowing he would respect their decision regardless of its effect on Amelia or his own conscience.

Radford shrugged. "Common sense tells me to side with Boyd."

Duke pushed away from the wall. "I agree, but you've always done a good job of managing our business. I'll trust your judgment."

Kyle had no idea what he would do, but he knew one thing for certain. He was going to visit Amelia Drake and find out what she knew about her father's debt.

Chapter Seven

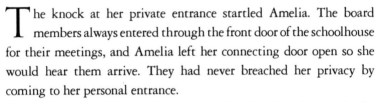

T he knock at her private entrance startled Amelia. The board
members always entered through the front door of the schoolhouse
for their meetings, and Amelia left her connecting door open so she
would hear them arrive. They had never breached her privacy by
coming to her personal entrance.

Maybe it was Eva coming to warn Amelia that she was in for
an hour of chastising because of the scene with Richard at the bank.
Amelia sighed and opened the door, just wanting the meeting over
with so she could figure out how to support her mother without
succumbing to Richard's proposition.

To her shock, Kyle Grayson planted his hands against the
doorframe and angled his powerful body toward her. "We have to
talk," he said, in his straightforward manner.

Amelia blinked, unable to believe he was really standing in her
doorway when he knew perfectly well his presence at her apartment
would be viewed as the ultimate sin. Concerned for both of them,
she peered over his shoulder to see if Eva and Philmore Bentley were
leaving their house yet. "You can't be seen here, Kyle."

"I know. I'm sorry for putting you at risk, but we have a problem
to discuss. Did you know that your father's mill is nearly bankrupt?"

She honestly hadn't until a few hours ago. Believing Kyle had
come to rescind his offer on the mill, Amelia opened her mouth to beg
him not to do it, but the rattle of carriage wheels sounded in the street.
Knowing Kyle could be seen from the road, and that she would end up

losing the only income she had, she grabbed his arm and tugged him inside. Despite his surprise, she shut the door behind him then tried to calm her pounding heart.

He towered over her, standing so close that she could see the dark flecks in his eyes. She could smell fresh-cut wood and evening air emanating from his clothing along with a hint of aftershave. Whiskers speckled his jaw, and his thick hair was swept off his forehead as though he'd repeatedly shoved it back with his fingers. Even tired and work-worn, Kyle Grayson was disgustingly attractive. Amelia lowered her lashes, appalled that she would notice something so trite during such a catastrophic crisis. To her further dismay, her gaze riveted on the hair peeking from his open collar. The queer thrill in her stomach stoked her frustration as much as his news had.

"My brothers are ready to kill me for making such a bad investment, Miss Drake." His quiet statement spelled doom. He stared directly into her eyes. "If one of them had done this, I would fire them. I'm sorry, but in their interest, I have to cancel our agreement. The mill is debt-ridden. It could drag my own business into bankruptcy. I can't ask my brothers to take that risk."

"But I already used your draft to pay off the mortgage on Mama's house."

"Your father mortgaged the house, too?" Kyle pinched the bridge of his perfect, proud nose and shook his head. "There isn't any hope of saving the mill." He sighed and looked away, his gaze perusing the stark little box she lived in. "Jeb doesn't know what's going on, either. Do you think your father might have talked to your mother about his debt?"

Amelia shook her head and braced herself against the solid bulk of the table. Her father would have never worried her mother with his financial troubles. She wouldn't, either. Her mother was suffering enough heartache and worry without knowing the precarious state of their security.

"Do you have any relatives who can help you?" Kyle asked, oblivious to the panic drowning her.

"No."

"There isn't anyone anywhere that you and your mother can depend on?"

"My mother has a widowed sister in Georgia, who's as poor as a church mouse. She's our only living relative that I'm aware of."

"You're serious?" She nodded and his gaze darted through the room as if searching for something to punch his fist through. "What was your father thinking?"

"If you don't know the circumstances, don't blame him for this."

Kyle stared in disbelief. "Who do you think is responsible for this mess?"

She shrugged. "There could be a million reasons for Papa's financial problems. It may not be his fault at all."

"It most certainly is his fault! His bad decisions drove his mill into debt, and it could drag mine with it." Kyle grabbed her wrist and tugged her away from the table. "If you need proof of that we can take a trip to his mill right now and I'll show you the mess he has made."

The absurdity of her situation washed over her, and Amelia's emotions spiraled out of control. It would be so easy to sink to the floor in a laughing, weeping mess, but something stronger burned inside her and shoved aside self-pity. She'd had enough. She refused to be a victim any longer.

Every man in her life had manipulated her or let her down. From the moment of her birth, she'd lived her life under someone else's rules. She'd adored her father and appreciated his support, but she'd lived by his standards, not her own. After her affair with Richard she traded her freedom for a minuscule monthly stipend and a pristine reputation as a teacher. Now, because of a mistake in her past, one man's arrogance, and another man's bad decisions, her reputation and security were on the verge of destruction.

She tried to jerk her arm free, but Kyle kept her wrist captive. "Leave my apartment!" she demanded, refusing to be pushed or manhandled ever again. When Kyle still didn't release her wrist, she swung her foot straight into his shin.

Air whistled in between his clenched teeth and a sickly expression washed over his face as he swayed on his feet, but it was the low groan of pain and his hand clutching for the bedpost that made Amelia realize what she'd done.

"Your leg! Oh, Kyle... I'm sorry."

His entire body trembled and perspiration covered his face as she guided him onto her bed, but he didn't say a word. He clenched his fists in his lap until his knuckles turned white. His chest heaved and he squeezed his eyes shut, but the suspicious sparkle of moisture on his dark lashes rent Amelia's heart.

"Kyle," she said softly, touching his taut, damp cheek. "I'm so sorry. I forgot about your injury." He didn't respond and Amelia wasn't sure if it was because he was so angry or because he was in too much pain to do so.

She grabbed a freshly laundered towel off her linen stand and soaked it in the bucket of water she'd just drawn from the well. When she turned toward the bed, Kyle was sitting with his head tipped back against the wall, his eyes tightly closed. "I'll need to lift your pants leg."

He didn't respond.

Amelia raised the lightweight denim as gently as possible. When she saw Kyle's shin covered with black tissue and swollen to the point of deformity, she nearly wept with remorse for her rash behavior. How stupid she'd been. Swallowing back her nausea, she applied the cold, dripping cloth and apologized for the discomfort when he flinched. Her eyes blurred with tears and she cursed herself again for her inconsiderate act. It wasn't his fault her father was in debt, that her life was falling apart.

He let out a shaky breath. "Do you have another wet cloth?"

His voice came out graveled and slow, and it was apparent he was in no condition to lean over and hold the compress to his leg. She glanced around the room, but there was nothing to use to pin the cloth in place. She plucked a pin from her hair and slipped it over the area where the two ends of the fabric crossed. With the reinforcement of four more hairpins the rag stayed in place. She crossed to her linen stand, unmindful of her hair trailing down her back.

She wet a fresh towel, wrung the excess into her potted plant, the only living thing allowed to share her tiny apartment with her, and then returned to Kyle's side. After folding the towel, she pressed it to his forehead.

"Thank you," he said, his voice strained.

She didn't answer for lack of an appropriate response. No matter how many times she apologized, it would not lessen the pain she'd caused him or the guilt she was suffering for kicking him.

Minutes passed while he sat stiff and silent. Unable to offer comfort, she knelt before him and removed the cloth from his leg. She soaked it with cold water then pinned it back in place. When she stood to freshen the towel on his face, Kyle captured her wrist. Startled, she glanced down and found herself gazing into a pair of hurting, earth-colored eyes.

"I'm sorry I acted like a fool," he said quietly.

She couldn't have been more shocked by his apology if he'd said he would pay off her debts and marry her to boot. "You're sorry? I kicked *you*, remember?"

"Vividly. But I prompted the action, and for that, I apologize."

It disconcerted her to stand so close while he shrewdly assessed her from beneath those long, dark lashes. "Why are you looking at me like that?"

"I'm waiting to see if you're going to faint on me again." Despite his obvious pain, his lips quirked and made her heart ache.

"I thought you might do the same a moment ago." Her shoulders sagged. "Your leg looks awful. Shouldn't you see the doctor again, just to make sure it's all right?"

"Is that concern from the lady who just kicked me?"

Amelia lowered her lashes and leaned over to change the cloth on his forehead. "I forgot about your shin."

"I shouldn't have grabbed you." He gently lifted her wrist to inspect it. "I'm sorry I hurt you." Her eyes met his. "And I'm sorry I offended you the day I said I wasn't interested in marriage. It wasn't meant as a reflection on you, Miss Drake."

She flushed over his unexpected apology. "The way I dress, I wouldn't expect any man to be interested in me."

He looked at her as if she were crazy. "You could be dressed in rags and men would still be interested."

Unable to speak past the thrilling sensation in her chest, she ducked her head. Her hair slipped forward over her shoulder and she reached up to brush it back, but Kyle stopped her hand. Their eyes met, his gaze intimate and heated as he drew her forward and kissed her.

Chapter Eight

Kyle knew the moment his lips touched Amelia's that he'd made a colossal mistake. Every cell in his body exploded with unadulterated lust. He hadn't meant to kiss her, didn't even know how or why it had happened. He'd tried to warn himself of the disastrous results in that split second before their lips met, but no force on earth could have kept him from responding to the answering touch of her tongue upon his own.

She sank onto his lap and draped her arms around his neck, drawing him deeper into the kiss.

Kyle was lost. He lingered, savored, floated in the euphoric thrill that shot through his body. Like the one and only time he'd ever kissed Amelia, nothing existed but her. Her mouth. The feel of her hands in his hair. As if the rest of his world had gone black, Amelia became that pinpoint of light that drew him forward, that beckoned him to reach, to touch, to bask in the warmth of her soft yellow glow.

He began to lay her back on the bed and lose himself in her touch, but streaks of pain ripped up his leg and made his fists clench. Reluctantly, he ended the kiss and sucked in a mind-clearing gulp of air.

Her eyes opened, lazy and dazed as she stared up at him.

Kyle struggled to control the combination of pain and lust ravaging his body. As the sharp ache in his leg slowly abated, he stared at Amelia, wondering how a schoolteacher had learned to kiss a man like she'd been making love with him for years. He eased his hand off her hip. "My shin isn't appreciating our position."

A quizzical expression crossed her face then her eyes widened with understanding. "Oh!" Her palms hit his chest and she shoved herself off his lap. In a flurry of embarrassed fumbling, she straightened her skirt and pushed her hair off her red face. "I didn't realize, I mean, I'm sorry."

⚔️

Thoroughly flustered, Amelia backed against the table and steadied herself against its solid bulk. Her legs trembled and she felt flushed from her ears to her ankles as she stared at Kyle. Even with a few feet separating them, she felt overwhelmed by his presence. His dark gaze beckoned her back into his arms, but she wasn't going near him. Despite the thrill of his touch, losing control of her mind and body had scared the life out of her. That had never happened with Richard.

Kyle leaned forward and braced his elbows on his knees. "We've got to figure out what to do about the lumberyard."

The what? She'd just experienced an emotional earthquake and Kyle was thinking about money? She gripped the table for support. If she had the strength, she would cross the floor and kick him in the shin again. Had he felt nothing at all during the kiss?

The abrupt clearing of a throat yanked Amelia's attention toward the connecting door of the schoolroom where, to her horror, Eva and Phil Bentley stood with Judith Morton and Clara Bortwick. "I'm afraid that discussion will have to wait, Mr. Grayson. We have a board meeting scheduled that Miss Drake has apparently forgotten about." The reddish hue of Eva's face clearly expressed the depth of her outrage. Judith Morton and Clara Bortwick glanced at each other with such stricken expressions Amelia thought their hearts had stopped beating. But it was the suspicion in Kyle's eyes, as if he knew Amelia had purposely trapped him that made her heart thud.

Her stomach slammed into her ribs and her knees weakened. She leaned against the edge of the table and braced her hand on the smooth maple surface. There wasn't a single suitable excuse that would explain Kyle's presence in her apartment, nor could she convince Kyle that she hadn't planned this, because in the back of her mind, she had considered this very thing the instant she had pulled him into her apartment.

Kyle lunged to his feet and grabbed at the bedpost to steady himself. He dwarfed the room as he faced the gawking board members. "This isn't what you're thinking."

"Then what is it, exactly?" Eva's accusing gaze told Amelia her time as a teacher was over.

Fearing the repercussions from both Kyle and the board, Amelia struggled to speak, to correct their misinterpretation of the liaison they thought they were witnessing, but not a word of explanation would squeak from her tight throat. Spurts of panic raced through her body, making her legs quake and her heart pound. She couldn't fix this.

Mortified by her own disheveled appearance, Amelia scooped her loose hair behind her shoulders with trembling hands.

"Phil, are you aware that I just bought Tom's lumberyard?" Kyle asked.

Phil nodded, his forehead creased as though trying to figure out what that had to do with Kyle lounging on Amelia's bed.

"I came by to discuss a problem we're having there, but I barked my shin on that stool." He pointed to a hard wooden chair sitting cockeyed beside the table. "If you remember what my leg looked like at the funeral then you'll know I couldn't have walked back out that door to save my life. I was resting my leg and trying to get my breath back when you arrived."

Eva glanced at the rumpled bed and their disheveled clothing and raised a censuring eyebrow. "I hardly believe it matters what circumstances caused you to be in Miss Drake's bed. The fact is, you were." With a pointed stare at Amelia's unbound hair, she said, "You are well aware of what is considered respectable behavior and why we must enforce the rules with unbiased diligence. Two weeks ago we made an exception in light of your father's passing. We will not bend our rules a second time to accommodate your behavior, especially after that incident at the bank this afternoon."

"This is ludicrous!" Kyle said, his hard voice demanding their attention.

Eva straightened as if Kyle had spit in her face. Amelia clutched her stomach and feared her supper would soon be on the floor.

"I understand that you all have a responsibility to enforce proper protocol for this teaching position," Kyle said, "and I respect that, but your unwarranted suspicions are humiliating Miss Drake and insulting my reputation."

"Unwarranted!" Eva pressed her palm to the scarred wood doorframe as she thrust out her jaw. "This young woman rode off with you in the night without a chaperone not two weeks ago! Now we find you in her apartment lounging on her bed! I would say our concern is warranted, Mr. Grayson."

"Miss Drake's virtue has not been compromised."

"I beg to differ with you."

Amelia had to agree with Mrs. Bentley. She would be ruined when the gossips got hold of this.

Kyle faced the board members, and one by one they looked away from his quelling stare. "Phil, do you have reason to doubt my integrity?"

"Of course not."

Kyle looked at Eva. "Do you have personal reservations about my character, Mrs. Bentley?"

Eva's nostrils flared and she glared at him without speaking.

"Would you mind answering my question?"

"Yes, I do mind! You are insinuating yourself where you don't belong, and I'm asking you to leave the school grounds this instant."

"I'm standing here because you are rudely speculating about my character, which I'm entitled to defend."

"Your integrity isn't at issue, Mr. Grayson."

"The devil it isn't!" Kyle banged his fist down on the table with a crack that made everyone jerk back a step. "Your concern for Miss Drake's reputation may be valid, Mrs. Bentley, but to imply I have damaged her after I gave you a logical explanation for my visit is not only absurd it's insulting."

"There is no suitable explanation for you being found on Miss Drake's bed." Mrs. Bentley pointed toward the door. "Now, I'm asking you for the last time to leave."

Kyle closed his eyes and pinched the bridge of his nose. Amelia suspected he was fighting the urge to choke the old nag glaring at him and feared he was about to do something drastic. Or worse yet, maybe he was considering walking out the door and leaving Amelia's job and her reputation in ruins.

"Wait a minute," she blurted. Everyone turned surprised expressions in her direction. Her heart pounded, but she refused to let another man ruin her and walk away. "Kyle came here to ask me to marry him."

Kyle's eyes widened. How he kept his jaw from dropping she would never know, but he stared at her as if she'd lost her mind.

Despite her churning stomach and quaking legs, Amelia kept her chin high as she faced Eva's glacial stare. Everyone seemed to be waiting for her to go on, including Kyle. "Kyle refused to leave without a positive answer."

Judith Morton sighed as if she were reliving the first time she'd ever fallen in love. Phil glanced at Kyle as if to corroborate her story, but Kyle didn't move a muscle.

Amelia looked at him and immediately wished she hadn't when she saw the storm brewing in his eyes. Evelyn had said Kyle was hard-edged and too aggressive for his own good, and Amelia believed it. But Evelyn had also said on several occasions that Kyle was a good man deserving of a woman who could truly appreciate him. He was the sort of man her father would have chosen for her. He was the only man with the drive and intelligence to resurrect her father's business, and he'd wanted the lumberyard enough to buy it. If Amelia let Kyle walk out, she would be ruined. If he backed out on his agreement to buy the mill, her father's business would die and so would his memory. The bank would sell everything, including their house. Any physical reminder of her beloved father would be carted off or left to rot. And she would have no choice but to become Richard's mistress until he tired of her.

Despite Kyle's aversion to marriage, the kiss he'd just given her said he was attracted to her. Respect and attraction would make a perfectly suitable foundation for marriage. That would be enough to start with.

Amelia faced Kyle, her chin high despite her churning emotions. "I accept your proposal."

His jaw clenched.

She silently beseeched him to understand and forgive, but he stood like a mountain, hard and unyielding. His rigid sense of honor wouldn't allow him to rebuff her. He would marry her because his own actions had put her in this predicament, but Amelia's heart ached knowing he would never forgive her for trapping him.

Eva turned to the trio behind her. "I believe our board meeting is unnecessary." She turned back to Amelia. "As you are well aware, teachers are not allowed to marry while under contract. Judith will take over your duties in the morning." Without a single word of well wishes or farewell, she led the board members out of the schoolhouse.

Amelia bit her tongue to keep from pleading with them not to leave her alone with Kyle. His dark eyes burned with anger. His fists were clenched at his sides.

"Am I to assume that you knew about your father's debt?"

"Richard told me this afternoon. I was as shocked as you are."

"But you still used my draft to pay off your mother's mortgage?"

Shame filled Amelia, but she'd had to do it. "It was the only way I could guarantee that Mama would have a place to live." She laced her fingers in front of her to keep her hands from shaking. "What would Mama and I have done with the mill, Kyle? You're experienced enough to save it. We aren't. I needed to protect Mama's security and that was the only way I could do it."

He was silent for so long that Amelia could hear the pounding of her own heart.

"Did you honestly forget about the board meeting?" he asked.

Her heart skipped and she shook her head. "No. Only when you kissed me."

His nostrils flared and the anger returned to his eyes. "Do you realize that you've just committed us both to a marriage we can't escape?"

Outrage swept through her. She hadn't done anything but answer the door! Angry and humiliated, she clenched her fists. "*You* did that, Mr. Grayson, when you knocked on my door."

Chapter Nine

Of all the stupid things Kyle had done in his life, kissing Amelia had been the dumbest. He should never have gone to her apartment. He shouldn't have provoked her to kick his shin or touch him with those soft hands or hover over him with her breasts in his face until his mind had turned to mush. The woman should have kept her hair bound! A teacher wasn't supposed to look all soft and seductive or melt across his lap like warm honey.

A dead man would have responded to that temptation.

The loud knock on his door startled him. If it was Boyd coming to demand money for his share of the mill, Kyle would throttle him. He banged his empty glass down on the kitchen counter then went to the parlor to answer the front door.

At the sight of Richard Cameron, Kyle's mouth dropped open. It astounded Kyle to see his oldest, dearest friend standing on his doorstep. "What are you doing here?" he asked, grabbing Richard's hand in a firm, welcoming clasp.

Grinning, Richard returned the handshake. "I'm looking for someone to share a mug or two with." He slapped Kyle on both shoulders. "It's good to see you."

Kyle assessed his friend, whom he hadn't seen in four years. Richard still sported his good looks and cocksure attitude. He was a blond, fair-skinned version of Boyd, but rather than irritating Kyle at every turn as Boyd did, Richard had always made Kyle laugh.

"Come on in," he said, clasping Richard's neck and pulling him inside.

"Is your lovely bride home?" Richard asked, glancing around the parlor.

"Evelyn married my older brother a few months past and is now the lovely Mrs. Radford Grayson."

The teasing glint left Richard's eyes. "I hadn't heard. I'm sorry."

Kyle shrugged and feigned indifference. Though he'd forgiven his brother and fiancée for falling in love with each other, his wound was still tender and he had no wish to discuss it. "If it's ale you want it's ale you'll get. Come on."

Richard closed the door behind him and followed Kyle to the kitchen. "I came to see if you've lost your mind. What possessed you to buy Tom's lumberyard?"

Kyle stopped and stared at Richard. "How could you know about that? You just got back from Philadelphia."

"Which is why you should have waited, Kyle. I could have warned you off this disaster. You can't go through with this purchase. The bank is ready to foreclose on that property."

Willing or not, Kyle had to go through with it. He had to marry Amelia, and tomorrow night he had to convince Victoria Drake that he wanted to marry her daughter.

Kyle shoved open the window to let in the cool evening air then took two mugs into the pantry and filled them from a small keg of ale. Wait until Amelia learned she'd just bound herself for life to the man who had caused her father's collapse. She would hate him—if she didn't already.

"Did you hear what I said?" Richard asked, raising his voice so Kyle could hear him in the pantry. "I'm telling you this as a friend, Kyle."

"I know." Kyle came back into the kitchen. "I appreciate the warning, but it's too late." He handed Richard a mug then raised his own in a mock salute. "I'm getting married."

"How many mugs of this stuff have you had?"

"Two. I'm marrying Amelia Drake a week from Saturday, and I'm resurrecting her father's lumberyard."

Richard's glass stopped halfway to his mouth, his expression stunned.

"What do I need to do to stop the foreclosure?" Kyle asked.

"Wait a minute!" Richard lowered his mug and shook his head. "What's going on? You just said you were marrying Miss Drake, but I saw her this morning and she didn't say a word about it."

Kyle shrugged. "I proposed earlier this evening."

Richard stared in silence.

"You're invited to the wedding." Kyle gazed out into the darkness. What was he going to do with a wife? Before he'd left Amelia's apartment, she'd requested that they tell everyone their romantic interest in each other had started the day after her father died. She intended to say that Kyle's compassion won her heart and that they wanted to marry. To avoid scandal and upsetting their mothers, Kyle had agreed. But the lie tasted bitter.

He didn't want a wife. He liked his life just as it was—unencumbered by attachments, free of emotional ties that would strangle him.

Maybe he should have walked out. He could have lived with the whispered speculation from the ladies and sly grins from the men. But if word got out that he had been found in her apartment, she would be ostracized. He couldn't do that to her.

With a silent oath, Kyle cursed society, propriety, and his pathetic inability to escape the shackles he'd just closed around his own wrists. Through his own stupidity he'd bound himself to a debt-ridden lumberyard and a woman who was going to hate him and make his life miserable.

Richard shook his head as if trying to clear his thoughts. "Catherine hasn't said a word about you seeing Miss Drake."

"Why should she?" Kyle asked, wondering if Richard was hinting that he knew about Kyle's recent affair with his step-mother. "Miss Drake is a teacher. We've had to keep our relationship private."

"Well, where does that leave Catherine then?" Richard asked.

"What you mean?"

Their gazes locked for several tense seconds until Richard shrugged. "I just wanted to know if I can bring her to the wedding." He gave Kyle a sheepish grin. "She hasn't gotten out much since my father passed away. She would enjoy the wedding... that is, if you're inviting me to your ceremony."

Kyle's stomach knotted. He'd been a fool to think things couldn't get worse. Although Richard had invited himself, Kyle really wanted his friend at his wedding. That meant he couldn't refuse to invite Catherine without being rude or causing suspicion.

"Of course, Richard. I'm sure Lucinda will be there, too." If Kyle remembered right, Catherine's youngest sister was one of Amelia's friends. At least she had appeared to be during their school years. Kyle didn't even know what company Amelia kept. Their marriage was going to be a disaster.

⚓

"Mama, do you remember asking if I ever wanted to marry?" Amelia asked.

A look of expectancy and concern etched her mother's face as she glanced between Amelia and Kyle, who were standing in the foyer. "I remember, why?"

"At the time, I didn't think I ever would." Amelia tried to smile, but her lips were too stiff. "I've changed my mind. I'm getting married."

For the first time in her life, Amelia saw her mother's bottom hit a chair without an excess of hoisting skirts and fluttering hands. "You what?"

"I asked your daughter to marry me last night," Kyle interjected, his statement straightforward but quiet and respectful.

Her mother's expression brimmed with disbelief. "You're getting married? The two of you?"

Amelia nodded and glanced at Kyle who stood beside her doing a terrible job of looking pleased about their engagement. He'd worn the same expression an hour ago when they'd told his mother about their wedding plans. Amelia had expected Nancy to be upset or suspicious of the circumstances, but she'd seemed sincerely pleased and had said it was high time Kyle shared his life with a good, loving woman.

"But Kyle has already paid for the mill," her mother said, glancing between Amelia and Kyle, confusion filling her eyes.

"He's not marrying me for the mill, Mama."

"He's not?"

Amelia shook her head, trying to keep her heartache from showing.

Her mother's brows furrowed. "You barely know each other."

Amelia gazed up at Kyle with what she hoped to be a convincing display of adoration, but inside she trembled. Unable to bear his stoic expression, she turned back to her mother. "Since Papa's collapse, Kyle's compassion and kindness have eased my heartache and given me someone to depend on. You were right about me needing a man in my life, Mama, so I've accepted Kyle's offer of marriage."

Her mother sagged against the back of the brocade chair and stared up at Kyle. "What is she talking about?"

"She's telling you that we're two adults who are old enough to understand the commitment we're making."

Amelia's heart ached because Kyle wasn't professing his love, but he was a man who wouldn't lie to anyone for any purpose.

Her mother laughed with a touch of hysteria then shook her head. "You two are serious?"

"Yes, Mama."

"Very serious," Kyle added.

Silence descended then slowly mushroomed through the room until the standing clock in the foyer sounded like an iron hand maul striking a stone. "Are you doing this for me?" her mother asked.

Amelia would never admit that her mother's security and peace of mind was a major part of her motivation for marrying Kyle, but a straight denial wouldn't convince an astute woman like her, nor would it be the complete truth. Knowing only one way to convince her mother, Amelia cupped Kyle's chin and planted a kiss on his mouth. "Does that answer your question, Mama?" The astonished expression on her mother's face matched Kyle's and made Amelia laugh, but she prayed she didn't sound as hysterically insane as she felt.

"Well, I... my goodness." Her mother pressed a hand to her chest and her eyes misted. "I'd always hoped for the day when you'd make this announcement, but I thought your father would be beside me and that we'd... that he would... oh, honey, he would have wanted to give you away." Tears spilled over her lower lids.

Amelia pulled her mother into her arms. She glanced at Kyle and saw compassion pooling in his dark eyes and was relieved that his heart wasn't immune to someone else's suffering.

Her mother patted her face with her handkerchief and straightened her shoulders. "So much has happened lately that I'm just overcome with everything."

Amelia bit her lip. She was overcome, too. With loss. With sorrow. With regret.

"When are you planning to wed?" her mother asked, stepping out of the circle of Amelia's embrace.

Kyle tapped his hat against his thigh. "A week from this Saturday unless it puts too much of a burden on you."

After a moment of surprise, her mother squinted at them. "There is something you're trying to keep from me, isn't there?"

"Yes," Kyle said.

Amelia's stomach flipped. They'd agreed not to concern her mother with any of the circumstances surrounding their engagement. If he broke his word she would kick him right in his sore shin again.

"We want to make sure there's no slight to Amelia's reputation because of my visit to the school yesterday."

Her mother's expression filled with horror and she looked at Amelia. "What did you two do?"

"Nothing, Mama. Kyle came to propose to me and the board members found him in my apartment. That's why we want to marry right away."

"Then you're marrying Amelia to protect her reputation?"

"Yes." Kyle glanced at Amelia, but she couldn't read the emotion in his eyes. He turned back to her mother. "I should have waited for a more appropriate time to talk to your daughter, but my impatience brought me to the school and has jeopardized her reputation. Amelia accepted my proposal last night. With your permission, we would like to move forward with our wedding plans."

"Well, I... I'm shocked by your announcement, but if you're sincere, Kyle then I'll welcome you as my son-in-law. Tom would have been so pleased by this." Her nostrils flared, but Amelia gave her mother credit for not crying. "We'll have the wedding here unless you object."

"Whatever makes Amelia happy," he said, but Amelia couldn't tell if he was being sincere or sarcastic.

Chapter Ten

On Saturday evening Amelia met Jeb in the upstairs hall of her mother's house. Because of her fabricated story, everyone waiting below would expect her to be happy about marrying Kyle. She wasn't happy. She was heartbroken.

"I'm sorry your pa's not here to do this," Jeb said, his face drawn and eyes tired as he held her hand. "He would tell you how beautiful you look and how proud you've made him. I will tell you the same thing."

"Thank you, Jeb. It means so much that you're doing this."

He angled his head to see her eyes. "Are you sure this is what you want?" he asked. "It's awfully sudden."

Amelia tensed, afraid that her apprehension was apparent in her expression, that Jeb could sense her reservations about marrying Kyle. Jeb and her mother had enough to worry about. "I'm just sad about Papa. That's all."

Jeb studied her with sharp interest and Amelia forced a smile. "Truly."

"All right then. Let's get down there before I embarrass myself and start blubbering." He hooked her hand in the crook of his elbow and guided Amelia to the top of the stairs.

She gazed down at her guests. Their faces were lifted to watch her descend the stairs. Her mother stood with Agatha Brown and Nancy Grayson at the front of the crowd. Evelyn glowed like an emerald in her deep green dress. Lucinda stood beside Duke, looking angelic in her gown of sky-blue satin, her pleasure at being Amelia's maid of honor obvious in her smile. Radford held Rebecca and stood at the back of the crowd with Boyd—and Richard Cameron.

Catherine Cameron stood beside Richard looking shy and uncomfortable, but it was the sight of Richard standing in her parlor on her wedding day, a mere week after propositioning her, that sent a brutal jolt through her. Her heart thundered as she fought her panic.

She had forgotten that Richard was Kyle's friend. Kyle didn't know about the brief romance she'd shared with Richard during his first summer home from college.

Amelia gripped the railing and reminded herself to breathe, to keep her legs beneath her. Whatever happened she would keep her chin in the air. She had to convince her guests and her mother that she was happy, that she wanted to marry Kyle, and she would die before letting Richard know otherwise.

With that thought in mind she kept her eyes on Kyle. She told herself it didn't matter that he was angry with her, that he was too arrogant and ambitious, that she'd had to marry him. It could have been worse. It could have been Richard waiting for her in some clandestine place, shredding her self-esteem each time he walked away without offering to marry her.

In that moment, Amelia knew she'd made the right decision. She was able to appreciate how handsome her future husband looked in his dark brown suit and starched tan shirt that closed at his throat with a matching bow tie. He stood tall and proud with his face lifted toward her as she descended the last steps. She dredged up a ghost of a smile, but his dark eyes revealed a hard, guarded businessman who was simply assuming a burden he felt was his responsibility.

Amelia had suddenly become an actress in a tragic play.

She would find a way to be gracious to Richard, a man she wanted to forget and to ignore Kyle's coldness so she could speak her vows with him. She couldn't imagine how deep she would have to dig to be able to consummate those vows, or to bridge Kyle's resentment and make their marriage into more than a mistake.

Her legs trembled as she and Jeb stepped onto the parquet floor then moved to stand next to Kyle and Duke. Pastor Ainslie climbed onto the first stair tread and turned to their guests. "Who gives this woman's hand in marriage?"

"Her mother," Jeb said. "And me." He placed Amelia's hand in Kyle's waiting palm then stepped back to stand beside her mother.

Kyle squeezed Amelia's hand and she glanced at him in surprise. Though she was expected to be sad because of her father's recent passing, she had to look at Kyle with love in her eyes, not dread.

She managed a tremulous smile and he returned it with an encouraging nod. They turned toward the pastor who asked her to love, honor, and obey her husband, and Amelia promised she would and prayed she could. Kyle vowed to love, honor, and protect his wife, and Amelia silently asked him to add the word *forgive* to his vows.

"Is there anyone present who has a reason to protest this marriage?" the pastor asked, and Amelia knew she was going to faint. She couldn't even breathe as she imagined Richard lifting his blond head to announce that she was a fraud, that only a few days ago, she'd been considering the proposition of becoming his mistress. The silence in the room deepened, lasting an eternity before the pastor smiled and closed his Bible. "You may kiss your wife, Mr. Grayson."

Kyle sealed their vows with a brief kiss.

Amelia pulled back, but summoned a believable smile for her husband. Her *husband*. Her stomach wrenched so hard it nearly doubled her over.

Kyle tightened his grip on her arms and pulled her close, making it look as if he were kissing her cheek. "Are you all right?" he whispered.

She nodded, but she was definitely not all right. How on earth would she convince her mind and body in the next few hours that she must become this man's wife?

"We'll leave early," he said, and her stomach took another wild turn.

"Quit mauling the bride," Duke said with a laugh. He and Lucinda offered their best wishes as everyone surged forward to do the same.

"Be good to each other, honey." Her mother gave Amelia a fierce hug then she turned to remind Kyle of his duty.

Amelia found Evelyn and they embraced, rocking in warm silence. "I'm so happy for you," Evelyn said, sincerity and joy flowing from her voice. "Kyle needs you in his life. He might seem hard-edged at times, but that's only a cover when he can't express what's in his heart."

Amelia drew back and stared at Evelyn, but before she could encourage her friend to reveal more about Kyle, Boyd hooked his arm around her shoulders. "Don't believe a word Evelyn says. I've known Kyle as long as she has and he's as stubborn as a mule. You'd have done better to marry me," he declared with a flirtatious wink.

For the first time in over three weeks Amelia found an honest smile. "I suppose you feel safe proposing to me now that I'm married to your brother?"

Boyd grinned and she almost felt sorry for the woman who would try to tame him. If he had ever turned that look on her with sincere interest, he would have owned her body and soul. His eyes twinkled and he gave her shoulders a light squeeze. "Welcome to the family, sis. Now, I'm dying to know what on earth attracted you to my brother."

Amelia couldn't deny being attracted to her own husband, but she found herself unable to expound on Kyle's virtues when he was staring straight at her.

Kyle joined the group with Duke and Radford in tow and Boyd lowered his arm, stepping back to stand beside Lucinda Clark and her sister Catherine.

Lucinda smiled at him, but it was a friendly exchange rather than flirtatious. "Actually, that's a very good question, Boyd." Lucinda's green eyes revealed a hint of mischief that Amelia had never seen before. "But I'd rather know what men find most attractive in a woman."

Instead of answering, Boyd grabbed Richard by the coat sleeve and pulled him into their circle. "We need your opinion on something."

Hearing the commotion, everyone else in the parlor turned their attention to the small cluster surrounding Kyle and Amelia, and the two of them exchanged a glance that suggested they'd both prefer to be anywhere else in the world.

"Lucinda wants to know what men find most attractive in a woman. I say it's her figure," Boyd said.

"That's not true," Radford interrupted. "A woman's hair is the first thing a man looks at."

He winked at Evelyn and she laughed, a bright smile lighting her beautiful face. "Let's take a census. Duke, what attracts you to a woman?"

"Her cooking abilities." His answer made all of them laugh and the heat that had branded Amelia's face began to lessen. Perhaps she was taking this all too seriously. Perhaps they were all just having a bit of fun to celebrate the evening.

Boyd nudged Richard in the ribs. "Well?" he prompted. "What do you think?"

Richard looked at Amelia and her breath jammed in her lungs. She pressed a fist beneath her rib cage, silently cursing Kyle for inviting him. How could Richard stand there looking so innocent while knowing he'd taken the gift Amelia was supposed to give her husband?

With a glance at his step-mother, Catherine, that seemed rich with unspoken meaning, Richard slowly shifted his gaze to her youngest sister Lucinda. The adoration in his expression was enough to make Amelia's stomach burn. The wretch! The traitor! He hadn't wanted her at all! Sweat prickled her neck and she clenched her fists. Richard had looked at her like that once, as if she had the power to take him to his knees, but Amelia had learned that Richard ultimately held the power.

Feeling protective of her friend, Amelia had to bite her lip when Richard kissed Lucinda's hand. "The most attractive thing about a woman is her smile," Richard said, but he didn't laugh, nor did he spare Amelia another glance. His eyes and his attention were for Lucinda whose soft laugh stayed in the circle of their group instead of ringing through the room like a desperate attempt to draw attention to herself. Lucinda didn't need to beg for attention. Men's eyes were automatically drawn to the petite, slender blonde with slanted green eyes and an angelic smile.

Boyd nudged Richard in the ribs. "If you're not going to propose, get out of my way so I can."

With a laugh, Richard released Lucinda's hand. "Spare your pride, Boyd. I think Lucinda would decline both of us. But perhaps Catherine would be kind enough to suffer our attention for a while this evening."

Catherine's smile faltered, but Evelyn saved her from having to comment, by asking Jeb, "What's your opinion on attraction?"

Jeb glanced at Amelia's mother, who had been quiet all evening, her heartache apparent despite her efforts to smile. "Their eyes," he said. "The way they show everything a woman is feeling."

Jeb's words touched Amelia, but it was the shadow of sadness in Boyd's eyes that intrigued her.

Evelyn tapped Kyle on the arm. "Your turn, and don't try to get out of answering."

He released an exasperated sigh. "All right. It's a woman's intelligence."

Boyd and Richard burst out laughing and the ladies pretended to swoon. Radford and Duke grinned like idiots, but Amelia looked at him in surprise. He valued intelligence?

He folded his arms across his chest and glared at his male companions. "What?" he asked through gritted teeth.

"Matt Carson claims he married Charlotte Ladamere because he loved her mind." Boyd hooted. "Every man in this town has loved more than Charlotte's mind, Kyle."

"I haven't."

"Well, there's one," Boyd said, not in the least chagrined at his crude statement in front of the ladies.

"Two," Radford said, slipping his arm around Evelyn's shoulders.

Duke arched a censuring brow at Boyd. "Three."

Boyd held up a hand. "Don't even say it, Jeb and Richard." He looked at Kyle. "You can't tell me a woman's intelligence is so attractive that her reputation doesn't matter."

Richard's eyes locked with Amelia's. As if someone had pulled a plug from her lungs, her breath rushed out so fast she nearly lost her supper.

"If the rumors are true about Charlotte," Kyle said, "then it obviously didn't matter to Matthew."

"Then you're saying it shouldn't matter whether a bride is pure or not?"

"I didn't say that," he countered, irritation filling his voice. "I just said it may not have bothered Matthew."

"Which implies that it would matter to you?"

"Of course it would!" Kyle said. "Now stop being an idiot. You're embarrassing the ladies."

Richard glanced away, but Amelia knew he'd seen the shame in her eyes. She could have killed him in that instant. Her hands trembled and her fingers itched to rake his handsome face. He'd ruined her reputation and would have thought nothing of doing it again, had she been inclined to accept his offer.

She stepped from the cluster of friends and family who were there to celebrate a marriage that would never be more than a business arrangement at best—a nightmare at worst. "I'll get some glasses for our toast," she said. Before anyone could offer to help, she hurried across the room, praying she'd make it to the kitchen before she threw up.

Kyle leaned in the kitchen doorway watching Amelia at the counter arranging glasses on a serving tray. She wore her hair in a loose twist up the back of her head. Though her gown of midnight black was fancy enough for their wedding while still being appropriate for mourning her father, it looked sleek and provocative to him.

His gaze swept from her magnificent hair to her midnight hem and he imagined sliding the gown off her shoulders and unpinning her hair. Soon they would be alone and he would sink his fingers into the autumn strands and pull her down beneath him. That was the only positive thing he could say about this whole wretched mess.

She turned toward him then and his heart jolted. She looked panicked and near tears, her gaze darting around the kitchen as if she wanted to escape.

He levered himself off the doorframe and shook his head to clear the image of her in his bed. "What troubles you?" he asked, crossing the kitchen.

She cast a nervous glance toward the kitchen door. "We've made a dreadful mistake. I'm not the right woman for you."

"Isn't it a little late to be having this conversation?"

She met his eyes, her own filled with fear. "What if you find out that you don't like me? What if we're miserable together? What if you hate the way I keep house, and I dislike your sense of humor? What if we're not suited at all?"

"If you're trying to tell me that I'm not the man for you, I'll walk back in there and end this now."

"No!" Amelia sagged against the sink. "It's not you, Kyle. I didn't mean that at all."

"Then what is it?"

"I'm not... I... I'm afraid that you'll regret this night for the rest of your life. I'm afraid that you'll never forgive me for... forcing our marriage."

Her fear was unnerving him. He drew her into his arms because he didn't know what else to do, but he couldn't calm her fears when she was expressing his own so eloquently.

She buried her face in his chest. "How will we spend our whole lives together if we don't even like each other?"

A loud knock on the wall jerked his attention to the doorway where he could just see Boyd's shoulder and his finger pointing toward the parlor. Whatever anger Boyd still harbored toward Kyle for keeping him from buying the tavern, he'd found a way to set it aside for the evening. Kyle still had three weeks to come up with Boyd's money, but he suspected they both knew it would never happen. Still, instead of being a pain in the neck tonight, Boyd was warning Kyle that someone was on their way into the kitchen.

"We've got company," Kyle said. He reached over and picked up the tray just as his mother walked in. "I'll take these in," he said to Amelia then turned and left the room.

"I thought you might need some help, but I think I've accidentally made myself an intrusive mother-in-law."

Amelia tried to smile at Nancy Grayson, but her lips were too stiff to respond. "I was just feeling faint."

"You look pale," Nancy said with genuine concern.

It was because Amelia had suffered an attack of conscience, but hadn't been able to fumble her way through a confession. Kyle lived by a rigid standard of honor. He believed he'd married a virgin and he would never forgive her for lying to him.

Amelia placed her palm on her jittery stomach. "I've been nauseous all day," she said, knowing it was from the thought of playing out their farce of a wedding.

"I raced from church more Sunday mornings than I could count when I was carrying the boys."

Amelia gasped. "I'm not expecting a child! Is that what you heard? Are people saying that's why Kyle is marrying me?"

Surprise filled Nancy's expression. "Of course not. I was just trying in my awkward way to say that I understand how uncomfortable it is to suffer stomach upset. I'm sorry I offended you, dear." She patted Amelia's hand then turned toward the parlor and called for Kyle.

A second later he appeared in the open doorway, his expression filled with concern.

"You'd better have your toast then take your bride home. She's not feeling well."

Amelia watched the color drain from Kyle's face and knew her own expression must mirror his. They had an unfinished conversation hanging between them like a primed powder keg.

Chapter Eleven

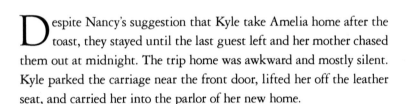

Despite Nancy's suggestion that Kyle take Amelia home after the toast, they stayed until the last guest left and her mother chased them out at midnight. The trip home was awkward and mostly silent. Kyle parked the carriage near the front door, lifted her off the leather seat, and carried her into the parlor of her new home.

"I'll be back after I take care of the horses," he said, standing her on her feet beside the sofa then he ducked back outside, leaving her with a low-burning lantern for company.

Thankful for a moment alone, she turned in circle to view her new home, but it was too dark to make out more than shadows. She thought about turning up the lantern, but felt too exhausted to care about anything other than putting her feet up and closing her eyes.

Twenty minutes must have passed before Kyle returned carrying her valise. He stepped inside and glanced through the dimly lit room before spotting her on the sofa. "Why didn't you turn up the lantern?"

"The dark felt peaceful after the noise at the reception."

Without commenting, he took her valise to the back of the house and returned a minute later, his limp more pronounced than earlier in the evening. He shrugged out of his suit coat and draped it across the back of a chair then faced her. The silence was awkward and she glanced away.

"I can show you the house if you like," he said.

"I'd rather wait until tomorrow, if you don't mind."

"I don't. I'd like to sit down for a few minutes before bed."

Instead of sitting in the parlor chair, he took her hand and pulled her to her feet. Without a word, he led her down the same hallway he'd disappeared into a few minutes earlier and then guided her into a room lit only by a smoldering fire. Two wing chairs were angled invitingly toward the fireplace and Amelia realized they were in his bedroom. *Their* bedroom.

Despite her trepidation, she absorbed the beauty of the room and wished she would have asked him to show her the rest of the house. "Where are your lanterns?" she asked, casting a nervous glance around the shadowed room.

"There's one on the chest of drawers and another on the bureau." Kyle stoked the fire, added a small log then stood as the flames began to circle the chunks of crackling wood. "I like it better without them."

So did she if he was planning to undress her. The darker the better. She eyed a thick afghan draped over the back of a padded chair. The evenings were still cool in late May and she longed to sit down, to bury herself in the yards of soft wool and just sleep for the rest of her life. Instead, she curled her sore toes, fighting the urge to remove her shoes and sink her feet into the soft rug beneath the chairs.

Kyle stepped behind her and slipped the wrap off her shoulders. "I'll be back in a minute," he said then laid her wrap over the footboard of his bed as he left the room.

Her neck ached with tension. She sat down and closed her eyes, trying to release the pain between her shoulder blades. Maybe if she told him now, before they made love, he wouldn't be as upset. Maybe he would forgive her. Maybe he wouldn't even care about something that happened so far in the past. But what if he did? What if he felt he'd been cheated and decided to annul their marriage? She'd be left with a ruined reputation and no security for herself or her mother. Worse yet, what if she told Kyle and he wanted the name of the man she'd given her virginity to? She could never tell Kyle that she'd given her virginity to his friend.

The clinking sound of metal against porcelain startled her and Amelia opened her eyes to see Kyle placing a tray on the table between them.

"I hope you like tea," he said, handing her a cup.

Surprised by his thoughtfulness, Amelia wrapped her fingers around the heat of the porcelain teacup and sipped the hot liquid more for diversion than from a desire to drink.

Kyle sat in the opposite chair and propped his elbows on his knees, cradling the cup in his large hands. "James Hale didn't cancel the shipbuilding contract he has with us," he said, reminding Amelia of why they'd had to wait a week to marry. Kyle had needed to go to Philadelphia to renegotiate a contract for deck beams that James Hale had set up with her father. "We have six weeks to get our deliveries straightened out. If we can't manage it, they'll cancel the contract."

She'd expected Kyle to bring up their earlier conversation, or try to ease her anxiety over consummating their vows, yet here he was on their wedding night talking business. Most women would have despised him for that. She could have kissed his feet.

"Can we do it?" she asked, glad to keep their conversation on business.

"We have to," he said, staring down into his cup.

He was so handsome when he wasn't frowning. The firelight warmed his hair to dark auburn and Amelia wished with all her heart that their situation were different. If only this night had been the result of a breathless first meeting where Kyle kissed her hand and asked permission to court her. She would have said yes, of course. Then they would have fallen in love and Kyle would have proposed and they would have married and he would kiss her as if she were the woman of his dreams. Amelia would slip into his arms, guilt-free and willing. That's how she'd always dreamed her wedding night would be.

But life didn't work like that. It moved too fast, swept away her dreams before she was ready to let them go, assaulted her senses and left her reeling. Like now, when she needed someone to hold on to and all she had was herself and a mountain of regret.

She raised her eyes and found him watching her, studying her as if trying to memorize her face. The intensity of his stare reminded her that they were alone and would be making love before the night was over. Soon, if his look was any indication of his intentions.

She inched back in her chair, her hands shaking so badly she was afraid she would spill what was left of her tea. Her stomach churned with apprehension and her shoulders tightened. She wasn't ready yet.

"Are you cold?"

Her arms were solid goose bumps, but she shook her head, her mind busy seeking a way to divert his attention and lessen the intensity in his eyes.

"I know you didn't want this marriage, Kyle, but I honestly had no other choice."

"I own as much of the blame as you do."

"I'm glad you're willing to admit it." His eyebrows lifted and her stomach tightened. "That wasn't meant to be insulting. I just don't want us to resent each other. I'm hoping that... you'll accept our marriage."

"We took our vows together, didn't we?"

She gulped a breath and forced herself not to look away. "I meant that I'd like us to find a way to be comfortable with each other."

He took the cup from her trembling hands and drew her out of the chair. "It's late. Why don't you get ready for bed?"

That he didn't want to talk was painfully obvious, but Amelia wanted to protest, to stall their consummation until they connected in some small way, but she couldn't speak, couldn't think of any other reason to delay him.

Although she was standing, she had to lift her chin to see Kyle's shadowed face.

He was studying her again, intently, his eyes dark, hungry. "I like your hair down," he said quietly, then left the room.

Chapter Twelve

Amelia yanked off her dress and undergarments on the way to the washstand. She needed time to make a plan, to figure out if it was possible to soothe Kyle's resentment and win his heart. Maybe if she feigned sleep he wouldn't wake her, wouldn't demand his husbandly rights. Tomorrow she could decide what to do, how to tell him, when to tell him. She would stall for time and when Kyle finally discovered the truth about her, he would care too deeply to hate her.

She scrubbed herself with the clean washcloth he'd left beside the wash-basin then with fumbling fingers, she pulled the pins from her hair. She dragged her nightrail from her valise and struggled into it on the way to the bed, but had barely turned back the covers when Kyle came into the room.

"Wait a minute, Amelia." His request was spoken softly, but she knew it was the second official order from her husband. She'd already taken her hair down. Now, ready or not, she was legally bound to follow the rest of his orders.

Her heart leapt and she folded her hands in front of her gown, feeling exposed and vulnerable in the flickering firelight.

His feet were bare. He'd pulled his shirt out of his trousers and it hung open in front. Droplets of water still speckled his collarbone. Golden-brown hair fanned across the muscled mounds of his chest. Amelia always wondered if the hair on a man's chest was coarse or soft, and she was about to find out. Richard had never taken his clothes off.

Kyle shrugged out of his shirt and tossed it over the back of the chair that she'd been sitting in earlier. He was tall, handsome, and breathlessly overwhelming. The tremble began in her stomach and bled outward until her legs quaked and her teeth chattered. She clenched her hands together and pressed her hip against the bed, but it didn't stop her shaking.

Suddenly, Kyle was standing in front of her clothed only in his trousers that were unbuttoned far below the level Amelia allowed her gaze to drop.

"Come here," he said, but it was an invitation this time instead of an order.

She stepped into the circle of his arms and leaned against his solid body to keep herself upright.

He rubbed his hands down her spine in long, bold strokes then across the tense muscles in her back, and up to the knotted cords in her neck. His fingers traced the curves of her back until she felt her body melting. He didn't talk to her, didn't try to calm her with words, but she hadn't expected him to. She'd expected anger. She'd expected punishment for trapping him into a marriage he didn't want. Not gentle hands and pleasurable feelings that were driving her out of her mind.

She tipped her head back to look up at him, to apologize, to beg for one night of abstinence, but he slipped his fingers into her hair and cradled her head in his large hands. Their eyes met as he lowered his mouth to kiss her. Soft, warm, unbelievably wonderful lips moved across hers. Amelia's eyes drifted closed. He deepened the kiss until she splayed her fingers across the bare skin of his back to steady herself.

She was lost and beginning not to care if she ever found her way back.

He drew her down onto the bed.

She went willingly.

He stretched out beside her.

Her heart pounded and her breath came in short spurts.

Still, he didn't speak a word, just looked at her from dark, passion-filled eyes. He brushed her hair off her face, his gaze roving over her as his fingers followed the crest of her cheekbone. He trailed his thumb across her lips. Rough skin and a hint of soap touched her tongue and her senses whirled.

He found her mouth again and kissed her. Suddenly, it seemed they'd both caught fire. Heat burned through her veins as he deepened the kiss. His hands fisted in her hair as he stroked her mouth with his tongue, pressing his hard-muscled body against her.

She was melting like wax in the sun.

He nibbled and caressed her breast through her gown. As he slipped his fingers between her thighs, she forgot everything but the feel of him touching her, of his warm, wonderful mouth on her breast and his fingers, oh, merciful heaven, his bold probing fingers...

Everything below her waist liquefied and she welcomed the throbbing pleasure spreading through her body.

She touched the glorious crisp hair and hard muscles of his chest, wanting to explore the textures of his skin, to learn the hills and valleys of his body.

"Lift your gown," he breathed near her ear, but he didn't wait for her to do so. He trembled and shifted off her then wrestled with something until the bed shook. An instant later he reached down and pushed her gown to her waist. He moved over her and settled himself between her legs, his bare skin brushing hers as he pressed himself into the juncture of her thighs.

That's when she realized he'd removed his pants.

His intense gaze left no doubt in her mind that he was ready to consummate their marriage. Now.

"Unbutton your gown," he said, his voice hoarse, his eyes so dark she was suddenly afraid not to obey him even though she knew she wouldn't. "I don't want anything between us."

It was more than her gown between them and Amelia knew without a doubt he wouldn't be able to accept it. He'd made it clear during their wedding reception that a woman's virtue mattered to a man—to him.

Despite his hard-edged manner and rigid standards, there was gentleness in Kyle, and she wanted a chance to know that private side of her husband. It felt too good to be held in his arms, to be touched and kissed and have glimpses of his tenderness, to risk losing it all because his opinion of her might change. She wanted more from him and from their marriage. If not love then at least respect.

He balanced his weight on his elbows, waiting for her to disrobe. She didn't move.

"We can leave it for tonight," he said, as the weight of his hips began pressing her thighs apart.

She stiffened her legs to hold him back. "I don't want to," she whispered, afraid to look at him, afraid to see his reaction.

He hooked her chin with his thumb and forced her to meet his eyes. "If it makes you uncomfortable, I won't ask that tonight. Just relax your legs for me."

In her heart, she wanted to please her husband, but to submit to him would destroy their future because he would know he wasn't her first, that she wasn't the pure woman he perceived her to be. She squeezed her eyes shut. "I can't."

"You can," he said quietly then shifted his hips to better accommodate himself.

She braced her hands against his chest. "This is too soon."

"I can touch you more" he said, his arms trembling from holding himself back, the hardness of him brushing her private place. She could feel the tension in his body like a drawn bow, waiting to be released.

She shook her head. "I just want to stop," she whispered.

"I won't hurt you," he promised, his breath soft against her ear.

His promise chilled her. Those were the exact words Richard had used before he'd annihilated her hopes. Kyle was her husband. He had a right to her body. But at the moment he was just another man who was going to take what he wanted. She couldn't stop him. Kyle could force the consummation and he would hate her.

She refused to spend the rest of her life trying to live up to his high standards without having a chance to win his love. No matter what mistakes she'd made in the past, she deserved a chance at happiness. She arched her back and shoved at his chest.

"What are you doing?" He grasped her arms to stop her from toppling them off the bed.

Tangled in the sheet with her legs straddling his hips and his hands gripping her arms, Amelia felt an endless wave of panic cut off her breath. She couldn't let him find out. Not yet. She *deserved* her one chance at happiness.

He pinned her beneath him, staring at her in shock, panting from the struggle as he sprawled across her trembling body. "What is the matter?"

His hips were still between her legs and there was nothing to stop him from pushing inside her. Her throat closed and tears of shame rolled down her cheeks. They hadn't even had a chance to talk yet, to become friends, to fall in love.

She didn't even know what he liked for breakfast.

She pushed his hand off her waist, knowing it wouldn't matter how many times she pushed him away. He was even stronger than Richard. She turned her head and buried her face in the crook of her arm.

"Amelia, I'm sorry." He brushed her hair off her face. "I'm sorry."

He lifted off her and she jerked her knees up, pressing her thighs together, but Kyle didn't pry them apart like Richard had done their last time together.

He moved to her side. "I didn't mean to frighten you."

He hadn't. It was her fear of his hatred that had made her panic. "I'm sorry," she said, meeting his eyes, her own blurred by tears. "I truly am, Kyle, but I... just can't do this yet. I know you can force things if you want to."

He jerked back as if she'd slapped his face. "I will never force you."

"I couldn't stop you." She turned her face away, despising the tremble in her voice. At seventeen she'd been too young to understand that an impassioned man could turn violent when a girl changed her mind about making love. She'd learned that lesson from Richard. Kyle's inflamed body was demanding release and it was cruel for her to deny him.

He cupped her jaw and forced her to look at him. "Who hurt you?" he asked quietly. "Was it the same man who taught you how to kiss?"

A horrified gasp burst from her and she stared at him, praying he hadn't guessed her secret.

"A woman doesn't kiss like this unless she's done it before."

She didn't respond, couldn't begin to tell him what Richard had taught her that summer, what mix of pleasure and shame he'd introduced to her life.

"I have never played with a woman's affections or taken anything they didn't willingly offer. I can't say it any plainer than that, Amelia. I expect us to be intimate, but when I take you to bed, I don't want to see your eyes filled with fear."

Her throat ached. This was supposed to have been the best night of her life. This was supposed to be a celebration of love and passion, not guilt and dread.

In her shame, she couldn't respond. Kyle heaved a sigh and rolled to his back, draping an arm over his eyes. The clock on the nightstand ticked in the silence and mingled with his ragged breathing.

"I'm sorry," she whispered. "I'm so sorry."

With a hard sigh, he turned away, giving her a shadowed view of his back and wide shoulders. "I'll wait a night."

Chapter Thirteen

Sunlight streamed in through the huge bedroom window and Amelia squinted as she braced up on an elbow. She rubbed her eyes, feeling disoriented and anxious. The room was wide and long and filled with light. Thick oak beams glowed warmly overhead. The bedcovers were dark and masculine beneath her curious fingers but wonderfully soft against her skin.

Her gaze settled on the fireplace, cold now, but familiar enough that she remembered where she was. She had sat in one of the burgundy brocade chairs the night before, drinking tea with her husband. Then she'd slept in his bed all night without consummating their marriage.

Shame burned through her and she glanced over her shoulder expecting to see Kyle stretched out beside her. He wasn't there, the coolness of the sheets indicating he'd been gone for a while.

She glanced at the clock on the nightstand and nearly stopped breathing. How long had he been waiting for his breakfast? She threw back the covers, leapt from bed, and yanked on her lightweight wrapper.

She rushed into the hall, but stopped outside the bedroom door, uncertain which direction to head. There was a door across from her and another to her right at the end of the hall. To her left and several feet down, the hallway appeared to open into a large room that Amelia assumed to be the main part of the house. She hurried in that direction and found herself in the parlor that Kyle had carried her into last night. Diagonally across from her was another open door and she rushed to it, praying it was the kitchen.

The room was occupied by a small bed and dresser instead of a stove and sink. Frustrated, she swept her tangled hair behind her shoulders, and turned back, her eyes frantically scanning the parlor.

Kyle leaned in a doorway across the room watching her.

She gasped and pressed a hand to her chest. "I had no idea it was so late. I was just looking for the kitchen."

"It's in here." He gestured with his chin toward the room behind him.

He was dressed for church, wearing a navy blue jacket and trousers with a white dress shirt and navy bow tie. Remembering how he'd looked last night with his skin bare and his hair mussed, his eyes stormy as his hands and mouth moved over her body made Amelia's insides melt. She'd lain awake for hours aching to finish what they'd started, knowing she couldn't. Seeing him now, so handsome as he stood in a swatch of sunshine angling through the parlor window, reinforced her desire to share a loving union with him.

"You should have woken me," she said, tugging the belt on her wrapper tighter as she started toward him. "I'll have breakfast ready in a minute."

"It's already on the table."

Her head snapped up and her footsteps faltered.

"Habit," he said with a shrug. "I'm used to doing for myself."

"I'm sorry, Kyle." Amelia hung her head. Not only had he been cheated out of his rightful wedding night, but he'd had to make his own breakfast. "I'd hoped to do a better job than this."

She heard the whisper of his clothing as he moved forward, saw his black Sunday shoes stop in front of her. He tipped her chin up until she looked at him. "I don't care about breakfast."

"You shouldn't have had to do this."

"You'll probably wish I hadn't when you taste my eggs. Come on. They'll be worse if they get cold."

Two plates filled with eggs and toast sat on a sturdy oak table in the middle of a gorgeous room. To her surprise the kitchen was accented by wallpaper in deep greens and rich burgundy swirls of color that brightened rather than darkened the room. A six-plate Acme stove was centered along the wall to her left, and straight ahead was a small icebox and a large sink surrounded by several feet of counter. Overhead a string of beautiful oak cabinets lined the wall. A small oak door, which she assumed to be the pantry, and a large window filled with sunshine, consumed the wall to her right. Awed by the beauty of the room, she stared at Kyle. "This is lovely."

"My brothers helped me build the house. Boyd made the cupboards and did most of the wood trim. I didn't have the patience for it."

He pulled out her chair then joined her at the table where they ate in awkward silence. Amelia inherently understood that Kyle wasn't one for small talk, but it rattled her that she knew nothing personal about her husband except that he had the ability to both frighten and excite her. She sensed a private, tender side that he guarded, but she also knew Kyle was every bit the tough businessman people believed him to be. How on earth was she going to find a way to appeal to both men?

The eggs were perfectly cooked, but her nervous stomach would only accept half of the meal he'd put on her plate. Kyle had finished ahead of her, but he waited until she'd wiped her mouth with the napkin and laid it beside her plate.

She glanced at him. "It was kind of you to do this."

He tipped his head in a slight nod of acknowledgment, but his gaze lingered, his eyes framed with an abundance of black lashes that she hadn't noticed last night in the shadows. His chest lifted and his lips parted, but whatever he'd thought to say stayed in his mouth.

Conscious of her mussed hair, she finger-combed it back and hooked it behind her ears. She stared down at her plate, embarrassed by her looks and by the awkwardness between them she didn't know how to lessen. "I should get ready for church."

As if eager to escape the tension, Kyle slid his chair away from the table. "I'll harness the horses. Will twenty minutes be enough time for you?"

"Yes. It'll only take a few minutes to clean up and get dressed." Amelia shoved her chair back and reached for the plates in one motion. She scooped up their silverware and stacked the plates together, but before she could straighten up, Kyle reached out and stilled her arm with a firm but careful grip. She clutched the plates and glanced up at him.

"I can wait for you, Amelia."

Her stomach flipped and her face heated. Was he purposely repeating the words he'd spoken last night to reassure her that she could trust him? Or was it his way of reminding her that he'd only promised to wait one night?

Surrounded by friends and family, Kyle sat in church beside his wife and new mother-in-law, feeling more alone than he ever had in his life. He'd always thought marriage would banish that empty feeling, but somehow it only seemed to emphasize it.

He didn't blame Amelia for needing time to settle in to their marriage and grow comfortable with him any more than he blamed Catherine for refusing to meet his eyes when he'd greeted her on the way into church. Even now, he could see Catherine out of the corner of his eye, sitting beside Richard with her face turned slightly away as if fighting the temptation to glance in Kyle's direction.

He knew it was respect and consideration that motivated her, not anger or resentment. Catherine still loved a man named Simon who'd died in the war. She'd confessed to Kyle after their first intimate engagement when he'd been so shocked by Catherine's unexpected virginity that he had proposed out of obligation. Richard's father, Alfred Cameron, had married Catherine, a woman twenty years his junior, in hopes of ending his sudden impotency. But Catherine's beauty and voluptuous body hadn't corrected his problem. The only thing they'd shared in their marriage had been friendship.

Though Catherine had been touched by Kyle's proposal, she'd never wanted more than friendship from him.

Still, he felt guilty for not having had the opportunity to tell Catherine he was marrying Amelia. Now he wished for a moment alone with her so he could thank her, so he could try, in his stumbling manner, to tell her what she'd meant to him. But all he could do was catch her eye and silently ask her to understand, to forgive his lack of tactfulness in ending their relationship.

He knew Catherine would want him to be happy in his marriage, just as he would wish the same for her. Unfortunately, he was learning that happiness was elusive and sporadic. There had been moments in his life when his laughter had come easy, when he'd felt a reckless burst of joy that fueled his passion for living, but mostly, life had been demanding and temperamental, sometimes even stingy.

His gaze slid to Amelia. Would she, too, prove to be demanding and temperamental? Or stingy? Would she ever evoke a natural burst of joy and laughter in him? Would she give him the passion he knew was bottled up inside her?

More importantly, what would he give her? Protection and security, for certain. Regardless of the circumstances of their forced marriage, Amelia deserved, and would have, his respect and fidelity, But emotionally Kyle had nothing left for anyone. Since the ordeal with Radford and Evelyn, Kyle had felt dead inside. Their betrayal had shattered his trust. He'd spent the past several months easing the ache in his chest, and now that he was finally breaking free of that weight, he wasn't willing to open himself again. Not even for his wife. They would share a house and a bed. That would have to be enough.

As if Amelia sensed his scrutiny, her lashes lifted and she looked up at him. Her eyes held unspoken feelings he couldn't read, a depth of sadness he knew he'd caused, a nervous shyness that warred with her curiosity to know him. He sensed her hidden desire to be touched, her fear of embracing passion, the unanswered questions she wouldn't ask.

What did she think of him? Was she really afraid of him or only apprehensive because of the newness of their relationship?

"Is something wrong?" she whispered, a delicate crease of concern forming between her eyebrows.

Should he tell her the truth? That she scared him? That he ached to make love with her? That he didn't want to wait until tonight? No. He couldn't tell her any of that. To confess that he burned for her would frighten rather than flatter her. For now, he would grit his teeth and wrestle with his urges in silence.

Chapter Fourteen

Instead of going home after church they visited for a long while in the Common, receiving hugs of congratulations and well wishes from their friends and neighbors. Finally, Kyle helped her onto their carriage and headed out Liberty Street. He slowed the horse in front of Evelyn and Radford's house. "Do you mind if we stop in for a few minutes?"

"Of course not," Amelia said, her expression shifting from anxious to elated. "I would love to visit a while."

She would love to delay spending the afternoon alone with him was more likely, but Kyle didn't comment. If they wouldn't be spending the time in bed, the long hours held little appeal for him, too.

He stopped the carriage in the driveway and saw Boyd near the barn dismounting from his horse. At the same time, Radford exited the livery with his daughter, Rebecca, riding on his shoulders. Though the eldest and tallest of the four, Radford could have been Boyd's twin. They both had dark coloring and gold eyes, but unlike Boyd, Radford was a quiet, happily married man who didn't break his neck watching girls all day.

Boyd opened his arms to Rebecca. "Come here, princess."

Kyle climbed from the carriage, his attention on the exuberant five-year-old who'd stolen his heart the day Radford brought her home. She'd been abandoned by her mother at infancy and was withdrawn and needy then. Now, with the healing love of her stepmother Evelyn,

Rebecca was as wild and reckless as her uncle Boyd who was twirling her in a circle.

"If she loses her breakfast, you're cleaning it up," Radford said, straightening his collar that Rebecca's skinny legs had crushed.

Rebecca clung to Boyd, weaving in his arms like a drunkard. He nuzzled her neck, making her squeal with laughter.

"Uncle Kyle, help!" She giggled and flailed her arms toward him. "Uncle Kyle!"

Kyle helped Amelia out of the carriage then turned and swept Rebecca out of Boyd's arms, glad for the excuse to pull her into a hug.

Rebecca hooked her arms around his neck and kissed his cheek. "You saved me!" She gave him a sloppy smack on his chin. "Put me on your horse."

"No." Radford caught her beneath the arms, but she clung to Kyle as if she were a bug with six legs hanging on for life. Radford plucked her away and planted her bare feet on the ground. "Tell your mother we have company."

She scrunched her nose and tipped her head way back to look up the tall length of her father. "Will she let us eat cookies now?"

Radford's eyes crinkled and he nodded. "Yeah, sprite."

"I'll go get 'em!" She skipped across the driveway then suddenly her head reared back and her face burst into a glowing ball of joy. "Miss Drake!" she yelled, and Kyle felt his stomach jump to his chest. It wasn't Miss Drake anymore. It was Grayson. Mrs. Grayson. Good grief, he really had a wife.

⊷⊱ ⊰⊶

Seeing Rebecca's bright face and waist-length curls bounce as she ran across the driveway made Amelia's heart lighten. She knelt and opened her arms in welcome.

"I'm five now, Miss Drake! And I can count over a hundred and do two cartwheels without falling over."

"Well, isn't that something!" Amelia exclaimed in a properly impressed manner before kissing Rebecca's dimpled cheek.

"Mama says you're my aunt now."

"That's right." Amelia felt her heart swell with love. "I married your uncle Kyle last night and now my last name is Grayson, the same as yours. You can call me Aunt Amelia."

Rebecca's eyes widened. "Really?"

"Yes, really." Amelia laughed and tickled Rebecca's ribs, loving the yelp of laughter that burst from the little girl.

The front door opened and Evelyn stepped outside. "I thought I heard your voice out here. Come sit a while." She gestured Amelia toward the porch with a welcoming wave of her hand. "I'm starved for company."

Rebecca babbled as they ambled down the driveway, and Amelia greeted Radford and Boyd with a smile. Kyle's inquisitive gaze seemed to inspect every inch of her. Amelia looked away. Every time she saw his gorgeous face, she felt a burst of excitement followed by a hard rush of despair. She wanted so deeply to have a loving marriage like Radford and Evelyn's, but the guarded look in Kyle's eyes made it seem impossible. He didn't even want to talk to her, much less fall in love with her.

"Mama made some cookies," Rebecca said, grabbing Kyle around the leg, her bare feet looking precious beside his large dress shoes.

He reached down and ruffled her hair. What a mystery he was with his abrupt manner that hid surprisingly tender actions.

"Missy's gonna have kittens again!"

Kyle smirked. "Is that so?"

"Yup. I'll get her for you!" Rebecca hopped across the driveway on one foot, scuffing up tiny puffs of dirt before she tromped up the porch steps.

Evelyn knelt in front of Rebecca and wiped a smudge of dirt off her chin. "I think Missy's in the barn, sweetheart."

Without a word, Rebecca wheeled around and pounded down the steps. Evelyn and Amelia exchanged a smile, but the desire for her own child gripped Amelia's heart and she struggled to keep her smile in place.

What would it feel like to have a child of her own, to sit on the porch swing with Kyle and their sleeping baby for a long, lazy afternoon of quiet conversation? She'd seen Radford and Evelyn on that swing, holding hands or cuddling their daughter, and Amelia envied their companionship and love.

"I'll bring out some tea," Evelyn said, drawing Amelia away from her private wishes. "Radford, why don't the three of you visit with Amelia while I get our drinks?"

Boyd started up the steps. "I'll keep her company."

Radford laughed, but Kyle just shook his head and followed his brothers onto the wide porch. By the time they had settled in comfortable chairs, Evelyn had returned outside with a tray of tall glasses. "I'm so glad you two stopped in. I figured we wouldn't see you newlyweds for at least a week."

Amelia forced herself to smile at Evelyn's teasing, but she didn't have the nerve to look at Kyle.

Boyd smacked his forehead. "That's why Kyle looks so grumpy today. No sleep."

Kyle scowled.

Boyd winked at Amelia. "If you don't want to live with a bear, you'd better make sure this boy gets some sleep tonight."

Though she tried to laugh, her throat closed and her eyes stung. Her mother had always called her father a bear when he was tired. The onslaught of her heartache came so unexpectedly, she couldn't quell the moisture blurring her eyes. Horrified to find herself on the verge of tears, she lowered her lashes.

Boyd groaned as if he'd been an idiot. "I didn't intend my teasing to be callous, Amelia."

She drew a shaky breath and met Boyd's concerned expression. "You weren't. You just reminded me of Papa, is all. Mama accused him of being a bear on Sunday mornings, and I... it was hard not having him at my wedding. I thought about him all night and... well..." Amelia shrugged because she couldn't force any more words from her aching throat.

Sympathy filled everyone's expression. "Of course you miss him," Boyd said. "How dense of me not to have considered how you might feel today. I'm sorry."

She nodded to let him know she accepted his apology, that she understood he'd just been teasing her, but she didn't dare open her mouth for fear the sob in her throat would roll out.

She hid her face behind her glass and pretended to sip the sweetened tea, but Evelyn's misty gaze brought a flood of tears rushing to Amelia's eyes. "I'm so sorry," she whispered, embarrassed to be teetering on the brink of a breakdown. "I'm having a rough day today."

"You're entitled." Evelyn patted the back of Amelia's hand. "After my papa died, I didn't sleep a full night through until I married Radford. It's good that you have Kyle to help you through this."

Amelia glanced at her husband. The tormented look in his eyes made her stomach drop. What on earth could he be thinking to make him look so... guilty? If it wasn't guilt, it was something equally strong, but definitely not love. No. Love was an emotion that radiated warmth and light. The look in Kyle's eyes held compassion, but there was something deep and painful there that chilled the warm May day.

She leaned back in her chair and drew a shaky breath. "Where did Rebecca disappear to?" she asked, desperate to change the subject, praying the little whirlwind would barrel up the porch steps and light up the dismal mood with her rambunctious enthusiasm.

"She's on the swing." Evelyn nodded to the huge oak tree in their yard.

Amelia turned in her chair and looked behind her. Rebecca sat on the board swing with Missy on her lap, talking away as if Missy understood every word she spoke.

Evelyn called to Rebecca. "I thought you wanted some cookies, sweetheart!"

Rebecca's face lit up and she slid off the swing. She lowered Missy to the ground then ran across the yard and up the porch steps. As if she'd brought the sun with her, the mood changed and it wasn't long before they were all laughing at Rebecca's antics and thoroughly enjoying the day.

They spent three glorious hours talking and laughing and lingering over lunch before Kyle insisted it was time to head home. But only minutes after they arrived, Amelia's mother came by and brought leftovers from their wedding, and by the time her mother finally left, Amelia didn't even feel capable of taking the food out of the basket.

"Would you mind having leftovers for supper?" she asked.

"No, but it's too hot in the house. Let's take the basket and walk down to the gorge."

It was only a few hundred yards from their home, but she was still surprised by Kyle's suggestion. She watched him disappear into the guest room and return a minute later with a dark brown throw that had hung over the foot of the bed.

Though she was tired, the fresh air felt great and she filled her nostrils and chest as they descended a steep wooded path. The peepers were waking up and the sun was a big orange ball hanging low in the sky. It cast a soft glow across the gorge and made the water shimmer.

"Is this all right?" he asked.

She nodded for him to spread their blanket in front of a bank of shale. The gorge was mostly loamy soil mixed with shale fragments and flat rocks, but in some areas the ground was smooth and fairly comfortable.

Kyle sprawled across the blanket and Amelia sank down with a sigh. She set the basket between them and rolled her shoulders. "All we need is for your mother to be waiting for us when we get home," she said then realized how her comment sounded and cringed. "Not that your mother isn't a lovely lady, Kyle, but one parent a day is plenty."

"I've had enough contact with relatives to last until next Sunday."

Despite the underlying unease between them, Amelia smiled. "You don't like making small talk, do you?"

"It seems like a waste of time."

"What do you like to talk about then?" she asked, curious what a man like Kyle would enjoy discussing.

He shrugged. "Business, I guess. I think about the mill a lot."

She'd figured as much. She glanced down the gorge and watched the water tumble and turn, gurgling as it twisted its way downstream. Birds swooped between trees, flapping and twittering, as if making their last-minute visits before the lights went out.

"It's so beautiful here," she said, wishing she could lean back on the blanket and just drift off to sleep. Kyle didn't comment, but she suspected he was enjoying the peacefulness, too. As the melody of the gorge wrapped around them, they watched the sun dip, noticed the swatches of orange widen across the banks of the gorge.

"Amelia?"

She glanced up at the softness in his voice.

"I'm sorry about this afternoon at my brother's house. I should have been more aware of your feelings and brought you home right after church."

A flush of embarrassment rolled through her and she wanted to return to that companionable silence they had shared a moment before. "I didn't expect to react so emotionally. I hope I didn't embarrass you."

"Of course not. I felt bad for you. Seeing your mother this evening made me feel even worse."

"Me, too." Her chest tightened. "Mama's so lost without Papa."

"So are you, Amelia."

Kyle's unexpected tenderness surprised her. He didn't reach for her, but to her own surprise, she yearned to lean against his broad chest, to feel the warmth and protection of his muscled arms. It would be wonderful to curl up beside him and surrender her heartache for one night.

As he leaned back on one hand and studied her, she did the same with him. Her gaze traveled up the angular plains of his face and tangled with his dark, liquid gaze. Something warm and ticklish somersaulted in her stomach and she knew it wasn't the idea of having to marry Kyle that troubled her so deeply. It was the thought of wanting his love and not being able to win it.

He held out his hand to her, but she clutched the blanket. If he touched her, she would be lost. One more second of looking into his hungry eyes and she knew she would fall into his arms and kiss him until tomorrow morning.

"I'm not going to pounce on you."

For the life of her, she couldn't think of a single excuse to keep her distance without offending him. She wasn't afraid of Kyle. She was afraid of herself.

He sighed and moved the basket from between them. "I just want you to sit beside me for a while. Why does that make you nervous?"

"It's not your request that makes me nervous. It's your expression."

"My face has a bad habit of reflecting my thoughts. Gets me in trouble all the time."

The teasing glint in his eyes shocked Amelia. Kyle was truly oblivious to the power of his own tenderness, the allure of his boyish charm, but it captivated Amelia, and she stared at him, wanting to see more of this side of her husband. Beneath Kyle's hard shield lurked a sensitive man with a sense of humor. What a surprising gift.

"Are there other bad habits of yours that I should know about?" she asked in a teasing voice, hoping to connect with this personable side of her husband.

"I sing."

The sound of her own laugh surprised her.

"That's why I don't have a dog. He would never put up with the abuse."

She gazed into his eyes, and though he didn't smile, she saw warmth there. Maybe he wasn't as serious as he pretended to be. Maybe he had a forgiving heart buried in that hard, muscular chest. Maybe he would understand her shame and accept her imperfections without blame.

Drawn to his warmth, and assailed by her own reckless need, she considered confessing everything and begging his forgiveness. But as the humor faded from his eyes, her courage waned.

"We should eat," she said, but she didn't care a whit about food.

"Later."

She didn't protest when Kyle drew her against him, but she kept her face lowered so he wouldn't kiss her. She felt the thud of his heartbeat against her shoulder, and his slow breathing added another voice to the song in the gorge. For the first time ever, she experienced the rhythm of her world from the circle of a man's arms, and she listened to the earthy sounds in awe.

After a long silence, Kyle leaned back against the shale bank and drew her with him. Her hair caught against the protruding edges of shale and loosened her chignon. She sat up to fix it, but he stopped her hand.

"Let it down," he said quietly, his gaze probing hers. Their eyes met, but she was too flustered by his request to comment. "We'll just sit here and watch the sun set."

That he was asking for so little when he could claim anything he wanted shamed Amelia. She pulled the pins from her hair, wishing she could give him more.

His eyes filled with appreciation as he looked at her hair hanging to the middle of her back.

The need in Kyle's eyes made her blush. When he slipped his fingers into her hair, she jumped. He didn't stop or comment, just kept dragging his fingers through her hair and across her scalp. The feel of his fingers spread delicious sensations across her head and down her neck. Finally, she closed her eyes and simply enjoyed it. "That feels so good," she whispered then wished her voice hadn't sounded seductive.

Not daring to look at Kyle, she kept her eyes closed, but to her surprise, he cupped the back of her head and drew her face to his shoulder, like he would with a tired child.

It felt wonderful to curl against his warmth and enjoy the feel of his hands on her body, but she wondered if his attention was leading up to lovemaking.

They sat in the silence for what seemed hours. It was probably only minutes, but under the caress of Kyle's hands, she felt her bones melt and her eyes grow heavy, and finally, she felt nothing at all.

⊶⊰⊱⊷

Kyle brushed Amelia's hair back, aching to make love to her, but knowing he wouldn't. She was exhausted and filled with grief over her father. He had wanted to hold her like this earlier at his brother's house when her eyes had filled with tears. To hear her voice break with grief, to watch her struggle not to fall apart when he knew she was dying inside, had torn a hole in his chest.

All he'd been able to do was sit there drowning in his own regret and guilt, knowing she would hate him when he told her the truth about her father's death.

Chapter Fifteen

A saw blade made a distinctive sound while slicing through timber; a plaintive whine underscored by buzzing, a breathless pause while the carriage gigged back then another screaming buzz as the blade made a second pass through a strip of pine.

Radford had once described the sound as the rhythm of home, and though Kyle agreed, he also recognized it as the true meaning of progress. The sounds of a busy mill meant money. With money came security and happiness, or so he'd thought until making that deplorable investment in Tom's lumberyard. He still considered it Tom's. Until Kyle and his brothers could drag Drake's sawmill out of debt and build it into a solid business like Grayson Lumber it was just another burden Kyle had hefted onto his own shoulders.

Standing beside Boyd in the middle of their lumberyard, Kyle realized that everything in his life had started falling apart when Evelyn broke their engagement. She'd said their bond of friendship wasn't enough to make a good marriage and their relationship was missing passion. She'd found that passion with Radford.

Kyle had found himself confused and lonely.

Marriage to Amelia hadn't relieved the emptiness at all, but he thought he might finally understand what Evelyn had been trying to explain about the power of passion. His physical reaction to Amelia was intense, a need that drove him recklessly forward despite his attempt to hold back. No errant thoughts had scampered through his head while kissing her. He'd been caught up in every nuance of Amelia's mouth, the intriguing scent of flower and soap in her hair and the softness of her body. She had captured his attention completely, and he'd wanted her with a desperation he'd never before felt.

By his own choice he had endured another night of lying beside his wife while his body ached for release. She'd been tired and grieving for her father, and though Kyle had wanted her, he knew she really did need time to heal.

A hard fist slammed into his shoulder and shattered his thoughts. Boyd frowned at him. "Will you answer my question?"

Kyle rubbed the knot in his right arm and stared at his brother. "What's wrong with you?"

"I've been talking to you for two minutes and you haven't heard a word I've said."

"Well, what do you want?"

"For you to pay attention." Boyd cocked his head and studied Kyle. "Have you slept at all in the past two nights?" Kyle opened his mouth, but Boyd raised his hands, palms forward. "Don't answer that."

"I haven't. So don't hit me again if you don't want to get knocked on your ass."

Boyd laughed. "Is married life that bad?"

Kyle rubbed his temples and closed his gritty eyes. "Don't ask." His head ached, and for the first time in two days, he honestly believed he could crawl into bed beside Amelia and actually want to sleep.

"I'm not trying to pry, Kyle, but I've been wondering why you and Amelia got married."

"We wanted to."

Boyd arched an eyebrow as if to dispute Kyle's comment.

Kyle sighed. "The school board found me in her apartment."

"What were you doing there?"

"Trying to break our agreement to buy her father's mill."

Guilt slowly replaced the shock in Boyd's expression. "I never told you to go there."

Kyle shifted his attention to the team of horses hauling a drag of logs into the mill building. "Why do you always say I'm an ass with women?"

"Oh, boy. This is bad." Boyd rolled his eyes. "Why couldn't you be having this conversation with Duke? Or Radford?"

"Because you're the only one who can tell me how to seduce my wife."

"What?"

Kyle thought he might have to pry Boyd's jaw off his chest. Knowing he'd finally managed to shock his brother made Kyle's day.

Boyd scrubbed his palms over his face, glanced around the yard then shook his head. "I must be sleepwalking."

Kyle would have laughed if he wasn't so miserable. "Welcome to my nightmare."

Rays of sun slanted across the side of Boyd's face, highlighting his expression of disbelief. A pine-scented breeze flipped his hair across his forehead, but he didn't even blink. Behind him, two men led a team of horses from the barn, yelling good morning as they passed. Boyd still didn't budge.

"Will you be over your shock soon? We have work waiting for us," Kyle said, barely able to squeeze the words past his pride.

Boyd laughed. "You're serious, aren't you?"

Kyle knew then that the stress had finally pushed him over the edge. Every ounce of his common sense had deserted him. He had to be insane to be discussing anything this personal with Boyd. To be talking about it at all was insane.

"You really want to know why you're an ass with women?" Boyd asked.

No. But if Kyle ever wanted to consummate his marriage, he'd better find out. "Try not to enjoy yourself too much while relaying the gruesome details."

"You promise to have my money for me in three weeks," Boyd said, "and I'll teach you every seduction trick I know."

"I can't even promise that we'll be in business next week, much less have money for you to buy a tavern that smells of smoke and piss."

"Then I'm going to ask Richard for a loan."

Kyle's gut clenched, but he resisted the urge to grab Boyd's neck and shake some sense into him. "You aren't going to let this go, are you?"

"No."

Kyle nodded, realized nothing he could say or do would change Boyd's mind. "All right," he said, finally swallowing the bitter reality that Boyd was going to leave the mill. "Don't take out a loan. If your business fails—"

"It won't fail."

"Well, if the building burns down and you lose everything, you'll still have to pay back the bank. And don't bother telling me about insurance. A simple fistfight can bust up a bar pretty badly. A windstorm is hard on a roof and windows, Boyd. There are all kinds of losses that can ruin you before you have half a chance to make a go of it. So just wait." Kyle huffed out a breath, knowing he couldn't change Boyd's mind. "I'll get your money, but I need some time." He met his brother's eyes. "I've just made the worst investment mistake of my life. Right now, I need your help."

Irritation filled Boyd's expression and he turned away.

"I can't manage all this on my own, Boyd."

As if ignoring Kyle would block out the fact that he was asking for help, Boyd stared across the yard.

"I have a wife and mother-in-law to support now," Kyle said to his back.

Boyd's shoulders tensed and he continued walking.

"Boyd, don't make me beg."

"Damnation!" Boyd kicked a thick slab of bark and it shattered against a log. He let loose a long torrent of cuss words that even Kyle had to admire.

He waited for Boyd's anger to burn down.

"It's driving me crazy spending every day of my life here. I need a change. I'm going to buy that tavern, so just get that through your thick head."

"Fine."

"And I'm going to restore the bar and tear up that scum-covered floor. I'm putting down oak and replacing the booze-splattered wallpaper. I guarantee you, Kyle, my bar won't stink like piss when I'm finished renovating it."

"Good. You can buy me an ale and I'll help you celebrate."

Boyd scowled, his face red. "How do you do this to me?" He jammed his hands in his pockets, his glare filled with disgust.

Kyle just smiled. "I think this is the part where you say you'll help me then reveal all your seduction secrets."

Boyd shook his head. "You're going to owe me for this."

"I know."

"All right, I'll stay for a while. Not forever, Kyle. You'd better live up to your part of the deal when I'm ready to go."

"I will."

"And you'd better wake up and realize there's more to life than this mill. You've got to stop living for this place. Take Amelia on a honeymoon or something."

"She's in mourning and I can't leave the mill right now. You know that."

"Then pretend you're on your honeymoon. Pay attention to her. Go home early and drag her into bed. Tell her you've been dreaming about her all day."

"Are you insane? I'm on the verge of bankruptcy. I don't have time to think about her." In fact, he didn't want to think about her. He wanted a simple, unassuming relationship, like the one he'd had with Catherine.

Boyd shook his head. "You're dense at times."

"I'm not going to lie to my wife just to get her into bed."

"You don't have to. Just flirt with her. Tease Amelia about distracting you, and don't tell me she isn't because you were so wrapped up in your thoughts a few minutes ago that you didn't even hear me talking to you."

"All right, Romeo. Fine. I was thinking about my wife. So what? Is this the extent of your worldly advice?"

"Walk around the house with your shirt off. It drives a woman crazy to see a man's bare chest."

Kyle laughed. He couldn't help himself. The idea of his bare skin exciting Amelia was absurd.

"It does," Boyd insisted. "But it really makes them sweat when you open your pants. Don't take them off, just let them fall open."

"What?" Kyle stared at his brother.

"Touch her as often as you can. Stroke her back when she passes by. Kiss her neck just below the ear. Women love their necks kissed. But whatever you do, do not kiss her on the mouth."

"You're out of your mind."

Boyd shrugged as if he were simply stating a fact that Kyle should know. "It diffuses the tension if you kiss her. You've got to tease Amelia, make her want to kiss you, but don't give in to her. It'll excite her and before you know it, she'll beg you to do it."

Kyle folded his arms across his chest feeling it spasm from silent laughter. This was really too much, but it was entertaining to hear Boyd's warped sense of romance. "Anything else?"

"Rub her feet."

"What do her feet have to do with what I'm after?"

Boyd grinned. "Trust me, if you can get a hold of her feet, you're more than halfway to the bedroom."

Kyle didn't believe a single word of it, but it felt so good to laugh at his miserable life, he could have hugged his brother right in the middle of their lumberyard.

He wasn't about to tempt fate by playing with Amelia's feet, but liked the idea of making her burn for him, making her long to consummate their marriage as desperately as he wanted to.

If he could just keep himself under control long enough to calm her fears, they might find a satisfying relationship in bed. But therein lay the problem. Kyle felt too reckless, too desperate to be reined by logic or compassion. No matter how considerate he wanted to be, he feared the instant he touched Amelia, his lust would trample his good intentions.

━━◆- -◆━━

Amelia surveyed the buildings at her father's lumberyard with new purpose, knowing this would be the best place to win her husband's heart. She would become his partner, his right arm, his confidante. Then his lover.

Several hundred feet across the yard, an immense, unpainted barn staked its claim on dry, rutted ground. Golden hay spilled out of the second story loft and sprinkled the ground in front of huge double doors. To her right, two long, single-story buildings sat parallel to each other, one of which housed her father's crew of ten men. The other contained the mess hall and an open area in the back of the building that her father had been converting to his new office. Knowing he would never experience the pleasure of working in it filled Amelia's throat with grief, but she turned away, reminding herself to keep a clear mind and steady nerves. She needed to remember every word her father ever told her about operating the mill, because she had no actual experience that she could use to prove herself to Kyle. She would just have to bluff her way and pray Kyle didn't catch on.

The instant she stepped inside the mill building, she slapped her hands over her ears to cut the noise of the screaming blades. Gads, she'd forgotten how deafening it was out here.

Several feet away Kyle was talking with Jeb, dwarfing the mill foreman with his superior height and wide shoulders. Though Jeb's medium build and kind, dark features made him passably handsome for a man her mother's age, he paled next to Kyle.

The instant Kyle spotted Amelia, his eyebrows lifted. He glanced at Jeb who shrugged and shook his head as if to say he had no idea why she was trespassing in a man's world.

Amelia tried to smile, but Kyle's displeasure was evident in the lowering of his brows, making her question her decision to come.

He sliced his hand across his throat, eliciting a return hand signal from Ray Hawkins, the head sawyer. A moment later, the blades stopped screaming and the mill quieted to a low growl as Amelia approached her frowning husband.

"Is something the matter?" he asked.

She shook her head, her stomach queasy. "I'm here to help you."

His eyes widened and he glanced at Jeb as if to ask what she was talking about.

Though she'd expected Kyle's reaction, it still insulted her. "I spent nine summers traipsing through this mill with my father, Kyle. I'm capable of helping here. I happen to know a good deal about our operation," she said, directing her statement to both men staring at her. She pointed to the iron platform of the sawmill that held a partially cut log. "That piece of timber is shuttled back and forth by the metal table beneath it. It's called a carriage, Kyle." She pointed at the heavy iron frame holding the upper circular saw. "We have a Top Rig mill with dual saws that cuts six thousand board feet a day. If Ray talks real sweet to her, she can put out eight thousand feet, or at least that's what he's always told Papa."

Hearing his name, the sawyer puffed out his thin chest. "Well, sometimes a lady needs a bit of encouragement to respond. Don't she, Jeb?"

Jeb frowned, but Kyle's gaze swung to Amelia. Heat exploded in her cheeks and she averted her face, knowing he must be wondering how much encouragement it was going to take to get his wife to perform her duty.

"Amelia," he said, his voice condescending enough to set her teeth on edge, "I appreciate your offer, but this isn't a place for a woman."

Unable to look at him and speak coherently, she eyed the mill. "Do you know why we use two blades, Kyle?" She strode toward the mill and turned to face him. "The lower one does the hog work and the upper blade speeds the cutting so we can get more output per day."

He sighed and propped his hands on his hips.

She ignored his obvious irritation and pointed to a huge iron bar that revolved when Ray moved the carriage. "That mandrel is driven by a leather belt and pulley contraption. When Ray gigs back, that log will move—"

"Amelia! I don't care how much you know about the mill, this is no place for a lady."

"But if I can help here then you'll be free to work the depot," she said. Though Grayson Lumber and Timber Works was the largest mill within twenty square miles, and her father had a sizable mill of his own, there were several small mills that dotted the countryside. It got confusing when referring to a sawmill unless you tied it to a last name. With fathers and sons in the same business, that didn't always determine whose mill you were talking about either, so Kyle and his brothers started referring to their mill as the depot. She smiled at her husband, hoping he would see the wisdom of her proposal.

He folded his arms across his broad chest. "You're not staying, and you'll not convince me otherwise."

Her heart sank. The outraged expression on his face spoke volumes. He was going to send her home before she'd even had a chance to prove herself helpful to him. Knowing she had lost her one and only chance to win his respect, she slumped against the cast-iron frame. Her shoulder bumped a lever and the sawmill jerked violently to life. The hum and wind from the saws blasted her ears as Kyle leapt forward and grabbed her arms. She felt a hard tug on her waist and heard a horrendous tearing of fabric as he hauled her away from the mill. By the time Ray slapped the lever in place, and Kyle had her back on her feet, Amelia's lower half was clothed only in her muslin underskirt. Her heart was pounding so hard it made her light-headed.

"What are you doing?" Kyle asked, fear making his voice raspy and harsh.

Burning with embarrassment and scared within an inch of her life, Amelia yanked her shredded skirt from the mill. Cursing herself for being careless, she wrapped the ragged scrap around her waist.

"Are you all right?" he asked.

"Of course I am," she snapped, her frustration so extreme she wanted to rip her skirt to shreds. This was the first breath of freedom she'd had since escaping the apartment she'd been imprisoned in for the past four years. The only difference between her lonely schoolroom and her lonely house was the amount of space for her to pace in. She couldn't bear to trade one prison for another. She had to stay! It was the only way to show Kyle that she could be of some value instead of just a burden he'd acquired. She wanted his respect!

"Before you lose any more of your wardrobe, I'm going to have Jeb take you home."

Her chin shot up and she faced her husband. If he was going to end up hating her anyhow, why hold back? Why go on pretending to be the docile little mouse she'd been forced to portray to keep her teaching position? If she was going to face a lifetime without his love and respect then she was going to insist on the freedom to be herself. At least she would be happy.

"Not to disrespect you, Kyle, but the only reason I'm going to go home is to change my clothes."

"It's unsafe here, Amelia. I don't want you anywhere near the lumberyard."

She propped her hands on her hips, ready to do battle if that was what it took to break the links chaining her. "Then I guess we are about to have our first marital argument, because I'm coming back."

She expected Kyle to rail at her, to command her to leave the business side of their union to him, but a spark of appreciation flared in his eyes before he turned and ordered Jeb to take her home.

Chapter Sixteen

Amelia returned to the mill garbed in one of Kyle's old shirts and a pair of trousers she'd borrowed from Evelyn, who wore a pair just like it while grooming horses in her livery. Amelia had also visited her friend to get some much-needed advice.

Her father's lumberyard thundered with activity. Horses strained at harnesses, pulling hard on drags of timber. Men with rolled shirtsleeves stacked wood on pallets and tossed scrap onto piles that fed the boiler. Saw blades screamed inside the mill building, and the smell of roasting beef drifted out the open windows of the mess hall.

Amelia strode boldly across the yard.

Seven startled men gawked at her from disbelieving faces. All activity screeched to a halt. They yanked their hats off, stuffed them back on their heads then hauled them off again, obviously unsure of how to greet a woman in men's clothing. Some nodded, some tried to mumble with jaws still hanging open, others respectfully dropped their gazes and shuffled their feet, but it was Kyle's stunned expression that made Amelia's steps falter.

He stood open-mouthed beside a team of thick-bodied Percheron horses he'd been using to move a drag of timber to the mill building. The horses snorted and tossed their heads, but Kyle ignored them, his gaze locked on Amelia as he inspected her from her hot cheeks to her boot-covered feet.

If she was reading his expression correctly, he was going to throttle her.

He lowered his hands and strode purposefully toward her, stopping mere inches from her. "What are you doing?"

Despite her nerves, Amelia lifted her chin, trying to pretend she wasn't cowed by his dark scowl. "I told you I was coming back after I changed my clothes."

Kyle put his back to the men and lowered his voice. "You can't be here, or *anywhere*, dressed like that. Where did you get that outfit?"

His shirt was huge on her, but unfortunately, Evelyn was thinner than Amelia and the britches were admittedly snug. Still, Amelia kept her jaw clamped shut, afraid Kyle would berate Evelyn for giving them to her.

"Most of these men aren't married, Amelia."

"What does that have to do with my clothes?"

His eyebrows shot up. "Have you looked in a mirror?"

"Of course not. I barely took time to change before hurrying back here."

"Well, you should have because you'd be as shocked as I am."

"I'll only wear my britches at the mill."

"No, you will not. You're distracting the men."

She glanced at their crew. They all ducked their heads and pretended to be working, but she knew they had been watching. "Kyle, I can't wear a dress for safety reasons."

"This outfit is a safety issue for the men!" he said, gesturing toward her britches.

"Nonsense. They're just surprised, but they'll get used to my trousers. Besides, I can't concentrate on my work if I'm preoccupied with catching my skirt in something."

Kyle caught her hand. "Let's finish this discussion in the office."

"First let me say hello to the men my father was so proud of," she said, her voice loud enough to top the distant buzz of the saws. Heads lifted and each man's eyes flickered with pride. "I haven't spent time here since I was sixteen, so I'll need you to help me remember what you all do here."

Without waiting for Kyle's approval, a short, balding man on her left stepped forward. "I'm Willard Barnes. I joined the crew last year. The gang calls me Willie and I do the skiddin' here. I pull the logs out of the woods, and also around the yard or wherever the boss needs it."

Amelia smiled. She knew what skidding trees meant, but appreciated Willie's consideration.

One after the other, the men introduced themselves by their first name and position. Jake drove and cared for the horses. Axle sharpened their saws and provided blacksmith services. Lonnie dragged the scrap lumber off the saw tables. Cyrus fed scrap wood to the boiler that produced steam and powered the saws. Merle stacked cut lumber and loaded their customers' wagons. A stocky little man named Shorty puffed up his chest and declared himself the best cook in the county. They were a gritty bunch of men, some of whom Amelia remembered, but she felt an immediate bond with all of them.

As they turned back to their jobs, Kyle locked his fingers on her elbow and guided her directly to the office. He closed the door and leaned against it, his jaw working. "This is not going to work. The men won't get anything done with you here. Neither will I. I need to squeeze every possible bit of production from this mill to have any hope of resurrecting it. I can't do that if I'm busy pulling you away from circular saws that will make you mincemeat before you can blink."

"I won't go near the saws."

"They aren't the only danger here. Chains snap in half and slice the air like swords. Logs shift and crush anything in their path. Horses trample our feet if we aren't paying attention. Boilers blow up and spray water that feels like molten lava. There isn't one of us who doesn't have a black fingernail or bruised shin. Tools break—"

"How is your shin?"

"What?"

"Your shin. I noticed you weren't limping as badly today."

Kyle closed his eyes and pinched the bridge of his nose. "It's healing, but we're not talking about my shin right now."

"I'm not leaving," she said firmly.

He opened his eyes. "We're this close to bankruptcy, Amelia." He held his finger and thumb an inch apart. "I have no idea how I'll keep that from happening, but I'd better find a way, because if I don't, my brothers and I are going to have a tough time keeping the depot operating. We've poured every cent we have into buying this place. Our new saw arrived yesterday and nearly drained my personal bank account. I don't have anything to fall back on except determination and a lot of hard work." He straightened his shoulders and hooked his palm over the doorknob as if impatient to get back to work. "I appreciate what you're trying to do, but you'll help most by going home and letting me get this shipment ready for the Hale contract."

The pleading look in his eyes encouraged her to agree, but Amelia was determined to build a relationship with her husband while helping him rebuild their floundering business. "Let me clean up the office then. It won't distract the men, or you, and there are no life threatening risks in here that would keep you from concentrating on what you're doing."

He opened his mouth.

"Please, Kyle. I need to be more than a burden to you." She lowered her lashes, desperate enough to beg, but refusing to grovel. "I need to contribute something to our marriage." She was a lousy wife. She hadn't even cooked for him yet and it shamed her. Kyle had made her breakfast yesterday morning then last night they had had leftovers from their wedding. This morning, he'd left without any breakfast.

He sighed.

"Please," she whispered. "I won't bother anyone."

"Why didn't your mother warn me that you were so stubborn?"

"Maybe she was afraid you wouldn't marry me."

The irritation drained out of Kyle's expression and he heaved a huge sigh. "You're worse than Rebecca when you want something."

"Better for me to plead and cajole than to kick you in the shin again."

To her surprise, a lopsided smile tipped his arrogant mouth. "I suppose that was your last resort if I insisted you leave?"

She shook her head. "Not even close."

Chapter Seventeen

It was the first time Kyle had entered his own house to find supper waiting for him, and though it smelled divine, all he wanted to do was wash the grime off his body and fall into bed. His back ached and his shin throbbed. Dirt and sweat covered his body in thick layers that made his skin itch.

His stomach growled, prodding him to get to the kitchen, but he ignored it, his gaze glued to the thick cushions on the sofa as he contemplated trying to steal a ten-minute nap before Amelia realized he was home. Even five minutes would be a blessing. Two minutes would suffice.

He shifted his weight to one leg, reached down and yanked off his boot then did the same with the opposite foot. Two steps and he would nose-dive into oblivion.

"I was beginning to worry about you," Amelia said, standing in the kitchen doorway watching him.

He jerked upright as if she'd caught him peeking in her undergarment drawer.

"I hope you're hungry." Her lips tilted in a warm, welcoming smile. "I think I made enough to feed our crew."

The warmth in her eyes made him ravenous. All he'd thought about during the evening was kissing her sassy mouth. She'd been smart to leave the mill before he yanked those awful pants of hers down to her ankles and consummated their marriage on the desk.

"There's a tub of hot water beside the stove. I thought you might want to bathe before supper."

"You heated a bath for me?" Kyle couldn't imagine Amelia struggling with the metal caldron and going to so much trouble for him. His tub was huge. It took forever to fill it with hot water. "I can't believe you wrestled that heavy tub into the kitchen by yourself," he said, unbuttoning his shirt as he crossed the parlor.

"Who do you think did all my lifting and heaving at school?"

He had never considered it. Before he could comment his stomach interrupted with an obnoxious growl.

"Maybe you should eat first."

"Not while I smell like a horse." He angled his chin toward the kitchen and shrugged the shirt off his shoulders. "I asked my mother to pick up a few things for you. Did you have everything you needed for supper?"

"Yes." She glanced at his chest then her gaze flickered back to his face. "The pantry shelves are sagging and the cupboards overflowing. I won't need to shop for anything but meat for the next two months." Her gaze dropped back to his bare chest.

Well, what do you know? Maybe Boyd had been right after all.

Kyle rolled the dirty fabric into a ball and dropped it beside the sofa. The evening had suddenly taken an interesting turn. He unbuttoned the waist of his pants.

Amelia didn't say a word as Kyle stepped into the kitchen, but her eyes grew large and she grasped the brass knob on the door between the kitchen and parlor. "I'll close this for you so you can have some privacy."

"Leave it open," he said, deciding to test his wife's starch. He freed the rest of the buttons on his trousers.

Her gaze dropped to his hips, her cheeks blazing. "You'd better hurry. The dumplings will be done soon," she said then moved farther into the parlor.

Kyle had no intention of hurrying. He turned his back to the open door and purposefully slid his pants and undershorts over his hips and down his legs, hoping Amelia would discover the mirror on the parlor wall before he got into the bath.

He greeted the ensuing silence with a long, loud yawn and lifted his arms overhead, tightening his leg and buttock muscles, arching his back as he leisurely stretched toward the ceiling.

A startled gasp came from the parlor.

He grinned and stepped into the tub then turned toward the open doorway for a few bold seconds before sitting down. If he had to share his house with her then she would have to put up with his bad habits. It was only fair.

Heat swirled around his fatigued body as he eased into the water. A hot bath to soothe his aching body, a good meal to satisfy his hunger, and a woman to warm his bed. Life would have been perfect in that moment if he could have looked forward to a night of bold, boisterous sex, but he worried that Amelia would continue to shrink from his touch.

It wasn't that he didn't appreciate the bath and supper. He did. But he would appreciate her naked and lying beneath him so much more.

He sighed and lay back in the tub telling his awakening body not to expect anything more pleasurable than a bath. His knees popped out of the water like small mountain peaks, but his aching shoulders were blessedly submerged in hot water. It must have taken Amelia two hours to fill the tub. Her back probably ached as bad as his from hauling the metal caldron out of the pantry and into the kitchen. The tub rested in a small wooden frame with casters, but was still a beast to move, not to mention heating enough water to cover him up to his neck.

He would thank her during dinner. He would tell her she'd done a nice job of cleaning up the mess he'd made in the office while looking through her father's files.

He wet his head then lathered away the specks of sawdust and dirt that coated his hair. He slid beneath the water to rinse. Completely submerged with only his knees poking out of the heat surrounding him, he vowed to repay Amelia for this gift. Maybe he would undress his beautiful wife and put her in the tub. She could sit in the bath and eat her supper while he rubbed her feet. The chance of Amelia going along with his plan was so absurd it made him snort.

He regretted the impulse the instant he inhaled. He levered himself into a sitting position and coughed the water from his lungs, his shoulders shaking and eyes burning.

"Are you all right?" she asked from the doorway, her expression a mixture of concern and embarrassment.

He was fine, but another hard cough cut off his answer.

She took a cautious step into the kitchen.

Kyle realized she would come to his side if she thought he needed help. The idea was too tempting to resist. He buried his face in his hands to hide his guilt. He shouldn't do this to her. Really. It would be unkind after she'd worked so hard to please him. It would be unfair to subject her to his state of undress when it obviously flustered her. But he couldn't resist testing Boyd's theory a bit more because he wanted a connection with his wife.

He heard the fabric of her gown swish past his ear then felt her clutch his shoulder. "Are you breathing?"

Not answering was unforgivable, but he had to see what she would do.

The flat of her palm struck the middle of his wet back. The crack was so loud it stung his ears as fiercely as it stung his bare skin. He gasped and jerked upright as if she'd rammed a poker between his shoulder blades.

Her breath rushed out and she sank down onto the chair, her hands pressed to her stomach. "I thought you were choking to death.

You'd been under water so long I thought you'd fallen asleep and... you scared me."

She had been watching him! Kyle's ego started doing somersaults. Amelia hadn't been able to keep her eyes out of the mirror any more than he could have if she had been the one bathing.

His conscience immediately chastised him for taking advantage of his wife's innocence, but with her sitting beside him trying not to stare at his water-streaked body, and failing miserably, Kyle refused to waste a moment on shame. He would suffer that bane later. Right now, he was too busy trying to decide if he should ask her to wash his back.

She would comply, believing it her wifely duty, but to his surprise, he realized he wanted more than a dutiful wife. He wanted the bold woman who had stood up to him at the mill earlier. He wanted a wife who would drop her dress on the kitchen floor and climb into the bathtub with him. A woman who would throw her head back and laugh as they sloshed water across her pretty oak floor.

"Are you all right?"

He hunched forward, his body aching. No, he was not all right.

"I'm sorry I hit you. It must hurt like the devil. I left a bright red hand print on your back."

Do not think about her in this tub! Do not think about her warm skin all slick with water and her nipples tight and... he was lost. Kyle held the washcloth in front of his eager body. "Our supper is boiling over."

Amelia vaulted from the chair. As she peeked beneath the lid, Kyle seized the opportunity to stand up and sweep the towel off the chair.

"The dumplings are perfect," she said, glancing at him before he could shake open the towel and cover himself. "Oh!" The lid clanged back onto the pot and she stumbled away from the stove. "Oh, I'm... I'm... oh, my goodness!"

If she wouldn't have looked so shocked, Kyle might have actually laughed at the expression on her face. But instead of embarrassment, he saw fear in her eyes.

A mixture of irritation and sympathy swept through him and he covered himself with the bunched towel. "Let me dry off before you dish that up," he said, nodding toward the steaming pot.

She backed out of the room without saying a word.

Well, that had gone well. He was going to kill Boyd tomorrow. Kyle scrubbed himself dry then yanked on his robe. Amelia had even brought his slippers to the kitchen. She'd done all of this to please him and he'd acted like a lust-crazed fool and scared her. But why was she so afraid of him?

A gush of steam spewed out of the pot and sizzled on the stove. Kyle sighed. He may as well enjoy his supper, because Amelia's expression told him it would be the only pleasure he would have tonight.

Her face was still flushed when she returned. She went to the stove and dished up two plates of chicken and dumplings then set them on the table without looking at him.

Kyle made sure his robe was completely closed and belted before he sat down. "Do you know if your father ever gambled?" he asked, and was immediately rewarded with direct eye contact.

"Of course he didn't. How could you even think such a thing?"

"I don't think that," he said, spooning up a gravy-covered piece of chicken. "I'm just trying to figure out where all his money was going."

"Probably to fix the mill and pay off his debts."

"Maybe, but I think he might have been earning enough to keep the mill in repair without going into debt." Kyle blew on his chicken before putting it in his mouth. He savored the flavor, grateful for not having to eat his own miserable cooking. "This is delicious."

"Thank you." She took a bite and stared at her plate while she chewed. "Why would Papa borrow money if the mill was able to support itself?"

"I don't know. I checked his record book before buying the lumberyard, and he appeared to be producing a fairly nice profit. That's why I asked if he gambled. Your father has acquired a ton of debt without a logical reason to do so. Initially, I thought it was because the lumberyard wasn't making money. But I think it is."

She glanced up. "That's wonderful news!"

He shrugged. "Maybe." It would take at least three years to pay off Tom's debts, and that didn't include replacing the saw, which wouldn't last much longer, and any other breakdowns or problems they might have.

He reached for the salt shaker. Missing money made him nervous. That money had been used for something that Tom didn't want shown on his books. And it had been important enough for Tom to bankrupt his own business in order to fund or support it.

"I'll add more salt next time," Amelia said.

Kyle glanced down and realized he was going to bury his food out of habit. "No. This is perfect." He returned the salt shaker unused. "Really. I've just gotten used to hiding my bad cooking beneath a heap of salt and pepper. Most nights it was the only way I could choke it down."

Amelia smiled, and Kyle finally began to relax. It felt odd to be sitting at his own table having a conversation. Most nights he sat alone with his head in his hand, gulping down his mother's leftovers or whatever he could cook the quickest. Occasionally one of his brothers or his mother would stop by, but they rarely ate with him. He'd been comfortable with that, but it wasn't a hardship coming home to a good meal and having more than the four walls for company.

He sat back in his chair. Amelia wasn't temporary company. Barring misfortune or odd circumstance, she would be his tablemate every evening of his life. And soon she was going to become more than that.

He glanced at her, but her gaze was settled on his chest. He looked down and saw that his robe had gaped open. His first urge was to jerk it closed and apologize, but when he glanced at Amelia, her eyes were brimming with shy curiosity. If he hadn't witnessed the fear in her eyes when he'd been climbing out of the bath, he would have sworn she wanted him to touch him. Her mixed messages were killing him.

"Do you think Papa could have been buying another mill?"

He saw her mouth move, but his mind was too busy seducing her to understand a word she'd spoken.

"Could Papa have used his money to buy another business?"

He gulped a breath of air and dragged his mind back to their conversation. He had to get out of the house. He absolutely couldn't spend another night lying beside her with his fists clenched and his body aching.

"Kyle? Are you all right?"

"Did your father have any close friends who might have asked him to participate in a deal of some sort?" he asked.

"No." She shook her head as if to confirm her statement. "Papa spent all his time at the lumberyard or with Mama. He came to see me twice a week at my apartment, but that was the extent of his socializing after I... when I started teaching." Her gaze dropped to her plate. "No. I'm certain he wasn't entering into any type of business with anyone else."

He feared as much, but hearing Amelia confirm it made his stomach queasy. If Tom Drake had been involved in something illegal it would come back to bite Kyle in the throat.

And Amelia was going to tempt him beyond his limit if he didn't find an excuse to get out of the house.

Chapter Eighteen

Instead of going to the mill the next day, Amelia stayed home and prepared a small plot in the backyard for a vegetable garden. Afterward, she straightened the house, feeling as if she were cleaning someone else's home instead of her own. No matter which room she dusted, or which chair she sat in, she felt like a nervous guest.

Desperate for the familiar warmth of her parents' house, and her mother's arms, she headed outside. It took half an hour to have one of the men at the depot rig a phaeton for her use, but as soon as she was seated, Amelia headed toward Shumla Road.

The silent darkness of her parents' home shocked her, but when she saw her mother sitting in the cave like parlor, gazing out of anguish-filled eyes, she panicked. "Mama, you need to open the drapes and let in some sunshine."

"I have a headache and it feels better with them closed."

It was a heartache her mother was suffering, but Amelia didn't blame her mother for wanting to shut out the world. She felt like doing the same thing. Still, it broke her heart to see her mother filled with grief and hurting so deeply that she couldn't bear the sunshine.

Amelia groped for a way to breathe life back into her mother, and knew that normal conversation wouldn't do it. "I think Kyle's sorry he married me," she said, and was immediately rewarded with her mother's full attention.

"If that young man has done anything to hurt you—"

"He hasn't, Mama." Amelia hid a smile of satisfaction and sat beside her mother. "It's just that I don't feel at home in our house," she said truthfully. "I think my unease makes Kyle uncomfortable, too. But everything in the house belongs to him. I feel like a guest who has overstayed her welcome."

Her mother's eyebrows lifted and she stared at Amelia. "Has he told you that?"

"Of course not, Mama. I just feel that way." Amelia sighed and smoothed her skirt over her thighs. "Did you have this trouble learning to live with Papa?"

"No. Neither of us owned a stick of furniture so whatever we borrowed or acquired always felt like it belonged to both of us. It took us years to fill our old house, and by that time we had started to build this one. Everything we've had or done has always been together."

"Well, how could I feel like that when Kyle has already furnished the house with beautiful things?"

"Add a few of your own favorite pieces to what he already has."

"I don't have any furniture, Mama. Everything in my apartment belonged to the school, and it was awful anyhow."

"You have those beautiful pillows that you embroidered on your bed upstairs."

"What difference will a couple of pillows make?" she asked, feeling more disheartened by the minute. It was going to take more than pillows and furniture to make a loving home with Kyle.

"Don't look so sad, honey. It takes time to make a home together."

"I don't have time, Mama."

Her mother patted her hand. "You have the rest of your life."

"Will you help me?" Amelia clutched her mother's hand. "Please. Come home with me and show me how to make a good home for my husband."

Before her mother could protest, Amelia stood up and tugged her toward the stairs. An hour later they were rearranging the furniture in Amelia's new home and adding articles from Amelia's life that brought her a sense of comfort.

"Put these on your couch." Her mother tossed the two embroidered pillows to Amelia. "This afghan will look beautiful on the back of your rocking chair," she said, draping it over the oak spindle back.

"I hope Kyle won't mind me moving that out of the corner," Amelia said, wondering if she'd gone too far by dragging the big rocker into the grouping of parlor furniture. It had looked so unappreciated stuck in the corner, as if Kyle had purposely tried to shove it out of sight.

"You'll need it to rock the baby."

"Mama! I haven't even been married a week."

"I know, but you and that handsome young man of yours will be having children before you know it. This chair is right where it belongs, and if Kyle tells you differently, you send him up to talk to me."

Despite the embarrassing conversation, her mother's spunk gave Amelia hope that her mother would eventually pull herself out of her depression.

After they finished transforming the house, they took a break for tea then Amelia took her mother home. She hadn't been back in her own house for more than twenty minutes before Kyle walked in the door.

He stopped dead, his shocked gaze taking in the changes that Amelia and her mother had wrought in his absence.

Suddenly the cozy arrangement of furniture and the feminine look of her pretty pillows and oval rug seemed intrusive for a large man used to space.

"I can change it back if you hate it."

Instead of answering, he continued to note the changes, the vase of flowers on the coffee table, the shiny oak coat tree beside the door, the picture of her father hanging prominently on the parlor wall.

"I'll just move this back now," she said, dragging the rocker toward the corner. "I'll move the rest after supper."

"Leave it!"

Amelia jerked upright at his snapped command, dreading the outrage she would see in his eyes. But instead of anger, his expression was filled with apology.

"I should have asked if you wanted to change things." He shrugged, his expression sheepish. "Do you need help moving anything else?"

"Only if you want to move everything back where it was."

"This is fine."

"You're sure?"

He nodded.

"It'll only take a few minutes—"

"It's fine, Amelia. Leave it."

He took off his boots, and they ate supper in the awkward silence that she despised but was growing used to. Only tonight she didn't know if it was Kyle's normal inability to converse about the daily details of life or if he was upset that she'd taken over his home.

"I'm heating water for a bath if you want one after supper."

He sighed and laid his fork on the edge of his plate. "Thanks, but I have to take my shift in the warehouse at the depot tonight. You go ahead and enjoy the water." He pushed away from the table. "I'll see you in the morning."

He headed for the parlor and put on his boots. She sighed with relief, unable to bear another night of his disappointment when they crawled into bed together and lay stiff and silent beside each other.

But by the fifth night of Kyle's leaving the house after supper, claiming it was his turn to keep watch in the warehouse at the depot, Amelia grew suspicious. Kyle and his brothers had decided to dry the deck beams for the Hale contract in the same warehouse they used for drying their railroad beams, but Amelia wondered if Kyle was using it as an excuse to seek intimate satisfaction elsewhere.

At four o'clock in the morning, she pushed open the door to the long wood building and stepped inside, gasping as the heat hit her in the face. Several feet away a huge cast-iron stove hummed and crackled. Farther back in the rectangular room a lantern burned low and illuminated the lone occupant.

To her relief, her husband sat in an uncomfortable wooden chair sound asleep. He leaned back against a pile of deck beams, his chin resting on his chest. His feet were planted on the floor on either side of the raised front chair legs, his muscled arms locked across his chest, lifting and falling with each long breath he took.

Despite her relief at finding him alone, shame filled her for letting her insecurity lead her to wild conclusions. She should have known Kyle wouldn't lie to her. Everything he did was about honor. He'd married her because of his ingrained sense of honor. Now, his honor was keeping him from forcing her to consummate their marriage even though she knew he was aching to do so.

Compassion filled her when she looked at her exhausted husband hunched in the chair. He should be home sleeping in his own comfortable bed. She debated whether to wake him, knowing he probably wouldn't go home even if she suggested it. He would just start his day an hour earlier. Deciding he needed his rest regardless of how poor or uncomfortable it was, Amelia caught the latch and pulled the door around. The rusty hinges groaned and vibrated the thick planks.

She glanced back just as the chair legs hit the floor with a hard thud. Kyle vaulted to his feet, eyes wild and confused. "What's wrong?" he asked, as if he expected the building to fall in on him any second.

"Nothing. I'm sorry I woke you."

He dragged out his pocket watch and squinted at it near the lantern then glanced back at her. "What are you doing here at this hour?"

Well, she might as well try to send him home. "I came to relieve you until your crew gets here. I can feed the stove for an hour or so while you go home to bed."

"You can't stay here alone."

"I was alone at home."

"There's a lock on our door. There isn't one here."

"Then I guess you'll have to stay and guard me." She moved toward the stove, unwilling to go back to her empty house. She had spent enough lonely hours in her apartment to last her a lifetime. "I'll watch the fire while you sleep."

Kyle scrubbed his palms over his face then stared at her as she opened the heavy stove door. When she reached for a piece of firewood, he stepped forward and caught her wrist. "Leave it." He pushed the door closed and pulled her toward the chair he'd just vacated. "Sit down and tell me why you're not home in bed."

"I don't want to sit if you're going to tower over me like an angry parent."

He grabbed the ends of two stacked beams and inched them away from the pile far enough to form a seat. He sat down with an irritated sigh. "All right. What's wrong?"

She reached to hoist her skirt and realized she was wearing the britches he despised. "Are you really here because you have to be?" she asked, perching on the edge of the chair. "Or do you just want to get away from me?"

"Both," he said, in his usual brusque manner.

Her chest constricted, but she forced herself not to look away from him. "You hate me for forcing our marriage, don't you?"

Instead of responding immediately, he studied her with his dark, perceptive eyes, his expression unfathomable. "You didn't force me into anything, Amelia. The repercussions of that meeting are a result of my own stupidity, not your manipulation."

"Then you don't hate me?"

"No." He didn't look away or roll his eyes or snort or do anything else to express the irritation she suspected he was feeling. He just sat and looked at her, his face dark with whiskers, his eyes red with fatigue. "Why are you afraid of me?" he asked quietly.

A rock of foreboding lodged in her stomach and she didn't know how to answer.

"I do intend to consummate our marriage, Amelia."

"I know," she said, but they weren't ready yet. They'd had almost no time together to develop a friendship or a caring relationship. Kyle's reaction to her lack of virginity would be the same now as it would have been on their wedding night.

"I'd like you to answer my question."

She wasn't afraid of Kyle, but it was the only excuse that would buy them more time. "You feel like a stranger to me," she said. "I don't know any more about you today than I knew a week ago."

Lantern light highlighted beads of moisture on his forehead and accentuated the shadows around his eyes. "What do you want to know?"

A million questions flashed through her mind, but one repeated itself and begged for her attention until it was the only thought she had. "Have you ever felt vulnerable?" she asked. "Even once? I know men probably don't experience fear, but—"

"Yes." His gaze locked with hers. "I've felt insecure and powerless before."

His face was so close, his look so intense, she felt her stomach lift in anticipation. "When?" she whispered, torn between wanting him to answer and wanting him to kiss her.

He eased back and sighed. "When my father died." He'd answered in his straightforward manner, but the pain was evident in his eyes despite his ability to keep it out of his voice.

She inhaled wood-scented air, but it didn't ease the sudden thickness in her throat. "I shouldn't have asked. I'm sorry. My papa was everything to me. I'm sure you felt the same about your own father."

Kyle braced his elbows on his knees, a habit of his that she was growing fond of. "My father had been ill a long time. I knew he wouldn't live to become an old man, but the morning he didn't wake up for church was a hard shock." Kyle stared at the floor. "He just went to sleep and never woke up."

Hal Grayson had contracted a disease as a young boy that had slowly crippled him, but several years before his death, he'd been a tall, handsome man who walked with a cane and flashed a gorgeous smile that he'd passed on to his four sons.

"I didn't mean to bring up painful memories," Amelia said, knowing it was a difficult topic for both of them.

"I was lucky to have the depot to manage. It kept me from dwelling on losing my father." His eyes met hers. "I guess it makes sense now why you want to spend time at your father's mill."

"I love being there. I want to be your partner, Kyle."

His lips tilted and he laughed.

"I'm serious. I promise to stay away from the saw, but there are a hundred other things I can do to help."

"I don't mind you coming by occasionally to clean the office. I can actually find the files I'm looking for now."

"I am not interested in becoming the mill maid. My brain would shrivel to the size of a raisin within a week. I need to be learning something, or teaching, or doing anything that will stimulate my mind."

"I'm willing to teach whatever you want to learn," he said.

Stunned by his boldness, she could only stare into his handsome face. The fire in his eyes told her he wasn't talking about the mill.

He was offering to be her instructor in the art of intimacy. If he only knew that she didn't need his instruction. Just looking at him made her want to pull his clothes off and devour him. She thought about sinking onto his lap and kissing him, but considered where it would lead and knew she had to get away from him before she was foolish enough to answer the craving in her body. She'd made that mistake once and it had nearly ruined her future. She wasn't going to fall into bed with her husband and mess up her last chance at love.

"I'm serious about helping at the mill," she said, tugging her hand free.

"All right, Amelia. I'll allow your help in the office. But that's it. You can look through your father's records and files and see if you notice any strange paperwork or odd spending patterns." He lowered his hand to his thigh. "I'm too busy helping the crew to do it myself."

Unsure whether to trust him, she studied his face, but he seemed sincere. "You'll have to tell me what I'm looking for."

"I'm stuck here until five o'clock and you don't seem in a hurry to go back home."

She ignored his hint to return to the house. She was just as curious as Kyle was to know where her father's money had been going. "Why do you think something bad was going on with Papa?"

"Experience. The whole situation at the mill doesn't make sense. I've learned not to take anything at face value. That's why I want you to look through his files."

She sat on her makeshift chair, eager to learn more about her husband, but aware that she was heading into dangerous territory. The affair between Evelyn and Radford had broken Kyle's trust and made him cynical. Eventually her lie would reinforce his cynical outlook on life.

He stretched his arms overhead and yawned then he propped his fists on his knees. "You ought to go home and sleep another hour or two. I'll pick you up later when I go to the mill."

"You have a bad habit of bossing people, you know."

"I know."

His honesty made her smile. "Does anyone ever disobey your orders?"

"My mother. The last time I made the mistake of giving her an order, she smacked me across the head with her newspaper and told me it was her house and that I was her son not her boss." Kyle laughed. "I haven't mistaken my mother for a mill hand since."

"You're lucky she only hit you with her paper and not a rolling pin."

"She saved that for Boyd."

Knowing Boyd's propensity for shenanigans, Amelia had no trouble understanding why Nancy Grayson might need to use her rolling pin to control her wild son. Their house must have been filled with life, noise, and laughter. What a wonderful way to live. "It must have been fun growing up with brothers," she said, her voice wistful. "I'll bet you got into tons of trouble."

"You can't even imagine."

Though his expression didn't change, the smile in his voice intrigued her. "What was the worst thing you boys did?"

As if he were recalling some fond incident in his past, Kyle's lips quirked. "We had a horse-turd fight in the barn."

"You did not!"

"We did. The four of us were supposed to get the barn cleaned before my aunt and uncle arrived from Buffalo. Boyd was mad that he was stuck shoveling stalls instead of swimming in the gorge with his friends, so he slung a shovelful of dried crap across the barn. Radford told him to knock it off, and I slapped him on the head on my way to the next stall. When I bent over to grab the handles of the wheelbarrow, Boyd dumped a whole load of dung across my back. I returned the favor and a ruckus broke loose. Next thing we knew, all four of us were winging dried turds at each other. That's when my father pulled in with my aunt and uncle."

"Your parents must have been furious!" Amelia said, laughter bubbling from her throat.

"They were, but Boyd got his wish to go swimming. My mother sent us to the gorge to wash up." Kyle met her eyes, his own sparkling from the memory. "We had a ball that afternoon."

Loving this private side of her husband, Amelia linked her fingers and tucked her hands against her stomach. "How wonderful it must have been to have brothers to fight with," she said, encouraging him to go on talking.

To her surprise, he laughed an honest-to-goodness laugh. "That's all we ever did. We drove my parents dotty." As his smile faded, he searched her eyes. "What's it like to be an only child?"

"Lonely." She didn't even have to think about it. It was dreadful not having someone to fight and laugh with. "I always wanted a brother," she said, surprising herself with her confession.

"If I had known, I would have given you Boyd."

"No you wouldn't," she said with a laugh. "Your life would have been too boring without him around to antagonize you."

"Probably."

"What is the wildest thing you've ever done?" she asked, ignoring the slivers of morning light slipping beneath the crack of the door. She wanted to hold on to the sudden warmth she saw in Kyle's eyes. She liked him like this.

"I rode my horse down Liberty Street in my underwear because Evelyn stole my clothes."

The image made her laugh. She leaned forward to ask what had happened, but the slow realization that Kyle had been unclothed with Evelyn seeped into her mind and didn't feel funny at all. She had never really thought about the intimate side of Kyle's relationship with Evelyn. Surely he'd kissed her. Maybe they had done a lot more than that.

Her curiosity overcame propriety. "Do you still love her?"

"Yes."

The truth cut through her. Of course he loved Evelyn. She had been the one to break their engagement. Not Kyle. He'd wanted to marry Evelyn.

"She's been my friend since childhood."

Amelia lowered her lashes to hide her reaction. "You don't have to explain. I love Evelyn, too."

"It's not—"

"What did Richard want when he came by the house last evening?" she asked before Kyle could embarrass her with his explanation. It didn't matter why he loved Evelyn. It only mattered that he did.

Kyle blinked at her sudden change of topic. "He came to invite us to supper."

The breath left her lungs and she sagged back in her chair. Though Richard had only stayed a few minutes last night before riding out of the yard with Kyle, she had hidden in the bedroom until they were gone. "You didn't accept, did you?"

"No. I invited him to our house instead."

"You what?"

"I didn't think you would mind. I was going to tell you when I came home for breakfast this morning that Richard would be coming to supper tonight."

"I'm in mourning, Kyle. I can't be hosting supper parties."

"It's not a party. It's just a private meal with a close friend."

"I can't do it." Realizing she'd spoken aloud, Amelia straightened up in her chair. "What will I make?"

"Anything. Don't worry about it. It's just Richard. It's no different than if you were cooking for me or one of my brothers."

It was worlds different, but Amelia kept her anxiety to herself. "Is he bringing Catherine with him?" she asked, praying Lucinda's oldest sister would come and help lessen the tension.

"I didn't invite her."

"Why not?"

"She's Richard's stepmother, not his wife."

"Well, they share the same house, Kyle. Catherine will eat alone if Richard isn't there. I'll send her a note today and ask her to come."

Kyle opened his mouth then clamped his jaw shut.

"What?"

He shook his head. "Nothing."

"What's wrong?"

"Nothing."

"Then why are you wearing that expression?" He didn't answer, and Amelia's stomach clenched. "Are you keeping something from me that I should know?"

His eyes became dark wells of regret. The pain in his expression was so raw it frightened her. Whatever he was hiding, it was killing him.

"I need to tell you something."

She stepped back, sensing that whatever he wanted to confess was going to hurt both of them. "Your crew is arriving, and I don't want to start a conversation we can't finish." She backed toward the door. "I'm going home to get your breakfast ready."

Chapter Nineteen

Later that day, Amelia closed her father's journal and rubbed her eyes. She'd spent hours in the office at the lumberyard looking for errors, but her father's books were accurate. The mill was earning a profit, just as Kyle had suspected. It wasn't much, but it had been enough to keep the mill operating without the need to mortgage anything. So where could he possibly have been spending his money?

She rubbed her temples, her bleary gaze resting on the contents of the open desk drawer while she racked her brain for ideas. Not only did she want to know for her own peace of mind, but she wanted to find the answer for Kyle, to feel proud that she'd helped him.

She dug out the dry ink bottle that had kept the drawer from closing, but before shutting it, she ran her finger across several old writing utensils her father had used at one time or another. "What did you do with your money, Papa?" she asked, longing to hear him answer, to hear the sound of his voice, which she missed so deeply.

Something shiny peeked from beneath the pens and she dug out a coin-like object. It was an engraved, flat piece of mother-of-pearl. She flipped it over and studied it from several different angles in order to read the inscription. *TLD* was engraved on the back side. *Thomas L. Drake*? That didn't make sense. Her father's middle name was Reginald, so why would he have an *l* stuck between his initials?

She dug through the drawer and found two more pieces, but they were more worn than the first piece she'd discovered.

The office door swung open and she glanced up, hoping Kyle or Jeb or whoever was coming in the door would know what the odd pieces were and what the l stood for.

To her amazement, her mother stepped inside, her expression tentative as she scanned the office. Her gaze lingered on a ragged old flannel jacket that Amelia's father had worn. It was lying across the top of a file cabinet now because Amelia couldn't bear to throw it away.

Her mother hugged her arms across her stomach, her eyes filled with pain. "Please tell me there is something here that I can help you with. I can't spend another minute alone in that house."

"Oh, Mama." Amelia slipped the mother-of-pearl pieces into her shirt pocket and hurried to her mother's side, ashamed that she hadn't been spending more time with her. "I'm sorry. I haven't considered how miserable you must be at home."

"I didn't come here to make you feel bad. I just need something to do. I can't stand being alone any longer." The dispirited expression on her mother's face broke Amelia's heart. Although she couldn't think of a single thing her mother could do, Amelia vowed to find some type of project for her.

"Come on, Mama. Let's make a cup of tea and visit a while." She took her mother to the mess hall and put the kettle on the stove. "Look in the pantry and see if there's any flour and brown sugar," Amelia instructed as she took baking tins from the cupboard. "I'm going to make a batch of oat streusel to go with our tea. I'm starving and in no mood for Shorty's cooking."

"Your father said the man's a terrible cook."

"He is," Amelia said with a laugh. "But he tries." She dragged out a cookbook and smiled when her mother looked over her shoulder.

"So this is how Elizabeth has known how to make all those wonderful dishes for us. I thought she was a brilliant cook and now I find out she's been cheating all these years."

"Everyone uses a cookbook if they don't know how to make something. I used one all the time when I lived in my apartment."

"I guess I hadn't considered that." Her mother took the spoon from Amelia's hand. "Let me do this." She read the recipe directions, measured the ingredients then stirred the mix. After a few minutes of silence, she glanced at Amelia. "Were you unhappy being a teacher?"

"No," Amelia said truthfully. She'd been worlds beyond unhappy, but she would never confess that to her mother.

"I always wondered why you never married Richard. You seemed quite taken with him."

Amelia looked away from her mother's probing stare. "Richard had to go back to college."

"Probably a good thing he did," she said, scraping the mixture into two baking pans. "You were too infatuated with that boy. He would have hurt you, honey." She shrugged. "There are some men you just can't depend on. Is that ready to go in the oven now?"

Glad to change the subject, Amelia checked the fire that the men had started earlier then told her mother to put in both pans. She poured two cups of tea and they sat at the table while the streusel was baking.

Her mother cradled the cup between her palms and sipped for a few minutes then she sighed and cast a hopeless look at Amelia. "I've been trying to think of ways to help you and Kyle, but I have no skills that would earn us a single dollar. How on earth am I ever going to be anything but a burden to you?"

"You don't need to do anything, Mama. Kyle and I can manage alone."

Her mother inspected the utensils on the wall then gazed at the line of cookbooks on the shelf. "I've spent my life trying to make a good home for you and your father. I thought that meant having pretty chandeliers and parquet floors, hosting dinner parties and church meetings." She raised her gaze to Amelia. "I didn't know I was supposed to teach my daughter to cook and help my husband with his business."

"Papa wouldn't have wanted you here. I think he felt guilty for spending so much time at the mill these past few years and that's why he showered you with gifts all the time."

Her mother's nostrils flared and she pushed away from the table. "I didn't need those gifts, Amelia. I would have rather he spent time with me." She stood up and put her cup in the sink with a clunk. "You said the streusel would be done in thirty minutes. Should we check it now?"

Her mother's sudden withdrawal made Amelia wonder if there had been something painful between her parents that they had kept to themselves. She didn't know two people who'd been more in love with each other, but there was honest pain in her mother's eyes when she turned back to face Amelia. "Why did Richard come to your wedding?"

Amelia flinched in surprise. "He's been friends with Kyle for years."

"No man would look at his friend's bride the way that boy was looking at you. Mark my words. Whatever you two started before he went back to school, he's looking to finish."

"Then he's too late, Mama. I'm married to Kyle now."

"You remember that when Richard conveniently forgets that fact."

Insulted, but unwilling to argue with her mother, Amelia bit her lip and removed the streusel. Any protestations or denials would only make her look suspect. She set the pans on the counter to cool.

"Honey." Her mother rubbed her palm across Amelia's shoulder. "I'm not trying to offend you. I know it's hard to let go of your first love, but Kyle's a good man and he deserves your loyalty."

"He's my husband, Mama. Of course he'll have my loyalty. I'm long past my infatuation with Richard," Amelia said, knowing she meant it.

"I hope so." Her mother picked up the knife and pointed toward the streusel. "Can I cut that now?"

Before Amelia could answer, Shorty and the crew of nine men came pounding through the door. "What smells so good?" Willie asked, sniffing his way to the counter. Every eye in the room focused on the streusel as the men sought the source of the delicious aroma.

Amelia's gaze swung back to the open doorway where Kyle stood frowning. Why couldn't the man smile more often? If it was the only thing she succeeded in changing about their relationship, she was going to teach him how to laugh.

"What's going on?" he asked, shifting his gaze between Amelia and her mother as if he'd caught them stealing the silverware.

Amelia straightened her shoulders and took a step closer to her mother. She needed to be here as much as Amelia did. "Mama made dessert for everyone," Amelia said, loving the way her mother's chin lifted a notch.

The men backhanded their mouths, but Kyle didn't budge from the doorway. To Amelia's surprise, her mother propped a fist on her hip and faced Kyle. "Quit frowning at me, young man, and sit down or you're not getting a slice of this streusel."

As if her mother had crossed the room and pinched him, Kyle instantly blinked the frown off his face. "Sorry," he said then to Amelia's surprise, he took a seat at the table with the rest of the crew.

The instant they got their plates, the streusel disappeared amid profuse groans of pleasure.

It was then that Amelia discovered how to make grown men grovel. Just give them sex or food and they were happy. How pathetic.

As if to confirm her thought, Jeb finished his slice and rubbed his stomach. "That was great, Victoria. It's a nice change from Shorty's gruel."

Shorty glared at Jeb, but her mother smiled, her eyes reflecting a new sense of pride that Amelia had never before seen.

"Mama's going to help Shorty with the cooking," Amelia announced. She linked her fingers in front of her hips, trying to look confident in the face of her mother's surprise and Kyle's scowl.

Shorty glanced at Kyle, his expression outraged. "What's she talking about?"

Amelia's stomach churned in the face of Kyle's authority, but she refused to back down. "With Mama's help, Shorty will be able to spend more time in the yard where you need him. If that doesn't make sense to you then I'm sure Mama can find more pleasurable pursuits to fill her time than helping us."

Instantly, Kyle's eyes scanned the number of bodies circled around the table and Amelia knew she'd won. Even though Kyle could depend on Boyd to run the depot, Kyle had his hands full with this floundering lumberyard. No matter how much he disliked the idea of having women at his mill, he needed every available man out in the yard.

Chapter Twenty

A melia prayed Catherine wouldn't notice her trembling as they exchanged a hug in the parlor, but to her surprise, Catherine felt just as tense.

"You look lovely, Amelia."

In the face of Catherine's smile, Amelia felt anything but lovely. All the Clark girls were gorgeous, but they were also genuinely kind and loving, so it was impossible to hate them for being so pretty. Still, Amelia wished she was wearing something more attractive than her black mourning dress.

She glanced at Kyle and Richard, who had just exchanged a handshake. That they were pleased to see each other was obvious in their beaming expressions.

"I hope you're hungry," Amelia said, groping for a suitable way to greet Richard.

"I'm famished. Catherine fairly starves me." Richard cast a teasing smile at his stepmother, who flushed and lowered her lashes. He laughed and gave her a side-armed hug then turned back to Amelia. "You look lovely this evening," he said, and then to her chagrin, he pressed his lips to the back of her hand.

Amelia summoned a believable smile, but tugged her fingers from Richard's grasp. "Thank you. Why don't you and Kyle relax in the parlor while I get beverages for everyone?"

"I'll help you," Catherine said, latching on to Amelia's arm as if desperate to escape the men.

Amelia had thought Catherine's presence would lessen the tension, but to her surprise it actually made the situation worse. Catherine had been different since she'd married Alfred Cameron. Before the marriage, when she still lived with her parents, Catherine had been happier, more talkative, and though Amelia had gone to their house to visit Lucinda, she'd enjoyed the teasing that went on between the four sisters. Catherine was still friendly, but her eyes were full of heartache and secrets now.

The instant they stepped into the kitchen Catherine gasped. "What a splendid kitchen!"

Amelia smiled, knowing her first reaction had been similar. "Kyle and his brothers built the house," she said then conveyed the details while pouring ale for the men and tea for herself and Catherine.

To Amelia's relief, they shared an amiable drink in the parlor then brought their light conversation to the table with them, which seemed to calm Catherine's unease and her own as well.

Kyle and Richard headed toward the beer barrel in the pantry for the third time. Amelia and Catherine exchanged a glance then flinched when a loud burst of laughter came from the pantry. Kyle and Richard came back out with grins on their faces and proceeded to wash down their supper with several mugs of ale.

"How many times did we fall from that vine before your father cut it down?" Richard asked, his face alight with laughter.

Kyle grinned, his own face flushed, his eyes alive with humor that mesmerized Amelia. She'd never seen him like this, almost boyish in his enthusiasm. Richard and Kyle were talking about a thick, wild grapevine that they had used to swing out over the gorge and drop several feet into the water. Apparently it didn't always make a full arc over the water, and whoever had taken the ride would come crashing back into the bank they had just jumped from.

"I think he chopped it down after Boyd busted a rib." Kyle shrugged and laughed. "I don't recall."

"Remember that fort we tried to build up there?"

"Yes! My father almost killed me over that."

Kyle laughed and Richard set his fork on his plate. He turned to Amelia and Catherine, his smile of remembrance genuine. "We helped ourselves to Mr. Grayson's lumber. Every night after chores I would meet Kyle, Duke, and Boyd at the mill and we would haul those long planks half a mile up the gorge. It about broke our backs, but we hauled, sawed, and pounded nails every night for a week before Mr. Grayson realized his lumber pile was diminishing. When he discovered we were using his prime lumber to build ourselves a fort, I thought he was going to whip us."

Richard glanced at Kyle and they both snickered as if they were still boys. Despite her anxiety over Richard's presence, Amelia leaned forward, intrigued by Kyle's childhood and his friendship with Richard. "What did he do?" she asked, directing her question to Kyle.

Kyle smirked. "Dad put us to work shoveling sawdust at the mill."

"We must have shoveled a hundred wagons full of that stuff before he let us off the hook." Richard took a drink of ale then laughed. "I begged my father to pay Mr. Grayson for the lumber, but he said the work would be good for my character."

"It wasn't that bad."

Richard gawked at Kyle. "I could barely stand upright for a week!"

"You just weren't used to shoveling. I was glad to make some money."

"That's right!" Richard hooted. "Mr. Businessman here sold the sawdust for insulation."

"We were able to buy the rest of the lumber we needed for our fort, weren't we?"

Richard lifted his glass to salute Kyle. "True. I got my first lesson in business from you. Do whatever you have to do to survive."

Amelia's gaze shifted between Richard and Kyle and she could see the enjoyment in their eyes, the smiles on their faces attesting to a long friendship and years of fun memories. Despite her misgivings and anxiety over Richard, she knew she wouldn't break that connection between her husband and Richard.

As Amelia cleared the last of their dishes from the table, Richard gestured toward the parlor with his glass.

"Catherine has been dying to see your home, Kyle. Would you show her the rest of the house?" he asked.

Catherine's face paled. "The house is lovely, Richard, but I'm not imposing on Amelia to give me a tour."

"That's why I asked Kyle show you through."

It seemed they all exchanged glances simultaneously, but no one said a word.

Richard lifted his glass. "Go ahead. I'll stay here and keep Amelia company."

Catherine cast a helpless at Kyle, eliciting Amelia's sympathy. Richard could be so pushy sometimes. Pity the woman for having to live with him.

"Go with them, Richard. I'm almost finished in here," Amelia said, carrying their stacked plates to the sink. She didn't care if they took a tour or sat and visited, as long as she didn't have to take part.

When Amelia heard the shifting of chairs and the sound of footsteps cross the kitchen, she breathed a sigh of relief to finally be alone. She filled a dishpan with hot soapy water and started to submerse the plates in the dishwater.

"Why didn't you tell me you were marrying Kyle?" Richard asked, his mouth so close to her ear that she squeaked and dropped a plate into the dishwater.

She clutched her stomach and turned toward Richard, who had trapped her between himself and the sink. She glanced toward the door that connected the kitchen and parlor, but Richard's quiet chuckle drew her attention back to him. "Don't worry, Kyle's giving Catherine a tour of your bedroom. They'll be a while."

Although they had been provoked into it by Richard, the thought of them alone in her bedroom put an uncomfortable knot in Amelia's chest. "Why aren't you with them?"

"I wanted a minute alone with you."

She stepped back and bumped against the sink. "You're in Kyle's home, Richard."

"I'm aware of that."

"Well, he trusts you."

"He should. Kyle's my friend."

"Then act like his friend."

His eyebrows lifted, but Amelia ignored his offended look.

"You manipulated Catherine and Kyle to get them out of your way so you could purposely put me on edge. And don't pretend you aren't aware of what I'm talking about." She drew a shaky breath and smoothed her damp hands down the front of her dress. "I don't want to come between you and Kyle, so please stop this nonsense."

"Is that some sort of a backhanded threat?"

"No, Richard." Amelia sighed with frustration. "I just want you to be his friend. Forget you ever knew me before tonight."

"Amelia." His voice was soft, contrite. "I know it's too late for us and I accept that. I just wanted to tell you that I'm sorry our past relationship is causing problems for you and Kyle."

"What?" She stared at him.

"Kyle has hinted that your marriage is under some strain."

She gasped at his audacity. "Kyle told you that?"

Richard ignored her question and squeezed her arm. "If you need to talk, you know where to find me."

⊷⊶

When Kyle returned to the kitchen and found Richard caressing Amelia's arm, his first instinct was to throttle the man. But Richard touched everyone like that; a slap on the shoulder, a jovial handshake, an arm around the shoulders. He'd just hugged Catherine in the doorway not two hours ago. It was just his way and it probably meant nothing, but Kyle knew better than to trust anybody.

His own brother had betrayed him with Evelyn, the woman Kyle was supposed to marry. That was Kyle's fault for not paying attention. He wouldn't make that mistake again.

In three long strides, he crossed the kitchen and grabbed Richard by the back of the neck. "I see I'd better keep this rogue in my sights," he said to Amelia as he forced Richard back two steps.

Richard laughed, apparently believing Kyle was teasing him. "I was just complimenting your lovely wife on her delicious cooking."

"Well, do it without the use of your hands."

Richard lifted his palms as if to protest his innocence, but Kyle nudged him toward the door. "Come on, you hound. Let's take Catherine home and stop at the Pemberton for a nightcap." Anything to get Richard out of his house and away from Amelia. "I won't be late," he said, glancing back at his wife's surprised face as he guided Richard and Catherine Cameron out the door.

Chapter Twenty-one

T hough Kyle had calmed his jealousy, and he and Richard had enjoyed a few mugs at the Pemberton, he felt an odd tension between them the next morning when Richard and Catherine greeted them in the churchyard.

Catherine smiled and exchanged pleasantries with Amelia, and gave Kyle a brief, intimate glance he hoped no one else noticed. It had been torture showing her through the house last night, pretending they barely knew each other, when the whole time Kyle's guilt was burning like acid in his gut. He'd hated bringing a former lover into his house and unintentionally playing Amelia for a fool. She had been so gracious and warm to Catherine, and though Richard seemed to make Amelia uncomfortable, she'd welcomed him, too. He'd also hated treating Catherine so callously. Even though she'd only wanted friendship, it still felt awkward and cruel to show her through the house he was sharing with another woman. The brief apology he'd given her in the bedroom seemed pathetically inadequate.

"Richard and I wanted to wish you a Happy birthday," Catherine said to Kyle, her cheeks flushed a soft shade of pink that nearly matched the overskirt of her dress. A tower of gold curls spiraled down her neck and over the crest of one plump bosom.

Kyle couldn't deny her beauty, but it was appreciation instead of attraction that made him notice.

Amelia's startled expression made him cringe. He'd forgotten about his birthday. It was just another day to him, but Amelia's hurt look made him sorry he hadn't remembered to tell her. "Thank you, Catherine."

An awkward pause ensued before Richard spoke to Amelia. "The meal and... companionship last night were both delightful," he said, but to Kyle's surprise Amelia's expression remained strangely blank, as if she were working hard to keep any emotion out of her eyes.

Amelia thanked Richard then turned to Kyle wearing a fake smile. "We really must get home so I can finish your birthday cake."

Kyle nodded to Richard and Catherine and then guided Amelia to the carriage. The minute they were out of the yard, she turned on him. "Why didn't you tell me it was your birthday?"

"I didn't remember until Catherine mentioned it."

"How on earth could you forget your own birthday?"

He shrugged. "It's not important to me."

"Well, it is to me, Kyle! I felt like a fool not knowing my husband's birthday. I felt humiliated. When we get home I want you to make a list of your brothers' and mother's birthdays so I don't have to suffer this embarrassment again."

"My mother's birthday is today."

"It is not."

"It is. She was hoping I would be born on her birthday so I entered the world two weeks ahead of schedule to please her."

"Typical of you to be an aggressive infant."

"When's your birthday?" he asked.

She crossed her arms over her chest, suspecting that Kyle was trying to derail her from chastising him. "I'm not telling you."

He smirked at her. "Is that supposed to be a pout on your face?"

She tried to glare at him, but his brows lifted and Amelia caught herself staring. It happened every time he looked at her, as if he could see right into her mind and read her thoughts. She didn't need to read his to know he was contemplating kissing her, that he was at the end of his patience with holding himself back, that they would be consummating their marriage today or tomorrow. During the week she'd sensed his reserve breaking down as clearly as she could now see the desire filling his eyes. Last night she'd been sound asleep when he came home, but today, the entire afternoon and evening stretched out before them without a thing to do.

"I have a surprise for you," she blurted, hoping her outrageous idea would jar Kyle out of his preoccupation with the mills and help her bridge the awkward gap between them. She didn't want to give him any more reason to fill Richard's ears with complaints about their marriage. "We have to change our clothes though."

He frowned.

Before she realized what she was doing, Amelia pressed her fingertips to the crease in his forehead. "Why on earth do you frown over everything?"

"I don't."

"Yes you do!" She lowered her hand. "You have a permanent crease between your eyebrows."

"That's from squinting in the sun."

"It's there because you're always irritated with something. Don't you ever have fun? Isn't there something you like to do that makes you smile?" She met his stare, challenging him to deny his perpetual frown.

"I've got a lot on my mind."

"Who doesn't?" she asked with a laugh.

"Why do we have to change our clothes?"

"You're not allowed to ask questions about a surprise. And you're not allowed to frown for the rest of today." He glanced at her and she put her hand on his arm. "It's your birthday, the sun is shining, and it's gorgeous outside. Can we just try to enjoy the day together?"

"Whatever you want." His shoulders lowered as though fatigued. "What am I supposed to wear?"

"Your work clothes. We're going to the lumberyard."

"What?" he asked, his expression appalled as he pulled into their driveway. Sunday was their only day off and by the look on Kyle's face the lumberyard was the last place he wanted to spend his birthday.

"Stop frowning. We won't be working," Amelia said, climbing out of the carriage before he could help her. She headed toward the house. "I have to change and put water on to heat for laundry, but I'll meet you out here in fifteen minutes."

Kyle nodded, but when he met her back at the carriage, his face was devoid of his usual frown and it lifted Amelia's spirits so much she hummed softly all the way to her father's lumberyard. No matter what she had to do, she was going to find a way to connect with her husband today.

She barely gave him time to put the horses in the barn before she caught his hand and dragged him out behind the mill. "Your surprise is down here," she said, picking her way along an overgrown path that cut down into the gorge. Silently, she scanned the rocky, tree-lined bank.

"What are you looking for?" Kyle asked, his forehead beginning to crease as he walked beside her.

"My boat. And stop frowning."

He relaxed his face, but only because surprise had lifted his ears and eyebrows. "You have a boat?"

"There it is!" Amelia hurried to a mound that looked like a fallen tree on the rock-strewn creek bank. She tugged it upright and huffed out a breath. "We'll have to dig the sand and dirt out of it before we can put it in the water."

"That boat won't float five minutes, Amelia."

"Where are the oars?" She knelt down and scraped the sand with a flat rock. "I always kept them in the boat. The wind must have tipped it up." Of course it had been four years since she'd used the tiny rowboat her father had given her, but she wasn't about to admit that to Kyle. This was the only beautiful gift she had left to share with him. "Here they are!" She dug her fingers beneath one oar and tugged it from the mix of sand, soil, and rock. "Tip the boat over for me so we can knock the debris out of it."

"We are not putting that thing in the water."

"Why?" She faced him. "What are you afraid of, Kyle? That you might get wet? Or that you might actually have some fun?"

His head jerked back as if she'd slapped him, but his eyes filled with challenge and he marched forward and grabbed the edge of the boat. Well, there was lesson number three. Give a man food, sex, or a challenge if you want him to do something for you. She was finally getting the hang of this.

"This is insane."

Amelia grinned and hauled the other oar out of sand. "I know, but it's better than working, isn't it?"

"You don't think this is work?" he asked, but to her surprise, the expression in his eyes was almost teasing.

It took them ten minutes to get the boat into the water, and another five before Kyle deemed it seaworthy and they climbed in. The plank seats were so close, he had to plant his feet on either side of her legs and gird her knees with his thighs. He reached for the oars and Amelia pulled them from his grasp. "This is your birthday present. Relax and enjoy the ride."

"I'm not letting you row."

"Kyle darling, shut up."

His eyebrows slashed down and Amelia burst out laughing. "I knew you couldn't go an hour without frowning."

"I wasn't frowning. All right, maybe I was, but you told me to shut up."

"That's not half of what I wanted to tell you this morning when I found out it was not only your birthday but your mother's, as well. What on earth are we going to give her for a gift?"

"I bought a necklace for her when I was in Philadelphia."

"Thank goodness. We'll have to take it by later."

Kyle grimaced. "The party starts at seven o'clock."

"What party?" Amelia asked, feeling her stomach tighten in anxiety.

"The one I forgot to tell you about." He had the grace to look chagrined and he sat back and braced his palms along the dirty edges of the boat. "Evelyn's having a surprise party for my mother tonight. I was supposed to tell you yesterday."

"What?" Amelia gaped at him. "Kyle, how could you forget something so important?"

His gaze perused her from her hips to her mouth. "I've had other things on my mind."

Heat burned up her neck, but she forced herself not to turn away. Sunlight and leaf shadows flitted across Kyle's hair and shoulders. His eyes caught sparks from the sun and Amelia admired her husband as she moved the oars through the water.

"Where are you taking me?"

"Down the river of truth," she said then smiled at him. "As long as I'm rowing, I get to ask you questions and you have to answer them honestly. If I stop rowing, it's your turn to ask questions."

He grinned. "You won't last for ten questions."

"I'm rowing downstream. Guess who's rowing back?"

He laughed and her heart flipped. "You should do that more often," she said, still mesmerized by his wide smile and beautiful teeth. "You have a wonderful laugh, and it's much more attractive than that frown you're so attached to."

"Is that a criticism or a backhanded compliment?"

"Both, but since I'm rowing that means I get to ask the questions."

He laughed. She could tell that he liked her sassiness. Kyle admired people with the nerve to stand up to him as she'd done that day at the mill when she refused to go home. He'd been sincere during their wedding reception when he'd said he appreciated a woman's intelligence. And ironically enough, for a staid businessman, he seemed to enjoy her outrageous behavior.

Thank goodness, because she felt wild today with the sun and breeze on her face. She would show Kyle her true personality today, and if it wasn't enough to ease his disappointment in her lack of virginity then in her heart she would have the comfort of knowing she'd tried to give him everything she had left.

"At this pace you're going to row all day," he said, but she knew he was picking on her.

"All right, who is the smartest person you know?"

"Boyd."

A laugh burst from her, and she propped the oar handles on her knees. "You're joking, of course."

The boat swung sideways and Kyle grinned. "You don't know my little brother. Since he was four years old, Boyd has been able to manipulate, swindle, or charm his way in or out of anything. That includes work and paying the bar tab when he's the only one drinking. You stopped rowing. It's my turn."

"What?" Amelia glanced down at the oars as Kyle dragged them into his hands, his face inches from hers.

"What is the most daring thing you've ever done?"

She could have said lifting her skirt for Richard, but that qualified as the stupidest. "Marrying you," she said, warning her heart to quit pounding.

His eyes locked on hers and the paddles floated to the surface.

"You're about to lose the oars, Kyle." She nodded to the paddles slipping from his lax hands.

She took back the oars with a sense of pride for besting him so quickly. "What is the most frightening thing you've ever seen?" Tiny dots of perspiration sprinkled his forehead and reflected the sunlight as he stared at her. "You have to answer, Kyle, or you lose the challenge."

He blinked and straightened his shoulders, but surprise still lingered in his eyes. "Watching Radford lose control and think he was back in the middle of the war."

Amelia reminded herself to pull on the oars. Radford was the only one of the boys who had gone to war. Evelyn had never said anything about his trauma, though, and Radford always seemed so happy and calm when Amelia saw him, it was hard to believe he was afflicted with something so awful. "Does he still suffer like that?" she asked.

"He seems better, but he might still have nightmares about the war. They don't say and I don't ask."

"I'm sure it's kinder not to," she said, scouring her mind for something to make Kyle laugh. She wanted to lighten the moment and break through his rigid control, but nothing crossing her mind seemed outrageous enough to work. "If you could visit any place in the world, where would you go?"

"California, to see the redwood trees."

She laughed. "Of course you'd take a vacation where you could look at more trees."

"Well, where would you go?" he asked.

"It's not your turn, but I'll answer anyhow. I would visit the ocean. I love the water. I spent my summers paddling down this creek in my boat, and when that got too lonely, I'd trail after Papa at the mill until it was time to go home for supper. What's your favorite time of the year?"

"That's a boring question."

"You're right," she said with a nod. "I meant to ask, what's my deadline for consummating our marriage?"

His eyes shot open and he gaped at her.

"I don't expect you to wait forever, Kyle. I just felt we needed time to get comfortable with each other. I want to laugh with you before I make love with you."

He braced his fists beside him on the plank seat. "Are you saying you're comfortable with me?"

"No," she said softly, "but I'm hoping to be soon."

"How soon?" He leaned forward, his eyes growing dark.

She met his intense stare, the oars forgotten in her hands. "How soon does it have to be?" she asked, praying he would give her a few more days.

His mouth hovered inches from her own. "*Now* would be a good answer."

She gripped the oars. "Then answer one more question for me. Do you think you can ever learn to care for me?"

"Yes." He slipped the oars from her hands. "Now answer my question. Are you afraid of me?"

She opened her mouth to say no, but she'd promised him the truth. She was afraid. With nothing more than a kiss or a touch, he had the ability to make her lose control. Her feelings were involved now and she was afraid of getting hurt again. She met his eyes. "Yes. I'm afraid. A little."

"Why?" He leaned forward and brushed her temple with his lips. "When are you afraid?"

"When you make me feel like this."

He lowered his mouth to her neck, and her eyes fluttered closed. "What are you feeling now?" he asked, his breath warm against her ear.

"Tense." Her chest shuddered as she drew a breath. "Shaky."

"I feel that way, too." He kissed the corner of her mouth. "My heart is pounding just as hard as yours, Amée."

She drew back, wondering if Kyle had just called her by another woman's name.

He clutched the oars in one hand and brushed the back of his knuckles across her cheek. "I think of a softer name when I look at you. Amée is a French name meaning 'beloved'. It suits you." He lowered his head, his lips a breath away from hers. "Am I entitled to a birthday kiss?"

"Yes," she whispered, and he kissed her.

The seductive swirl of his tongue made Amelia forget they were in a rotted little boat in the middle of Canadaway Creek where any passerby could see them.

His shoulders tensed as he dragged the oars into the boat, but he didn't stop kissing her. He took it deeper, slower, until Amelia felt her bones melt and raw, needy desire burn through her body.

He circled her waist and tugged her toward him. She half stood to shift herself onto his lap—and the bottom dropped out of her world.

Literally.

Her foot burst through the rotted bottom of the boat and she fell backward as water gushed in around her shin like a small geyser.

Kyle gripped her waist and glanced down to see what had happened.

Amelia struggled for a few frantic seconds before she was able to wiggle her foot out of the huge, gaping hole. She glanced at the shore and knew there was no way they were going to be able to row her boat ashore before it filled with water. "Please tell me you can swim," she said, glancing at Kyle, but he sat there staring at the burbling water like a boy who'd just had his favorite toy ripped out of his hands.

"I don't believe this!" he said.

Amelia couldn't hold back her laugh.

He swung a disbelieving look at her. "What's so funny? We're going to sink!"

She was soaked to her calves and the water outside the boat was within inches of sweeping over the sides, but she crouched there and laughed because Kyle's expression was so boyish and vulnerable it was precious. "Come on, Captain," she said, giggling. "It's out of fashion to go down with the ship."

"I told you this thing wouldn't float."

"Don't complain." She grabbed his hand and pulled him to his feet, trying to be careful not to break through the bottom of the boat again. "You got a birthday kiss out of it, didn't you?"

He grinned and jumped from the boat with her.

Chapter Twenty-two

"Gah!" Kyle gasped and swept his hair out of his eyes. "There's still ice in this water!"

Amelia laughed. The ice had melted over a month ago, but the lakes and creeks in New York were still cold in June. Despite the shock and discomfort, the adventure of the unexpected swim was exhilarating to her.

"Take off your shoes," she said, bobbing in the water, fumbling with the laces on Evelyn's hand-me-down work boots. As the first boot sank, she yanked off her stocking and tugged at her other boot. "Do you know how many times I've wanted to do something like this?"

Kyle swirled his arms at his sides to keep his head above water. "Our muscles will freeze up before we can make it to shore."

"We'll make it." She dropped the other boot into the cold depths and swam toward Kyle with her jaw quivering. "Every day of the last four years I've wanted to do something outrageous, to feel alive. Teachers aren't allowed to have fun." She stopped in front of him. "Lie back and lift your foot." When he hesitated, she shoved his shoulder. "Come on, I can't tread water all day. Your boots will only slow us down."

Kyle floated on his back, fanning his arms while Amelia jerked his laces open and tugged off his boots. He stared at her, unable to believe he'd let her get him into that rotting boat.

"Let's go," she said, her eyes sparkling and face radiant with the thrill of their unexpected adventure. "I'll race you."

He grinned and stroked hard to catch her, willing his cold arms and legs to function, praying with each hard stroke that Amelia would be able to make it on her own because he wasn't sure his muscles would function in the cold long enough to help her.

"Last one to shore fills the bathtub," she said, her breath coming in hard pants as she kept her body one stroke ahead of him.

"Do you have to talk about a hot bath when I'm freezing my... important parts off?"

Her laughter mixed with the sound of splashing water. If they made it to shore he would gladly fill the tub.

"I like my bathwater really deep and hot, Kyle."

The thought of anything hot and deep cramped his stomach and he was glad his privates were too numb to react. He stroked hard until he was beside Amelia. "Are you doing all right?" he asked, fearing the tightness gripping his own body might be affecting her, as well.

"Get that look off your face," she said, panting and moving her arms in jerky arcs through the frigid water. "I intend to get that bath and I'm not going to carry those buckets myself."

He laughed and got a face full of water that he blinked and coughed away. "Only a few more yards, Amée."

"I like it when you call me that." She sank down in the water, her face disappearing for a couple of tense seconds.

Kyle grabbed her elbow and lifted her, burning his precious reserve of energy. "If you do that again, I'm going to hog the bathtub all night while you shiver on the sofa."

She looked pathetic grinning through blue lips, but her eyes still sparked with determination as she slapped her arms through the water. "That was just a trick to tire you out before the last stretch."

He laughed, enjoying her teasing. His chest filled with admiration when she clenched her jaw and put her head down, flailing her way toward shore with admirable tenacity. He kept pace, but made sure he climbed onto the rocky bank behind her, glad he was alive to worry about hauling buckets of water for his amazing wife.

"Please tell me we aren't far from home," she said, crawling onto the shore. Sitting in the sunshine with her head hanging, her rib cage heaving, she watched him do the same.

Panting, he sat beside her. "Probably thirty minutes, but I know a shortcut that will get us back faster."

She lifted her face and brushed her dripping hair back. "The sun feels wonderful," she said, her eyes closed, her mouth parted and shivering.

In all his fantasies he'd never seen a more beautiful woman, never imagined that a prim little teacher would turn out to be his seductive, sassy wife. Droplets of water covered her face and body, sparkling in the sun, tempting him to kiss them off her skin.

"That was the most fun I've ever had in that boat," she said then laughed and met his eyes. "You should have seen your face, Kyle. That was worth every minute of the swim to shore."

He started to frown, but caught himself, and realized he had truly enjoyed the adventure with Amelia. Though he would have never guessed it, he liked her sassiness and her challenges and the outrageous things she said to make him laugh. The uninhibited side of her personality intrigued him.

His gaze roved over her wet clothing. The skin on her neck was speckled with goose bumps, her nipples erect and visible through his old shirt that she'd started wearing to the mill. A disk-like bump marked her rib cage and he touched his finger to the hard spot. "What's this?"

Curious, she looked down and considered the lump a moment then sat up and dug something out of her deep pocket. "I meant to ask you about these," she said, dumping three coin-like objects into his palm.

When he saw what they were, he glanced at her in shock. "Where did you get these?"

"From Papa's desk. Why? What are they?"

His gut clenched and he felt sick as he turned the pieces in his fingers, finally understanding where Tom's money had been going. "These are gaming counters," he said, unable to lie to her, but wishing he didn't have to tell her. "They use them at gambling houses in place of money."

Her brows furrowed. "Why would Papa have them?" she asked, but as soon as the words were out of her mouth, understanding filled her eyes and her shoulders sagged. "Oh, no." She pressed her fingertips to her mouth and stared at Kyle. "You were right, weren't you?"

"Maybe there's another explanation."

She shook her head. "There isn't. I checked his books for you." She shivered and hooked her arms around her drawn-up knees. "Jeb said Papa went to Philadelphia every few weeks to see James Hale about the deck beam contract we have with him, but he never said anything about Papa gambling."

"If your father was spending his time in a gaming hall he wouldn't have told a soul. Not even Jeb."

"Probably not," she said, staring at the water where she'd just lost her little rowboat. "Papa kept his troubles to himself." Her body trembled and she lowered her head to her knees, looking so lost and hurt that Kyle couldn't stop himself from drawing her into his arms. She put her head on his shoulder and hooked her arms around his waist, and for the first time in his life, Kyle felt completely connected with another human being.

⊷⊶

When they entered their woodshed twenty minutes later, their clothes were still dripping wet and Amelia was shivering. Kyle peeled off his

169

shirt and tossed it over a stack of firewood. He unbuttoned his pants and her eyes widened.

"What are you doing?"

"Keeping our floors dry." Too cold to worry about modesty, either his or Amelia's, Kyle slid his pants and undershorts down to his ankles then stepped out of the wet clothes.

Amelia gasped and turned her back.

Kyle grinned. "You can undress while I get us some towels."

"You're enjoying this, you skunk."

He was. Absolutely. "Do you need help undressing?" he asked, fighting back a laugh as she blindly swatted at him.

"Get me a towel before I freeze to death."

Kyle laughed all the way to the linen closet in the bathroom. He pulled out a towel, opened it up and wrapped it around his hips. The next towel he opened was much smaller and he'd nearly shoved it back into the cupboard before a wicked little voice told him not to do it. He shook open the towel again and held it up, estimating how much of his wife's lovely body it would cover. Not much by his guess.

Perfect. He tucked it under his arm and headed back to the woodshed.

"Where are you?" he asked, scanning the deserted room.

"Behind the woodpile."

Kyle fought back a laugh. Typical woman. She was freezing to death and was more worried about modesty than survival.

"Here's your towel." He tossed it across the woodpile.

"Thank you." He heard movement then a gasp. "Kyle Grayson, this isn't a towel, it's a washcloth!"

Kyle bit his lip and counted to three before he could speak through his laughter. "It's the biggest linen I have," he said. "My towel is small, too."

Her head inched above the woodpile and she peeked at his hips. "We are ordering new linens from Agatha's store tomorrow."

"Order whatever you like, Amée." She was going to kill him when she found out they had towels as large as a horse blanket. "I'll go put water on the stove for our bath."

"Use the water I have heating for laundry. I'll do the washing tomorrow."

"All right, but you won the first bath."

"Well, I'm not coming out until the tub is filled. That's your job."

Kyle shook his head and went to the kitchen. He dragged the tub out of the pantry, filled it with hot water, added enough cold water to make it comfortable then headed back to the woodshed.

"Are you still out here?"

"Y-yes. Please tell me the b-bath is ready."

What a goose she was! Before she froze to death, Kyle marched around the woodpile, intending to drag her out if necessary. Amelia shrieked and scrambled to close the towel around her torso. Her slender legs looked a mile long. His gaze traveled from her ankles up every beautiful inch of skin until the small scrap of towel hid what he wanted to see most. His gaze drifted upward to the creamy swell of her breasts partially concealed by blue fabric and the sash of her dark, wet hair.

Despite her discomfort, Kyle grinned and swept her up into his arms.

"Stop! My towel is coming off!"

He glanced down and saw her beautiful breasts. Tempted beyond his resistance, he hurried through the parlor and into the kitchen. Before he lost control, he plopped her into the tub, towel and all.

Amelia gasped and blinked water from her eyes, still scrabbling to hang on to the towel. He raked his hair back with shaking hands, wondering what he was going to do. He honestly couldn't stand the abstinence any longer.

Suddenly, his towel was yanked completely off his hips.

He stood with his bare ass facing his wife. "I would suggest you return my towel," he said, knowing if he turned around in his current state of arousal he'd ruin his chances of ever consummating his marriage.

To his shock, Amelia giggled. "What an interesting place for a birthmark."

Kyle slapped a hand over his left buttocks. He hated that mark. If she said one word...

"It looks like a little turtle."

He held out his right hand. "Give me my towel."

"Can't. It's wet."

"Then I might as well join you in the tub." He turned to face her and Amelia shrieked and ducked her face. She huddled beneath both soaked towels while Kyle stood boldly before her, waiting for her to open her eyes. She kept her eyes squeezed shut and shoved a sopping wet towel at him. "Here. You can have it back."

"Too late." He put his hands on her shoulders and her eyes sprang open. "Hold your breath." Before she could ask why, he pushed her under the water to douse her hair.

She came up blinking and brushing water off her face. "What are you doing?"

"I'm going to wash your hair."

"What?" She coughed and glared at him.

He glanced at the small shelf on the side of the tub and picked up the most feminine bottle he saw. He sniffed it then poured a handful of what he hoped was soap into his hand. The second it began to lather he plopped it on Amelia's head and started kneading it into her hair.

"You're insane!" She hunched forward and gripped her towel, giving Kyle a wonderful view of her exposed back. She was submerged from the waist down, but the water was clear enough for him to see the exquisite peach shape of her backside.

"You don't have a birthmark anywhere back here," he said. She swatted at him and he laughed, thoroughly enjoying himself.

"Get out of here."

He knelt beside the tub and massaged her scalp. "Relax, Amée."

"I would if you'd leave the kitchen."

He wasn't budging.

"Please," she said, her voice close to begging.

He sighed and rinsed his hands in the bathwater as slowly as possible, brushing her back until she squirmed away. Finally, he stood up, unashamed of his desire, but he knew Amelia would keep her eyes downcast anyhow. "I'll be back in a few minutes with a dry towel for you."

"Make sure you get one for yourself, too."

He grinned as he left the kitchen, but a second later he tripped over the jutting rocking chair leg that Amelia had moved into the middle of the parlor. He cursed and limped down the hall, reminding himself why he hated the rocking chair. He'd bought it for Evelyn. He'd built her this house, furnished it for her, and offered her a life of security, but she'd chosen his brother.

"Are you all right?" Amelia called from the kitchen.

"I'm fine." Kyle dug through the linen closet until he found a large, thick towel for Amelia, and another one for himself. After concealing his lower half, he sat on the sofa and let his wife enjoy soaking in the hot water.

"Are you ever going to bring me a towel?" she called, and he considered telling her no, but he'd teased her enough.

He took her towel to the kitchen and laughed when he saw her shielding herself with the two towels she'd dragged into the tub with her. "I'll close my eyes," he said, opening up the dry towel and holding it like a blanket.

"Kyle Grayson!"

Kyle opened one eye and peeked at his wife's outraged expression. "You gave me this... this *washcloth* on purpose!"

He grinned.

To his surprise, she laughed and stood up in the tub. Water streamed down her bare skin as she let her tiny towels fall into her hands. Kyle's jaw dropped and his heart careened into his ribs.

She smacked him right in the face with her sopping wet towels. "You rat!"

He laughed and swept the yards of toweling around her, lifting his beautiful, playful wife into his arms.

She gasped as he cradled her against him. Water dripped off his hair and nose, but he lowered his mouth and kissed her anyhow. To his delight, she didn't protest. She put her arms around his neck and kissed him back, the water from their bath mingling with their kiss.

Just when he considered carrying her to the bedroom, she drew back. "You're so fun like this. Thank you for a wonderful day," she said, and Kyle felt his heart swell. It *had* been wonderful. He hadn't enjoyed himself this much since he was a kid raising hell with his brothers.

Amelia had a terrific sense of humor and was a good sport. She had a way of drawing him out, of tugging at him until he responded. Despite her fear in the bedroom, she wasn't afraid to speak her mind, to stand her ground with him, and he respected her for that.

"You'd better take your bath before the water gets cold," she said. "We have to leave for your mother's party soon."

He didn't want a bath and he didn't want to go to a birthday party. He wanted to lay Amelia on their bed and make love to her, but it looked as though he would have to wait a few more hours. But that was all he was willing to wait. He had given her time to get comfortable with him. He'd even laughed with her. It was time to make her his wife.

Chapter Twenty-three

When they arrived at Kyle's mother's house, Amelia's discomfort flared. She was welcomed with smiles and hugs, but even when the fun of surprising Nancy and sharing cake together was over, and after they had all settled into relaxed conversation, she still felt like a guest amid Kyle's close-knit family.

It wasn't their fault. There couldn't be a home that was more open and loving than the Graysons' nor one filled with more laughter and good-hearted teasing, but Amelia had kept herself outside the family by keeping herself from Kyle. She didn't feel like his wife or Nancy's daughter-in-law, because in her heart, she hadn't yet earned that special distinction.

Amelia drained her third glass of wine and glanced at her handsome husband, wishing their relationship was as relaxed and natural as Radford and Evelyn's. Evelyn had said that she and Radford shared everything, that they snuggled on the couch together in the evenings and talked about their day, their business, their dreams. Amelia couldn't imagine Kyle snuggling anywhere, or talking to her about his private dreams. Sure, they talked and laughed and Kyle answered any question she asked him, but he didn't offer himself willingly. She had to drag him out from behind his shield of cynicism and distrust every time she wanted a peek at the real man she'd married. She wanted to know his private side, the vulnerable part of himself that he kept hidden and protected.

Amelia refilled her wine glass as Radford guided Evelyn to the front of the room with Rebecca perched on his arm.

"I would like to make a toast," Radford said. Everyone quieted and raised their glass. "To Mom, for always giving us a place to come home to, for welcoming our stray dogs, our lovely wives, and my wild daughter who is going to have a brother or sister in about six months."

Nancy gasped and Radford winked at Evelyn, his expression so full of love it made Amelia ache to witness it.

Everyone clinked glasses and laughed and offered best wishes. As Amelia brought her glass to her lips and emptied the burgundy liquid into her mouth, her eyes met Kyle's gaze over the rim of her glass.

She'd expected his look to be condemning, but it was filled with desire and the same intense longing she'd seen during their boat ride. It jolted her to see how desperately he wanted a child of his own. She wanted a baby, too. For years she'd sat alone in her apartment imagining how it would feel to have her stomach round in pregnancy, to hold her newborn infant, to feel the heat of that tiny body against her breast.

She lowered her empty glass and wondered if the longing in Kyle's eyes was because he'd wanted that child with Evelyn. Nancy had said their broken engagement hurt Kyle more deeply than he let on. Kyle had said he still loved Evelyn, but it didn't appear he was still harboring ill feelings toward her or Radford when he embraced them and wished them well.

Finally having an opportunity to congratulate them, Amelia stepped forward and prayed she wouldn't lose her balance when she hugged Evelyn. The wine had taken the edge off Amelia's nerves, but it was making her light-headed. "What does Rebecca think about having a little brother or sister?" she asked, hoping her words didn't sound as awkward as they felt in her mouth.

Evelyn reached up and patted Rebecca's back. "She can't wait to mother someone other than our cat. Missy doesn't like wearing bonnets or nappies, does she, Rebecca?"

Rebecca's eyes widened. "She scratches me when I put the bonnet on her."

"I don't blame her," Kyle said, slipping his arm around Amelia's waist then turning to speak to Radford as if it were the most natural thing in the world to stand with his wife in his arms. "Remember when Duke used to tie Dad's old handkerchief around our dog's neck? How many times did Rex bite you for that, Duke?"

Amelia couldn't take her eyes away from Kyle's face. He was so incredibly handsome when he laughed. In that instant, she could vividly picture their children. She and Kyle would have big, hearty boys with wide smiles and dark eyes like their daddy. Their daughters would be tall, with Kyle's thick hair and her nose. All their children would laugh from the belly like Kyle did when he was with his brothers. They would be beautiful children full of ambition. The house would echo with the sound of feet pounding up and down the stairs, with children roughhousing and giggling in their beds when they were supposed to be sleeping. One would always be snuggled against Amelia, nursing an earache or begging a story or just wanting the security of her mother's arms.

The fact that she was holding a wine glass instead of a baby filled her with a desperate urge to start her own family. It would be wonderful if she and Evelyn could raise their children together. If Amelia conceived right away, her baby would only be a few months younger than Evelyn's.

Amelia wanted to make love with Kyle, but she didn't want to risk losing the new closeness she felt with her husband. She'd loved hearing him laugh and she relished the new expressions that had replaced Kyle's usual frown. Already her feelings for him went far beyond attraction and desire. They went to the center of her soul, a knowing so deep that she felt it in her bones. She was falling in love with her husband.

Amelia found the wine bottle and refilled her glass. She would have one more drink to keep her relaxed. Maybe if Kyle had a few more drinks he would relax, too. Maybe if he had enough wine they could consummate their marriage and he wouldn't even notice her secret.

"Where's your glass?" she asked, lifting the wine bottle toward Kyle and giving it a tempting slosh.

His eyebrow quirked and he shot her a curious look, but he held out his glass without commenting. Throughout the evening, she kept a firm hold on the bottle and a sharp eye on Kyle's glass, keeping it filled as he joked with his brothers. Her mind grew foggy, but Kyle's laughter came easier and his touches bolder until he finally tossed her light wrap around her shoulders and told her it was time to go home.

A mixture of excitement and fear filled her stomach, but to bolster her courage and cloud Kyle's thoughts, Amelia slipped a nearly full bottle of wine beneath her wrap.

⊷⊶

The fresh air cleared Kyle's head, but his persistent little wife insisted he share her bottle of pilfered wine. With a laugh at her daring, he helped her finish it off on their short drive home.

"How did that second verse go?" she asked, squinting over at him, making him laugh. He couldn't believe she'd gotten him to sing the raunchy songs most women would have swooned over.

"'She had long, long legs and—'"

"No. Tell me the part about the man." She wrinkled her nose. "I'm not going to sing about some woman's legs."

Kyle laughed.

She hit his arm then fell against him. "Come on."

"All right." He inhaled and opened his mouth. "'My head grew light and my knees turned weak. She held me so tight I couldn't even squeak.'"

"Why the devil would you want to squeak?" Amelia asked, wobbling on the seat beside him as she tried to stare into his eyes. "Do you squeak when that happens?"

His chest felt as if it were going to burst from holding back his laughter, but he didn't want to hurt her feelings. "I don't squeak. I might moan some."

"Really?" Her eyes widened. "Does it hurt you, too?"

The laughter drained out of him as he turned the carriage into their driveway. "No. It feels good. Really good."

"Oh..."

He stopped the carriage and climbed out. His face was warm and his legs less than steady, but Amelia could barely stand up. He left the carriage in front of the house and carried her inside.

She hooked her arms around his neck and giggled as he stumbled through the front door. "Kiss me like you did in the boat."

He looked at her, their noses only inches apart.

Amelia swung her feet and laughed. "Kiss me right here in the parlor with the door open." She pulled his head down, but missed his mouth and kissed his eye. She laughed and tried again, but got his chin. "Hold still, for Pete's sake. How do you expect me to kiss you when you keep moving your head?"

He loved this silly, playful side of her. "I think your head is floating from all that wine you drank."

Amelia covered her ears. "Don't mention that word right now."

Kyle laughed and carried her into their bedroom. He leaned down and laid her on the bed.

She squeezed her arms around his neck and kept him from standing up. "Make love to me."

"What?"

"I want a baby, Kyle."

So that was why she was doing this. He had thought she was finally ready, that he'd finally earned her trust. He cautioned himself not to be hurt by her words. She wouldn't mean to be callous. She'd had too much wine. She'd die of embarrassment tomorrow if she remembered any of this.

"Please." She tugged at his neck. "We have to do it tonight while you're... while I'm ready." She released him and fumbled with the buttons on her dress. "This is going to take too long. Here," she said, reaching down to grasp a fistful of her skirt in each hand. "I'll pull up my skirt."

Kyle stared at her stocking-clad legs and felt every drop of wine rush through his blood, leaving him dizzy and shaking.

She bent her knees.

His own knees buckled and he knelt beside the bed. The sharp ache in his shin did little to clear his mind or ease the ache in his groin. He clapped his palms over his face and gulped a breath of air. He wanted to make love to her. His body begged him to. But he couldn't. Not like this. Not with Amelia barely conscious. Not their first time.

His hands shook as he unbuttoned her dress and slipped it off her pliant body. He unhooked her garters, rolled down her stockings, and took off her shoes.

"Ummmmm... what are you doing to my foot?" she asked, her voice so mellow and breathy, his heart began thudding. He kept her foot in his hand and rubbed his thumbs across her arch in long strokes that made her moan. He would give Boyd credit for knowing the art of seduction. Figures his own timing would stink.

Amelia shivered and Kyle didn't know if it was from the foot massage, from fear, or simply from the cool air, but her discomfort helped him regain his common sense. He tugged her stockings off and dropped them beside the bed then pulled the covers over her shivering body. She sighed and turned on her side, drawing her knees up like a small child. "Get in here and warm me up."

Kyle didn't climb in. He stood by the bed for several minutes to make sure she'd fallen asleep then he went outside to his carriage and drove to the Pemberton Inn. There was absolutely no way he could sleep with Amelia tonight and not make love to her, and the only way he could abstain was to stay out of the house.

⊷⊶

"Are you already sneaking out?" Boyd asked, as Kyle dropped onto the barstool beside his brother.

Kyle nodded to Richard who was on the other side of Boyd, and then signaled the bartender to bring him an ale. "Amelia's sleeping off the wine you gave her."

Boyd held up his hands. "Don't blame me for that last bottle. She stole it on her own."

Kyle stared at him. "You saw her do that?"

"Yes!" Boyd laughed and slapped Kyle on the back. "I fell in love with her right there in the parlor. I figured you were going to be in for quite a night."

"I was." Kyle dropped his forehead into his palm.

Boyd laughed. "This is exactly why I'm not married."

Kyle picked up his mug and drained it, liking the way it revived the wine already in his body. "Bring me another one, Pat." The bartender nodded and grabbed Kyle's mug.

Richard grinned. "Did you and Amelia have your first lover's quarrel tonight?"

"No. My wife was too inebriated to talk, much less argue."

Richard's brows lifted. "Amelia was inebriated?"

"To her eyebrows, but I doubt she'd appreciate anyone else knowing." Kyle rubbed his temples. "Remind me not to let her drink."

Richard and Boyd exchanged a glance then burst out laughing. "Well, don't keep us in suspense," Boyd said. "What happened?"

"Nothing. That's the problem. Nothing happened." He drained his second ale and shoved his mug forward for a refill even though his fuzzy brain tried to tell him that he didn't need any more.

"Richard, I think you and I are going to be carrying Kyle out of here tonight."

"I'm sleeping right here on the bar." Kyle drank down half of the golden-brown liquid in his mug then let the heavy bottom thunk back on the bar. "Why are women afraid of sex?"

"They aren't." Boyd glanced at Richard. "Are they?"

He shrugged. "Some don't like it much, but I don't think they're necessarily afraid of it."

"Why should they be? It's not like we drag them by their hair to the bedroom," Kyle said, glad he could commiserate with his own gender.

"Maybe that's your problem, Kyle." Boyd wiggled his eyebrows. "Amelia might like that."

Richard's laugh irritated Kyle. "What's so funny, Cameron?"

"Nothing, I was just... listening. I'm sorry you're having problems."

"Not as sorry as I am." Kyle lifted his mug to salute his friend. "I'm the sorriest wretch here. Somebody shoot me and end my misery."

A pair of handcuffs clanked onto the oak bar beside Kyle and he looked up to see Duke standing beside him with a badge on his chest and a revolver strapped to his hip. "I would help you out, but I'm still on duty." Duke's sharp gaze surveyed the tavern as if trouble might be lurking somewhere in the shadows. "What am I missing?"

"Kyle hasn't consummated his marriage yet."

"Great. I get to be humiliated here, too." Kyle pinched the bridge of his nose, his thoughts growing duller by the drink. "What am I going to do?"

"Don't ask me," Duke said, leaning against the bar, crossing his arms over his wide chest. "I stay away from virgins and marriage."

"Good advice." Kyle eased back on his stool. "Thanks for offering it too late."

"What's Amelia afraid of?" Boyd asked.

"I don't know." Kyle glanced to either side to make sure they weren't being overheard. Satisfied his personal life was being shared only by his brothers and his friend, Kyle rested his mug on his thigh and spoke to Boyd. "She was scared to death on our wedding night. I couldn't force the issue with her, and I haven't been able to since."

"I couldn't stand it," Boyd said, his voice sympathetic. "I'd visit one of my affectionate friends."

"No you wouldn't."

"I would!" Richard declared. "You have rights, Kyle. If Amelia isn't performing her wifely duty, you're entitled to seek comfort elsewhere."

Kyle dismissed their comments. He didn't know about Richard, but Boyd wouldn't cheat on his own wife any more than Kyle would.

"Maybe you're too aggressive," Duke said. "Maybe you just went too fast with Amelia."

"I told her I'd slow down."

Duke braced his hand on the bar. "Well, maybe you need to be less threatening and just, I don't know, lie on your back and let her take control of things."

"I'd bind my hands and hang from the bedpost if that's all it would take." Kyle leaned his elbows on the bar and set his glass down. It clinked against the handcuffs and he nudged them aside with the bottom of his mug. The cool metal glimmered up at him, glowing and shimmering in the lantern light until he couldn't seem to draw his gaze away. "Duke, do you have another set of cuffs?"

"Of course. They're at the office."

"Give me the key to this set."

"What for?"

"Just give me the key." He turned toward his brothers and Richard. "Keep your fat mouths shut about this."

A wide grin broke across Boyd's face. "What I wouldn't give to see this show."

Chapter Twenty-four

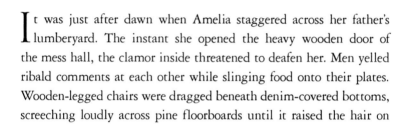

It was just after dawn when Amelia staggered across her father's lumberyard. The instant she opened the heavy wooden door of the mess hall, the clamor inside threatened to deafen her. Men yelled ribald comments at each other while slinging food onto their plates. Wooden-legged chairs were dragged beneath denim-covered bottoms, screeching loudly across pine floorboards until it raised the hair on Amelia's neck. Serving ladles whacked plates then clanked back into the pans before they were hoisted and banged in front of the next man at the table.

To Amelia's surprise, her mother stood by the stove with her apron on seemingly oblivious to the painful din. She'd been helping with lunch and supper, but Shorty had been the king of the breakfast hour. By the look on his face, he viewed her mother's presence as the ultimate invasion of his privacy.

"Good morning," Amelia said, sagging against the doorframe, praying she wasn't going to embarrass herself by losing her stomach in the mess hall. She felt awful.

Not one person heard her.

"What's going on?" she asked.

No one acknowledged her because none of them heard her. She may as well be talking to the door.

As the ache in her head mushroomed, she walked to the stove, removed two lids from steaming pots, and turned to the rowdy group before her. She slammed the lids together with the force of a lead cymbal man in a marching band.

Ears that were accustomed to screaming saws and crashing lumber were not as fatigued at five-thirty in the morning. Heads jerked up and forks clattered to the table as every man present sought the source of his abuse.

Her husband stared at her in shock, his eyes as round as the sausage patties in the middle of the table. "I guess I won't ask how you're feeling," he said.

"Too awful to listen to all this noise." Amelia placed the lids back on the pots then finger-combed her hair back, realizing with dawning horror that it was still hanging loose down her back. She'd been so preoccupied with wanting to know if she'd pleased Kyle last night, if he'd learned her secret, that she'd just yanked on her clothes and begged one of the men at the depot to take her to the lumberyard.

Mortified, by her behavior and state of undress, she turned away from the room full of shocked stares and filled her bowl. She could barely swallow the first bite of her breakfast, and it wasn't because of her sensitive stomach. "What is this?" she asked, her eyes tearing from an effort to choke down the gooey lump.

"Sagamite," Shorty answered. "It's Indian meal and brown sugar all fried up together."

"I did the measuring and mixing," her mother added proudly.

Amelia glanced around the table. "Have any of you tried this?"

"Not yet."

"Nope."

"I'm fixin' to."

She waited patiently while Jeb, Ray, and Willie spooned the lumped-up gruel into their mouths. As the pasty glob registered on their taste buds, faces turned red and one by one each man repeatedly gagged on his food. Jeb and Ray got theirs down, but Willie returned the gruel to his bowl with a disgusting splat.

"What is that?" Willie demanded, backhanding the drool from his lips.

"I just said it was sagamite, ya fool!"

"It tastes more like sh—"

"Willie! Wouldn't you say it has yeast in it?" Amelia asked, trying to keep the men from killing each other.

"There ain't yeast in sagamite," Shorty argued.

Amelia stuck her spoon in the middle of the lump where it stood like a flagpole on a prairie. "There's yeast in here. Mother, who showed you how to mix this?"

Victoria pointed straight at Shorty.

Insulted by her accusing finger, Shorty thrust his jaw out. "I told you three cups of meal to each cup of brown sugar."

"You said to each spoon of yeast."

Shorty's eyes rounded. "You poisoned my delicious sagamite with yeast?"

"Well, you cut my beautiful pie to pieces yesterday!"

"I was trying to help you serve it."

"Well, I was trying to help you make breakfast, you ingrate!"

"You keep your bustles and clumsy fingers out of my kitchen!" Shorty bellowed, his face red.

Kyle slammed his fist on the table and stood up. His expression was dark and stern and Amelia knew he was going to order her and her mother to leave the mill.

"Kyle, wait! Mama just wants to help us. Please. This is the only way she can do that." Before he could comment, Amelia turned back to Shorty. "Would you and Mama please make the crew something they can eat so we can all get back to work?"

Without another glance at Kyle or her mother, Amelia pulled open the door. "Wait a minute," Kyle commanded. With her heart in her throat, Amelia ignored him and stepped outside. If he was going to chastise her, she didn't want it to be in front of the crew.

He followed her outside and closed the door behind him then guided her around to the side of the building. "I thought you would spend the morning in bed, which is obviously what you should have done. What are you doing here?"

Coming to see him, to see if she'd passed muster as his wife, but she couldn't blurt out her question like a harlot waiting for payment. "What time did we finally go to bed?" she asked, hoping his expression would answer the question she couldn't ask.

"About ten o'clock for you. I was with Boyd and Richard until around midnight."

"What?" Amelia pushed away from the building. "We went to bed together, didn't we?" His eyebrows lifted and her stomach flipped. "You carried me into the bedroom, Kyle. You took my dress off and we... you... didn't we?"

Kyle shook his head. "We didn't consummate our vows last night if that's what you're asking. You'd had too much to drink."

She sagged against the worn wallboards, unable to believe nothing had changed between them. She'd wanted that first time over with. Now it loomed in her future like a disease. Even though she'd asked him to make love with her, Kyle hadn't taken advantage of her. Some men would have jumped at the opportunity. But not Kyle. She should have known.

"We have to consummate our vows, Kyle."

"I agree."

"Then let's just do it."

"All right."

"Tonight."

A grin tipped his lips. "Go home and sleep for a few hours and I'll come get you at noon."

"Noon? Won't it be better to wait until tonight?"

"No." He put his finger across her mouth to stop her question then kissed her on the forehead. "I have a surprise for you, Amée. Just be ready at noon."

Chapter Twenty-five

Amelia could barely return Kyle's smile when he swung her up into their carriage and drove to a wooded area a mile or so north of her mother's house. She'd been expecting him to pull off her clothes and drag her into bed the minute he entered the house, but he hadn't even glanced toward the bedroom before rushing her outside.

Kyle secured the horses then took her hand and guided her into the woods and down a long narrow path. She stepped over a fallen tree limb then nearly bumped into Kyle's back when he stopped suddenly.

He released her hand then tested his weight on his injured leg before bracing his good foot against a huge boulder. Hooking his toes and fingers in the small crevices, he slowly scaled the side of the rock then climbed on top of the massive stone. He disappeared for two or three minutes then returned and dusted his hands on his trousers. He squatted on the balls of his feet and looked down at her. "Give me your hand," he said, reaching for her. "There's no other way around."

Amelia glanced to her left where the bank dropped several feet into the gorge. To her right was another bank rising high overhead. Though she hadn't realized it, Kyle had been leading her along the wide shelf of a cliff that swept down into the gorge. "Are you serious?"

"It's the only way to see what's on the other side."

Amelia lifted a brow. "Do I really want to know?"

"I sure hope so," he said, his voice filled with quiet desperation. "Come on. I won't let you fall."

She hiked up her dress, grasped Kyle's hand, and hooked her toe in a wide crevice. "How are we going to get off this thing?" she asked, hoisting herself up to the next foothold.

"We're not. We're going to live in a cave and drink wine and forget about sawmills and contracts and obligations that wear us out."

"Sounds wonderful," she said, and immediately lost her footing.

"Whoa!" Kyle wobbled above her before regaining his balance. "I'd like to experience a night or two in our cave before you kill me."

Amelia giggled as she grasped a protruding shank of rock and anchored her foot. She tipped her head back and met Kyle's twinkling eyes. "If you keep making me laugh, I'm never going to make it up there."

"I'll fill the bathtub tonight if you do."

Amelia laughed and scanned the side of the craggy rock then took a cautious step.

"There's a ridge about eight inches above your left foot," Kyle said, leaning over the edge, a tense expression on his face as she worked her way toward him. "Hook your right hand in that hole."

"What hole?"

"Two feet to your right."

Amelia studied the side of the rock until she found the hole. "What's on the other side?"

"Something special."

"It better be worth scraped shins and broken fingernails."

"One more step. There you go. I've got you." Kyle reached behind her, cupped her bottom, and hauled her over the edge. He fell backward and Amelia yelped as she slipped between his knees, her body sprawling across his. He scooped her hair back and captured the length in one hand. "I'm glad you made it."

"Of course I made it. I climb like a monkey," she said, lifting her nose in haughty arrogance.

He laughed. "I noticed your tail wagging while you were climbing."

She swatted his shoulder. "You owe me a bath, Mr. Grayson."

"My pleasure. I'll even wash your back if you like." He sat up and pulled her up beside him. "Your hair fell down."

"I noticed." She reached up to fix it, but he caught her hands and pulled them away.

"I like it loose."

His beautiful mouth was only inches away. She could tip her face back and simply lean in to a kiss. Their gazes held for several seconds, but he didn't kiss her. He sat beside her with a relaxed, serene expression on his face. He was leaning back on one hand, his other arm resting on an upraised, bent knee. The breeze lifted his hair and ruffled the sleeves of his tan shirt. Amelia took in their peaceful surroundings then turned to Kyle. "You're happy out here, aren't you?"

"I like the woods."

She tilted her head, searched his face. "That's what's different about you today. You're not a lumber boss out here or a tense husband. You're just Kyle."

"What's that mean?"

Despite his smile, she sensed sincerity in his question and she lowered her guard. "You're relaxed and easy to talk to."

A length of hair blew across her face and Kyle tucked it behind her ear then drew her into his arms. He felt like a rock and smelled like the forest. No wonder he was at home here. The thrumming pulse in his neck beat softly against her forehead. He was strong and vibrantly alive, his body warm and vital against hers. Touching him ignited her senses and she yearned to discover his secrets, to know the real man inside.

They sat in silence for a long time, listening to the birds, the splashing water, the breeze, as he stroked his fingers through her hair.

Slowly, he tilted her head up and looked at her. "You're so beautiful," he whispered. Then he kissed her so tenderly it made her heart flutter. A voice inside her told her she wasn't worthy of Kyle or his affection, but she clung to him anyhow, giving him what she could, taking what she desperately needed.

Finally, he eased her away and stood up. He took her hand and guided her across the boulder then they stepped down into a cave.

Amelia stopped in astonishment. Two rows of lanterns burned softly and formed a glowing walkway that illuminated both walls of a cave. "How did you manage all this?"

"I brought them up this morning."

The stone walls shimmered in the lantern light. "This is magnificent. I had no idea all this beauty was hidden in the dark."

She explored the jagged ceiling, but when she made it to the other end, Kyle asked her to wait. Before she could turn back, he reached down and lifted her into his arms.

"What are you doing?" she asked with a surprised laugh.

"Carrying my bride to her future." He stepped out of the cave and turned her to face the sparkling majesty of the falls.

"Oh, Kyle," she whispered, staring at a blanket of falling water.

He stepped into a wide shaft of sparkling sunlight and lowered her to her feet. "We're behind the falls."

She glimpsed daylight and trees through the funnels of cascading water that dropped into a frothing pool far below them. "How did you know this was here?" she asked, awed by the beauty of the deep green pool below and the slick gray shale that glistened in the afternoon sun.

"My father cut timber for the man who owns this land back when I was ten or so. Boyd and I found this place by accident."

"It's beautiful," Amelia said, overcome by an urge to thrust her hands beneath the crystal water. "It's so peaceful." She noted the shelf they were standing on was a good six or seven feet wide and stretched twice as far on either side before disappearing into the cave they'd just exited. "What a magical place."

"It made a good hideout for two restless boys."

"I'll bet." Amelia lifted her face and felt the light mist from the falls kiss her cheeks. "It's so mystical, I can almost see water fairies with glittering wings and long golden hair."

Kyle chuckled and stepped behind her, drawing her against his chest. "You're more likely to see a bat with beady eyes."

He circled her waist with his arms, and she realized she needed his touch, his love. For this one precious moment, she was going to pretend that her father was alive and her parents were happy and that she was a wholesome girl worthy of Kyle's love.

"Boyd and I were pirates that day," Kyle said, a smile in his voice. "We captured enemy ships, stole their women, and robbed them of priceless jewels." He laughed softly then grew quiet. "It seems like a thousand years ago now."

Amelia envisioned Kyle as a carefree boy with a vivid imagination and she liked the mental picture of a young, adventurous Kyle. "Did you play here often?"

"No. I haven't been back since."

She tipped her head back to see his face. "Why not?"

"I guess I got busy and forgot it was here."

Sunlight danced over the writhing water, sparking like brilliant fireflies. "I could never forget something this magnificent," she said reverently. "It feels so safe here."

"It is, Amée." His arms tightened around her waist and they stood quietly, watching the sparkling water rush past, listening to it drop into the churning pool below.

She turned to face him, knowing they'd earned this moment of closeness, of wonder and joy. "Thank you," she whispered.

He kissed her. His tongue stroked hers in slow, deep sweeps. She swayed in his arms and he lightened the kiss, until finally he simply eased away and looked into her eyes. "It's dryer over there." He nodded toward the far side of the falls where the ledge was deeper.

She followed him then glanced at a large cloth sack leaning against the wall. "What's in the bag?"

He tensed, his expression uneasy as his gaze locked with hers. "It's our wedding bed, if you want it to be."

Chapter Twenty-six

Amelia's eyes widened. "Here?"

"Only if you want to." He glanced from the bag to Amelia. "This morning it seemed like a great idea. Maybe it's not?"

She looked at the bag then at the falls then finally at Kyle who stood before her waiting for her answer. She knew he wanted this day to be special for her, and somehow it made sense that they should share their first intimate experience in this magical, private world. "All right," she said quietly. "What do you want me to do?"

Kyle released his breath. "Whatever you feel like doing. You lead. I'll follow."

She nodded because she didn't know what else to do. How could she lead when she was filled with nerves and memories? How was a woman supposed to make love to her husband if he just stood in front of her waiting for her direction? "I think I want you to lead."

He reached for the bag at his feet. "Let's open this first." He knelt beside it and pulled out a thick roll of bedding that he laid on the warm slate. June sunlight slipped through the crevices in the rocks above Kyle's head, splashing across his shoulders and the blankets as he opened them to make their bed. He pressed his hand into the springy thickness and turned to Amelia. "I hope it's soft enough for you."

For her. He'd done this for her. The lanterns, the falls, the bed he would love her on, everything was for her. She moved forward then knelt beside her husband, wanting to love him. She kissed his cheek then turned the top cover back to open the bed. "I'm ready to become your wife."

His eyes grew dark and his hands shook as he reached for the buttons at her neck. "Would you rather do this?" he asked when his fingers kept slipping and bumping her chin.

"It might be faster."

She reached up to help him, but he trapped her hands in his. "I don't need fast." He brushed his thumbs across her fingers. "Your pace, Amée, not mine."

Touched by his consideration, she released the buttons down the front of her dress. She slipped the soft fabric over her shoulders and let it fall to her waist.

"Will you be cold?" he asked with concern.

She shook her head. She couldn't feel anything but heat pushing through her veins. She'd never undressed for Richard. "Your turn," she said.

Kyle shrugged off his tan shirt and tossed it onto the cloth bag that had contained their bedding. "The undershirt, too?" he asked.

She nodded, admiring the flex of his broad shoulders as he pulled his arms from the sleeves then stretched to lay it aside. A swath of dark hair covered his chest and contrasted with the intriguing shadows of rib and muscle tapering across his flat stomach.

"I can put it back on," he said, a question in his voice.

"No." She met his eyes, embarrassed for staring at him. "I mean, it's not necessary. Is it?"

He eyed her suspiciously for a moment then said, "I prefer it off."

She nodded and waited then realized he was waiting for her. "Oh! Sorry." She reached up to untie the ribbons on her chemise, glad that she'd forgone a corset and spared Kyle's trembling fingers the task.

"Amée?"

She stopped plucking her ribbons and looked up.

"It doesn't need to be this awkward."

She let her hands fall to her lap. "I thought I was the only one who felt this way."

"We're both nervous."

Apprehensive and excited seemed the more appropriate words, but when she thought of the final act of lovemaking, it was nerves that tightened her stomach. It had hurt the first time with Richard. And she'd felt violated and dirty the last time they'd been together. It wouldn't be that way with Kyle. She knew that. What she didn't know was if she could keep her mind anchored in the present instead of the past when Kyle consummated their union. "I think we should just do it," she blurted then nearly swooned from the heat of embarrassment that hit her face.

Kyle grinned and arched a dark brow. "All right."

She buried her face in her hands. "I meant, we should quit being so serious about everything."

"Good idea," he said.

The sound of metal clinking made her lift her head. When she saw what he had in his hands, she gasped in disbelief. "What are you doing with handcuffs?"

"Easing your fear, I hope."

"What?"

He closed the cuffs around his wrists. "I want you to feel safe, to be relaxed with me." He showed her a small key dangling from a blue ribbon then slipped it around her neck.

She could only stare into Kyle's gorgeous eyes. "Tell me you didn't ask Duke for those cuffs." Kyle's expression grew sheepish and Amelia groaned. "He knows about this?"

"Not exactly."

"Oh, Kyle, how am I ever going to face him again?"

"I was hoping you'd return the cuffs for me."

"What?" Kyle burst out laughing and Amelia lunged at him. He howled with laughter as she pushed him backward onto the blankets.

Amelia couldn't stop herself from kissing him. She loved him like this, playful, charming, irresistible. She kissed the laugh lines by his eyes and bit his arrogant nose then smothered his laughter by covering his mouth with her own. She felt his bound hands trapped between them and knew he was making a joke of the cuffs to distract her from the real reason he'd chained himself. He honestly believed she was afraid of him. Her proud, arrogant, controlling husband was making his final surrender. He was giving her his power to help her quell her fears.

Shame filled her for misleading him, and her eyes misted as she sat back. She gazed down at Kyle as she finished undressing for him.

His eyes devoured her as she knelt beside him, clad only in the blue ribbon around her neck, but he didn't move. Her lead, he'd said and he was keeping his promise. Amelia lifted his bound hands and brought them to her breasts, loving the feel of his warm palms and the way his nostrils flared when he stroked her there. Her stomach lifted like a hot-air balloon, filling her chest with joy.

Seeing the need in his eyes, she moved his hands to the fastenings on his trousers. Obediently, he opened them, but was unable to pull them off with his wrists chained. Locking gazes with her dark-eyed husband lying on his back, willing to do anything for her, brought tears to her eyes.

"I can't, Kyle. Not like this." She pulled the ribbon necklace over her head and reached to release the metal clasps at his wrists.

He caught her hands before she could unlock them. "I want you to be sure."

She turned the key. She slipped them off his wrists then tossed the key and Kyle's bonds onto her pile of discarded clothing.

She lay down beside him and they turned to face each other. He cupped her chin and drew her mouth to his. She slipped her arms around his neck and pulled him closer. He skimmed her side and her back with his palm then lower, over her bare hip and thigh. Gooseflesh rippled across her skin from the coolness of the air and the heat of his hand.

"You're chilled," he said then sat up and pulled off his shoes and stockings. He lay back on the blankets, braced his shoulders and feet on the bedding, and lifted his hips to slide off his pants and undershorts. Amelia looked away as he slipped his feet out of his trouser legs, but she knew her husband had every right to be proud and arrogant. "Climb in," he said, drawing the blanket over them.

Amelia lay wrapped in his arms, drawing warmth from his hard body, praying this act would bring them closer and bond them for life.

He brought her fingers to his lips and kissed them then placed her hand on the crisp hairs of his chest. "Lead the way," he whispered then kissed her until her mind reeled and her heart pounded. She moved her hand over his ribs, and Kyle's palm caressed her side. She felt his sleek, hard hip, and he felt hers. As she grew bolder in her exploration, he returned each of her caresses with his exquisite, tender touch, stroking her until Amelia felt breathless and hot and urgent. Finally, she drew her fingers over his hardness, and he sought her softness until she arched and shuddered into his palm, gripped by waves of pleasure that made her gasp and bury her face in his chest.

The airy roar of the falls mixed with Kyle's hot breath on her neck as he rolled on top of her and braced himself between her thighs. "Now?" he asked, his voice ragged.

Amelia nodded and welcomed her husband, her future.

Pleasurable pressure filled her as Kyle slowly began to join them as husband and wife. She cupped his firm hips and felt his muscles flex beneath her palms as he tried to hold back. It didn't hurt. It didn't feel dirty. She didn't feel violated. She felt reborn!

He moved, gently at first, his face a mask of concentration that changed to confused surprise as he pushed and she welcomed him with ease.

His arms trembled as he held himself still, the question growing in his eyes. Amelia lowered her lashes and pulled him closer, deeper, until her own passion mounted beneath his rolling hips and she soared toward the wondrous sensation she'd experienced earlier.

He looked different with his jaw slack and his eyes glazed with passion. He was as open and vulnerable in that moment as she was. Waves of pleasure rippled through her, she cried out with love for her husband. Kyle lunged, the sound of his voice filling her ears as he followed her into that blissful moment of release.

Their breathing mingled with the sound of the falls and the splash of water on the rocks below. Soft light slipped through the rock ceiling and brought out the auburn strands in his brown hair as their hearts slowed to normal. She pushed her fingers into the thick strands at his temples, holding his head between her palms, and looking into his sated eyes. "You have no idea what this meant to me," she whispered.

His gaze locked with hers, his unspoken question brimming in his eyes. She knew he was waiting for her to tell him, to offer an explanation, but thick, choking shame filled her throat and cut off her words. Her hands slipped from his hair and fell to her sides as she lay beneath him feeling too unworthy to even touch him.

Kyle's lashes lowered, but she glimpsed the pain in his eyes as he withdrew and lay on the bed he'd made for her. He turned onto his back and covered his eyes with his arm. He didn't move a muscle or make a sound for so long, Amelia's fear nearly swallowed her.

"I loved him," she said quietly, not wanting him to think the worst of her character. She knew now that what she'd felt for Richard had only been infatuation, but at seventeen, she'd believed it was love.

The roar and splatter of the falls suddenly seemed intimidating as she lay there waiting for Kyle to ask questions, to ask why, to hear her apology for keeping the truth from him.

He laughed instead—the mirthless, bitter laugh of someone who suddenly realizes he's a fool, the unsuspecting victim of a cruel joke he's played on himself.

Chapter Twenty-seven

Kyle pressed his forehead to the front door, loath to go inside and face Amelia. He'd spent two grueling evenings trying to act as if nothing had changed, but in his heart, everything had changed.

He had thought making love would be the beginning of their marriage, but it felt like the end. The shame in Amelia's eyes had confirmed his suspicion, but it wasn't Amelia's lack of virginity that had been tearing him up inside. Sure, he'd been surprised, disappointed even, but he hadn't thought less of her because of it. It was that she'd lied about being afraid, that in her need to conceal the truth, she'd let him make a fool of himself.

He'd been so relieved when he'd finally turned Amelia's nervousness to laughter. It hadn't mattered in that moment what it had cost him in pride to ask Duke for his handcuffs. Making Amelia laugh had been worth it. For her, Kyle had held back and experienced the beauty of making love slowly, of watching a woman explore his body as if she'd never touched a man. When she'd cried out with pleasure, his body rejoiced, but his mind fought the truth as he followed her over the edge in a state of shock and disbelief.

Perhaps it was selfish of him, but he had wanted to introduce his wife to the act of lovemaking. He had wanted to teach her about intimacy and passion. Kyle had owned Evelyn's friendship, but she'd given her passion to his brother. Catherine had only allowed his friendship. Kyle wasn't willing to settle this time. He wanted it all. Companionship. Passion. Trust. A woman who could commit herself to their marriage body and soul without betraying him by keeping secrets.

Still, he had been keeping his own secrets, and maybe the real crux of his problem was his own guilty conscience. It was eating a hole in his gut and he couldn't stand it any longer.

"Kyle?"

He spun toward Amelia, who stood behind him with an empty laundry crate under her arm and a worried expression on her face. "Are you all right?"

He shook his head, knowing he was going to confess everything, that he was going to lay himself bare and ask her to do the same. Then, God willing, they might stand a chance of reconciling, of living together with respect and friendship, and maybe something more someday. "We need to talk," he said, dreading the painful discussion ahead of them.

Her face paled, but he pushed open the door and waited for her to step inside. The parlor was dim after the bright sunshine, and Kyle caught the toe of his boot on the rocker leg as he passed it. He stumbled and cursed, but kept himself from sprawling across the pretty little oval rug Amelia had placed in front of the rocking chair.

"I'm going to move that back into the corner," she said, setting her crate on the floor between the sofa and chair.

"It's fine there. I just wasn't paying attention." Indecision filled her expression and Kyle sighed. "Forget the chair, Amelia. I have something to tell you that's going to be difficult for both of us. Maybe you should sit down."

Instead of sitting, she stepped behind the parlor chair and rested her hands on the back as if it would shield her from what he was about to say. "Are you trying to tell me that you want me to leave?" she asked, her voice unsteady. "I can stay with Mama if you don't want me here."

Regret consumed him, made him ache because his cool silence had allowed her to think he didn't want her. He'd just needed time to ease the shock and sort through feelings.

He met her eyes. "I don't want any more secrets between us, Amelia. They'll only cause problems later on."

Her face flushed and she lowered her eyes. "I was only seventeen, Kyle. I believed he was going to marry me, but I learned too late that he didn't want a wife." She looked at him, her eyes filled with regret. "I'm truly sorry. At our wedding reception you said it mattered whether your bride was pure. I should have told you right then and there, but I was afraid. I needed to marry you. Now I need you... in other ways."

He needed her, too. That's what scared him so much. Somehow Amelia had cracked open a door he'd sworn to keep closed. Not only had she rearranged his home and his daily routine, she had invaded his life and shaken him wide awake. As much as he wanted to keep her at arm's length, he felt an intense need to pull her close, to hold her and protect her and make her laugh again. But he wouldn't make her laugh today. He would break her heart and it was going to kill him to do it.

He rubbed his eyes, having no idea how to explain his own stupidity and express his regret. "Your father and I had words the night he died," he said, deciding to get right to the heart of his confession. "If I had known he'd been having chest pains, I never would have gone to see him, Amelia. But I swear I didn't know. The night your father collapsed, I'd stopped by his mill to ask when he was going to pay me for the timber I'd sold him. He'd been putting me off for three months, and that night he claimed he still couldn't pay me"

"He probably couldn't, Kyle. We both know that everything Papa had was mortgaged to the bank."

"I wasn't aware of his financial situation that night any more than I was aware he was ill. I'd heard he just made a large deposit at the bank. I needed the money he owed me so I could pay for the new sawmill I'd ordered."

"There wasn't any money in Papa's accounts. I verified it myself."

Her anger surprised Kyle and he held up a hand to calm her. "I had no way of knowing that. I thought your father was railroading me. He'd been acting strange and I wasn't sure what to think anymore. He'd even been undercutting prices to take business away from the smaller mills."

"Given his financial situation I would think Papa was probably trying to save his business from going under."

"At the time I thought it was his way of keeping me from expanding my own mill."

"Oh, Kyle. You didn't accuse him of that?" Her shoulders drooped. "Papa would have never held you back or cheated you out of money. He thought the world of you. How could you even think such a thing about him?"

"He'd been acting strange, Amelia. I didn't know what to think anymore." Kyle flexed his fingers, wishing for the hundredth time that he'd never gone to see Tom Drake that night. "I didn't realize how my words were coming across, but believe me, I regret ever saying them and upsetting your father. When he collapsed it was the worst moment of my life."

The blood drained from her face. "Are you saying my father collapsed over an unpaid bill?"

There was no need to respond.

"You made cruel accusations and upset Papa because you thought he was standing in the way of your ambition?"

Kyle suffered her condemning stare knowing he deserved it. "I admired your father, Amelia. I would never have intentionally hurt him."

She stared at him. "You caused this whole mess, Kyle. You caused Papa's collapse. You came to my apartment and got me dismissed from my position. All because of your ambition!" She struck her fists against the top of the chair back. "My father never would have betrayed you. You knew that, but you were too concerned about your own interests to consider it."

Knowing he couldn't dispute her claim, Kyle sighed. "Maybe I was. I don't know."

Her glare left no doubt what she thought.

"Amelia, I'm sorry." He sighed again, but it still felt as if he were carrying two hundred pounds on his shoulders. "There's nothing I can do to change what happened, but I'm deeply and sincerely sorry for everything I've done that's brought pain to you and your family. I made a terrible mistake with your father, and I know it."

"Then why didn't you tell me this before I married you?"

His heart cramped, and he wondered if she was suggesting she wouldn't have married him if she had known what happened. "I couldn't tell you because it would have only deepened your pain."

"I don't think that's possible." Tears pearled on her lower lids as she scooped up her laundry crate and walked into the kitchen.

Kyle let her go, not because he wanted to but because there was nothing left he could say. He'd wanted to confess everything, to tell Amelia about her father and Catherine, to apologize for both situations, but after seeing the pain in Amelia's eyes, he knew he could never tell her about Catherine.

Chapter Twenty-eight

As the month of July crawled by, the temperature soared and Amelia and Kyle sweated through their days at the lumberyard. Though Kyle still wanted Amelia to stay home where it was safe, he had allowed her to do some light physical labor because she seemed to need an outlet for her heartache. In addition to doing office work, she shoveled sawdust, pulled slabs of scrap wood from the cut-off table, and helped her mother in the mess hall. Shorty had finally relinquished his cooking duties to her mother, who was slowly learning to laugh again, but Amelia's own laughter was painfully absent.

Though she hadn't put her back to him at night, Kyle knew she needed time to work through her resentment and heartache so he hadn't pushed her to make love with him. There was a vast emptiness in their relationship that he didn't know how to fill. He longed to resurrect the adventurous, spirited side of his wife that inspired him to laughter, but Amelia had shut that part of herself away. She was quiet and serious, so far removed from the sassy woman he'd married that Kyle wished he'd never made his confession.

Even now after a rewarding, productive day at the lumberyard, she sat in the rocking chair in the parlor, sipping cold tea with him without speaking a word. Her hair was still wet from her bath and it reminded Kyle of the day they sank her little rowboat and how they'd played afterward.

Tonight he'd considered slipping into the kitchen to tease Amelia while she was bathing, but he knew she would have resented the intrusion, that she wouldn't have laughed no matter what he did. So he sat on the sofa wondering how they were ever going to bridge her heartache and his inability to express himself.

If he could just hold her, it would help. Even if it didn't soothe her discomfort, it would be a connection. He stood, intending to pull her out of the rocking chair and bring her to the sofa with him, but the knock on the door turned him back with a sigh of frustration.

When he opened the door, Lucinda Clark's brilliant smile greeted him, and after assuring her that Amelia was home and that it was perfectly fine for her to visit, Kyle escaped and headed for Radford's house.

He came back three hours later wondering if he'd lost his mind. It was bad enough having a rocking chair in his parlor that continually attacked his toes, and prissy pillows on his sofa he didn't dare to touch, now he was about to add two banshee kittens to the mix.

"Stay put, little tigers." Kyle tucked one kitten back into his shirt pocket, but a tiny paw took a swipe at his finger for the umpteenth time. "Ouch! You little..." He glanced at the wound and cursed. He'd stopped counting the pricks and scratches halfway home. "If it wasn't for my wife, you two would be going right back to Evelyn and Rebecca." Missy's litter of six kittens had been born three days after Kyle's wedding and Evelyn was thrilled to send the two female terrors home with Kyle. Rebecca had given Kyle the evil eye all the way out of the yard. Just remembering her scowl and those tiny fists propped on her hips made him chuckle. Radford would have his hands full when that girl got old enough to speak her mind.

Kyle breathed a sigh of relief to see that Lucinda's buggy was gone. He wanted to give Amelia the kittens in private. If she hated the little devils, he would gladly take them right back to the livery. But if she liked them, if they brought even a spark of joy to her eyes, he wanted to try in that moment to reach through her resentment.

He stepped into the parlor and nodded to Amelia, who was still sitting in that cursed rocking chair.

"You didn't have to leave just because Lucinda was here," she said, but Kyle only shrugged, his mind too busy planning how to present the kittens.

Several tiny needles sank into his chest and Kyle yelped as the kittens announced themselves. Amelia's eyes widened, but he was occupied with the squirming tyrants that were attacking him through his thin shirt. "Ouch!" He reached for his pocket and felt another set of claws pierce his skin. "You little demons!" He grabbed each side of his open collar and yanked. Buttons flew in all directions.

"What are you doing?" Amelia asked, her shocked gaze jumping between Kyle and the buttons rolling across the oak floor.

"Saving what's left of my skin." Gripping his shirt above the pocket, he worked his arms out of the short sleeves then shoved it toward Amelia as if it were a soiled diaper. "Here," he said, scrapping his plan of trying to romance his wife. The little hellions would flay him alive before he could get one of them out of the pocket.

The instant she took the shirt, her eyes registered the squirming mass in the pocket and she shrieked. She would have dropped it if Kyle hadn't cupped his hands and saved the kittens' miserable lives.

"It moved!" She glanced at Kyle with a horrified expression and he knew he'd totally destroyed any romantic effect he'd hoped for. "What is in there?"

"Demons." He lowered the shirt to the floor and stepped back, not trusting the miniature maniacs. "Don't ask me what I was thinking to bring them home."

One fuzzy little head poked from beneath the shirt and eyed Kyle as if deciding whether or not to attack. "Don't even think about it," he warned.

Amelia gaped at the kitten, but it ducked back under the shirt. "You brought home a kitten?" she asked. Before Kyle could answer, two furry heads peeped out at them. "Oh, look! There's two of them." Amelia glanced at Kyle with warm surprise in her eyes. "Are they Missy's?"

"Yes, but stay back. They're miniature female warriors."

Amelia laughed and knelt beside the shirt. "They're precious." She tapped her finger on the floor and the kittens barreled out from their hiding place to follow the winding trail she drew across the floor.

He watched with a mixture of surprise and gladness. He hadn't heard Amelia laugh in weeks.

The joy in her eyes made it worth having his chest shredded. So what if his fingers were filled with more holes than a sieve? It was a small price to pay for the joyful expression on Amelia's face.

"I can take them back if you don't want them," he said, fighting the urge to beg her to exile the rat-sized terrors.

"You got them for me?" she asked, warmth radiating from her eyes.

"I thought you might miss Missy. Evelyn said she used to belong to you."

"She was a stray that made the schoolhouse her home, but that was my fault for feeding her."

"If you'd rather have Missy back, I'll see if Rebecca will trade her for these two... kittens," Kyle said, his hopes soaring that he might yet find a way out of his own bad decision.

"Of course not. Rebecca loves Missy. I would never ask her to give her back. Besides, these babies are adorable." Amelia swept her fingers across the back of the darker colored kitten and it rolled onto its back, paddling her fingers with its paws. "What are we going to name you two?"

"How about Demon and Hellion?"

Amelia laughed and tickled the kitten's belly. "Did you give my husband a hard time on the walk home?" The kitten squirmed and nipped at her fingers. "Well, I don't blame you. I wouldn't want to be stuffed in a pocket, either."

"I would have wrung their scrawny necks otherwise."

Amelia sat back on her heels, her smile slowly fading as she met his eyes. "No you wouldn't."

Because he didn't know how to respond to the soft assurance in her voice, Kyle just shrugged.

"Thank you for the kittens." Her gaze shifted to his bare chest that was lined with scratches then back to his face. "I love them."

That's all that mattered. The demon twins could have the house, just as long as they continued to light Amelia's eyes with happiness.

"I'll call you Cinnamon," she said, finger-wrestling the dark brown kitten. She swept out her free hand and chucked the other kitten under the chin. "You're Ginger."

The kittens were the color of the spices she'd named them after, but Kyle still thought Demon and Hellion were more appropriate names for them.

After playing with the kittens all evening, Amelia turned on the mattress to face her husband, her heart aching with emotions that were still raw. She loved Kyle. She knew he regretted pushing her father into a collapse, but the fact remained that he had. No matter how she turned it, the situation made her ache. She wanted to forgive and forget, to love Kyle and enjoy their marriage, but every time she turned toward him, she felt she was turning away from her father.

"If those scrawny rats don't stop their crying, I'm going to haul them right back to the livery."

She knew Kyle wouldn't do any such thing. "The kittens don't like it out in the woodshed."

"Well, they're not sleeping in the house."

"It would stop them from crying."

"No."

"They can't climb out of my laundry crate."

"I don't care."

"It's their first night away from their mother."

Kyle sighed.

She knew his resistance was weakening. "If they aren't quiet in here, I'll take them back to the livery myself."

Kyle tossed back the sheet and climbed out of bed.

She smiled as the sound of his feet thudded across the floor. She heard the door open into the woodshed and the sound of angry mewling increase.

"Where do you want them?" Kyle asked, returning to the bedroom.

The moonlight coming through their huge window washed across his naked body, and Amelia stared in admiration. He stood before her, godlike, all sinew and muscle, broad shoulders and narrow waist, with long, hard legs planted two feet apart. He was so handsome, so incredible, and so oblivious to his own perfection.

"I can take them back to the livery now if you like."

She smiled. "Bring them over here by the bed."

"Are you insane?"

"If they don't quiet down in a few minutes, I'll take them back to the woodshed."

Kyle plopped the crate on Amelia's side of the bed. "If I ever do something this stupid again, shoot me."

She laughed and reached over the side of the bed to stroke the kittens. They curled together and purred and after less than three minutes of having their soft fur stroked, they had fallen asleep.

They were so precious she had to resist the urge to bring them into bed with her. Instead, she turned toward Kyle, who lay on his back with his arms folded behind his head. That he'd been trying to please her, that he was willing to do anything to make her happy, melted her resentment. The sadness and pain lingered, but the anger had finally dissolved.

"Thank you for bringing the girls inside," she said, trying to do her part to heal their marriage.

"Thank *you* for putting them to sleep."

"I love them, Kyle." She slid her palm over the muscles and mounds of his chest, letting her fingers slip through the coarse hair. "They're a wonderful gift."

His chest shuddered and he gripped her hand to stop her from moving it farther down his abdomen. "I don't need to be rewarded, Amelia. I just wanted to make you happy." He lowered his arms and slipped one around her shoulders, her head pillowed by his thick muscle. "Get some sleep while you can. The demon twins will be raising hell before you know it."

⊷⊱ ⊰⊶

The kittens lived up to Kyle's prediction, and he'd spent two grueling weeks thinking he was going to pull his hair out. While one kitten was mewling and swiping at him with her sharp little claws, the other was darting from beneath furniture and giving him heart seizures thinking he was going to accidentally step on the little fur ball.

But Amelia loved them and she was always playing with them. Her laughter filled the house and her eyes sparkled again. She took the kittens, or the *girls* as she called them, everywhere, including the lumberyard, and to Kyle's disgust, everyone ended up fawning over the little rats.

Even now she cradled them in her lap, petting them as they pulled into Radford's driveway to attend a picnic Evelyn was having.

Rebecca tore across the lawn, running toward their carriage. "Did you bring the kitties?" she yelled, and when Amelia smiled and nodded, Rebecca whooped. "I'll get Missy!"

While dodging the swipe of kitty paws, Kyle helped Amelia from the carriage. Evelyn immediately took one of the kittens and nuzzled its soft fur as they stood on the front lawn. "They've grown so much already."

"That's because Amelia feeds them all the time."

Amelia wrinkled her nose at him and Kyle grinned, glad to see her spirited personality returning.

Rebecca skidded to a halt beside them with Missy clutched in her arms. "Are they hungry?" she asked. "Their mama can feed them now."

"Let's see if they still know each other." Amelia knelt and put Cinnamon in the grass.

Rebecca lowered Missy. "Do mamas forget their babies?" she asked.

Kyle's heart jolted as Evelyn and Amelia exchanged a heartbroken glance. Although Evelyn treated Rebecca like her own daughter, another woman had given birth to her and abandoned Rebecca at infancy. With the help of nannies, Radford had raised Rebecca alone until he'd brought her home a year ago. For the first time since Evelyn had broken their engagement, Kyle could honestly admit that he was grateful Evelyn had chosen to love Radford and his daughter who desperately needed her love.

Missy sniffed at Cinnamon, but the little rascal was too busy swatting at a piece of grass to pay her mother any attention. Evelyn laughed and put Ginger in the grass beside her curious sibling.

Rebecca flopped down beside them, giggling as the kittens hunched their little backs and pounced on old dandelion stalks. They played with Rebecca's fingers, and crawled over her stomach as she lay in the grass beside Missy.

Watching Rebecca made Kyle's chest ache. She was so innocent, her child's laughter so beautiful. He would have his own daughter someday. She would be silly and playful like Rebecca. She would have her own personality and a laugh unique to her, but she would share the natural, carefree spirit that Rebecca possessed.

Amelia possessed that natural playfulness, too, he thought, looking down to see her and Evelyn sitting in the grass with Rebecca. Though Amelia's pain had suppressed that part of her nature, it was beginning to rise to the surface again, and hopefully soon, Kyle would have back the woman he'd married.

"Kyle!" He lifted his head and saw Boyd waving him out to the backyard. "Help us get this horseshoe pit set up."

Kyle's spirits lifted for the first time in a month, and he gladly headed toward the backyard where Radford and Duke were working with Boyd.

"You can thank me later for rescuing you," Boyd said then shoved a mug of ale into Kyle's hand.

As they finished digging out the pits, Kyle drank and talked with his brothers. Soon the yard would be filled with the crews from both mills. Their neighbors, Tom and Martha Fisk would come. Their mothers would come, too, and maybe even some close friends like Agatha Brown and Richard and Lucinda.

By mid-afternoon they were all there and Kyle enjoyed one of the best days he'd had in years. Shouts and cheers came from the men surrounding the horseshoe pits. Giggles and screams came from Rebecca and all her little friends who were chasing through the yard with her. The women stayed mostly on the porch, but their roars of laughter told Kyle they were having a grand time.

Occasionally, he would spy Amelia through the cluster of women, and the joy in her expression would ease his mind. He could see that she was finally beginning to feel at ease with his mother, who sat between her and Evelyn, talking. Kyle couldn't hear what she was saying, but he would wager a dollar it was a story about some stupid thing Kyle and his brothers had done when they were boys. Amelia laughed again and Kyle could tell she wasn't thinking about her father today, or the problems in their marriage. She was relaxed and enjoying herself with her family the way she should be.

The ale and the food made him drowsy, and he simply couldn't keep his eyes open. With feigned nonchalance, he ambled to a quiet area of the backyard and stretched out beneath a huge birch tree. The shade and the light breeze made it the perfect spot for a nap. Kyle closed his eyes and drifted, the sounds echoing through the yard growing more distant with each slow breath he took.

The feeling of something wiggling on his chest startled him out of a half-sleep, and he lowered his chin to see what critter had mistaken him for a nest.

Cinnamon stared back at him with curious green eyes.

Kyle tensed, waiting for the demon to sink her claws into his chest, but to his utter shock, she sprawled across his shirt and started to purr.

She was purring! She wasn't swiping or hissing or sinking her razor teeth into his fingers. She was purring.

"If you even think about trying something while I've got my eyes closed, you'll spend the rest of your life in the woodshed," he warned.

Cinnamon blinked up at him as if she hadn't a care in the world.

Kyle grinned and closed his eyes. Little minx.

⟨⟩ ⟨⟩

Rebecca giggled, and Amelia put her finger to her lips, grinning as she approached her sleeping husband. If he woke up and found Cinnamon and Ginger curled up on his chest there was no telling what he would do.

Slowly, stealthily, Amelia reached down to lift the kittens off his chest.

"If they sink their miserable little claws into me after they've spent the last half hour rattling my chest with their purring, I'm giving them back to Rebecca."

Amelia gasped and jerked her hands back, making Rebecca giggle. "You scared the stuffing out of me, Kyle. Why didn't you tell me you were awake?"

He opened his eyes. They were filled with warmth. "I was hoping you'd join me."

"I will, Uncle Kyle!" Rebecca plopped her small bottom beside him then leaned over and laid her head on his chest, her face only inches from the kittens. "Did you two take a nice nap?" she asked, like a little mother.

Amelia laughed and joined them in the soft summer grass, feeling more relaxed than she had in weeks. Even Richard's presence hadn't disturbed her today. Other than a polite greeting to her and the other women, he'd stayed with the men, tossing horseshoes and drinking ale like the rest of their friends.

Cinnamon stretched and yawned, her mouth gaping open as her pink tongue curled. Kyle rolled his eyes and Amelia smiled at him. She would never have imagined him like this, lazing under a tree on a warm day with a little girl and frisky kittens climbing all over him. How could she not love him?

"We should head home soon," he said, and she nodded.

It had been a wonderful, but long, day. Everyone had been relaxed and grateful for a day of freedom from their usual routine of worry and hard work. Even her mother and Shorty had managed the day without killing each other. In fact, their taunting had an edge of humor to it now, as if they both secretly enjoyed their sparring. Jeb hadn't interfered, but Amelia knew he had stayed beside her mother in case she'd needed him.

Amelia's gaze shifted back to Kyle. He'd stood beside her, too, when she'd needed him to marry her. Though he'd been disappointed when he learned the truth about her, he hadn't turned away from her as she'd thought he would. Instead, he'd been honest about his involvement with her father's death in hopes of eliminating any remaining obstacles that would hinder them from making their marriage work. She hadn't done anything but condemn him for his honesty.

Shame washed through her and she lowered her lashes. Kyle hadn't even asked her to forgive him, as if what he'd done was beyond forgiving. But it dawned on her that it wasn't a matter of forgiving but one of understanding. Kyle and her father had been friends. They'd respected and admired each other. Her father and Kyle may have gotten upset with each other, but both men had enjoyed competing and challenging one another to grow. Amelia even remembered a couple of occasions at the lumberyard when their faces had gotten red and their voices had been raised, but neither Kyle nor her father had been angry. They were just two stubborn men trying to make a point. More than likely that's what had happened the night of her father's collapse. She was willing to believe that it was misfortune rather than aggression that caused her father's death.

"What are you thinking about?" Kyle asked.

Amelia met his eyes. "I'm thinking I need to tell you that I forgive you." Surprise lit his eyes and he glanced at Rebecca, but Amelia knew their niece was preoccupied with the kittens and was too young to understand their conversation. "I'm sorry I hurt you," she continued softly. "I should have tried to understand instead of cast blame. I never meant to wound you, Kyle, or deepen your regret. I'm sorry I did."

Emotion filled his expression and he took Amelia's hand. "Let's go home."

⊷⊶

Moonlight and shadows softened the contours of Amelia's face. Kyle knew he would never tire of looking at her. She was different than he'd expected, stronger than he would have surmised. He'd assumed she would be every bit the prissy schoolmarm he'd once considered her, but Amelia was tough, intelligent, and stubborn. She was also sensitive and forgiving.

She could angle that proud chin of hers and goad him into stepping out of his business boots to try something ridiculous like paddling a rotted boat down the creek.

She burned with an inner energy that raced through his body every time he touched her. It excited him, and scared him.

His need for her was too strong, his emotions too out of control for his comfort. Healthy male need was one thing. But a soul-deep craving was another thing altogether.

Lying beside her made him ache for her. It had been so long since that day at the waterfall. He brushed the hair off her face, longing to pull her into his arms and love her, but he wanted her to come to him willingly.

She sighed and turned her cheek into his palm.

Kyle drank in the vision of her serene face, the gentle arch of her eyebrows, the sweep of her cheekbones.

"I want you," she whispered.

He lowered his head and brushed his mouth across her parted lips.

Moonlight slanted in the window, brushing her face with pale light, turning her eyes into shimmering dark pools that mesmerized him as she sat up and turned back the sheet. She worked the gown over her head and tossed it to the floor. Her hair spilled over her shoulders and swept around her rib cage like a waterfall of autumn colors. Not daring to speak, knowing he wouldn't have the words to express how he felt, Kyle slipped his fingers into the colored silk and pulled her mouth to his.

They sank back on the mattress and he kissed her, softly at first, more passionately as the seconds turned into minutes and their breathing mingled with the heartbeat pulsing in his ears.

He moved his lips to her neck, her collarbone, her breast. She whispered to him, telling him how wonderful his kisses felt. He moved his mouth lower, over her ribs and down to her hipbone then to the place that made her gasp and lift up on her elbows.

He reached up and cupped her breast with his hand then lowered his mouth again. She moaned and fell back on the pillows, lifting herself to accommodate his intimate caress.

As he listened to the rising pitch and tempo of her moans, blinding heat surged through his body.

"Kyle!" she whispered, her voice urgent. He covered her body with his own and she cupped his face with her palms. "I love you," she said, and Kyle's world shifted. He had so much to say, so much in his heart he wanted to give her, but he didn't have the words.

So he kissed her with a hunger that overwhelmed them, their passion bursting into a reckless and frenzied fire as Amelia cried out in the heat of their lovemaking.

Kyle followed her, and for the first time in his life, he let the moment own him.

Chapter Twenty-nine

A melia and her mother watched Kyle direct the crew, his eyes brimming with enthusiasm as the men disassembled and dragged out the old mill that had seized up for the last and final time. They had just completed their shipment of deck beams to James Hale, and Kyle was eager to get their new saw up and running before he negotiated the next contract for beams.

The men began hauling in the new sawmill that Kyle had originally ordered for the depot. It was still in the crate because the depot crew had been too busy cutting railroad ties to build a structure to house the saw in. Kyle said it made more sense to replace her father's old mill with the new saw. So the men fashioned a sled with plank runners and attached it to two heavy-muscled Percherons, whose sides heaved as they pulled the crated mill inside.

Her mother hooked her arm around Amelia's waist as they watched in fascination. "I'm beginning to understand why your father loved those men," she said, watching them trail alongside the sled with excited expressions.

Amelia did, too, and her new sense of contentment with Kyle filled her with happiness. Although he rarely expressed himself with words, she was learning how to read his actions. To hear him talk about Cinnamon and Ginger one would think he despised the kittens, but to see them sleep on his chest or scamper after his bootlaces in the evenings when he played with them told another story.

"Hold up!" Kyle yelled. "We've got a runner board coming off on this side!"

"Whoa, boys. Easy now." Jake stopped the horses. Jeb and the crew crouched on the left side of the sled. "It'll rip off if we try to move it."

Jeb slapped his thighs and stood. "Muscle up, boys, and grab some pry bars. We're going to lift the edge of this sled." When the men ran for the iron rods, Jeb turned to Amelia. "We need Jake's help in lifting this runner. Can you manage the horses for him?"

Amelia glanced at Kyle, but he didn't even lift an eyebrow to stop her. "I'll try," she said, but her nerves were crackling with tension when she moved forward to stand beside the massive beasts.

"Victoria, we need someone to drive the board back under the sled once we lift it," Jeb said. "Can you swing a maul?"

"Of course," she said, her eyes lighting up as she moved to Jeb's side.

Amelia saw her mother and Jeb exchange a warm look of friendship. She suspected it would deepen and become more someday, but surprisingly the idea didn't bother her. As her mother's heart healed and Jeb grew more comfortable, they would naturally turn to each other. Her mother would always love her father regardless of how many years passed. But she was too young to live the rest of her life alone, and both Jeb and her mother deserved to find happiness again.

The men came back with bars and a twelve-pound hammer that her mother could barely lift. Amelia saw Kyle's lips tilt, but to her surprise, instead of taking over, he stayed with the men. They squatted side by side, gripped the iron handles of their pry bars and heaved until cords stood out in their necks.

"Now," Jeb grunted, his face red with the exertion of lifting the edge of the sled three inches off the ground.

Her mother rocked the maul like a pendulum until she got enough momentum to swing then she swatted at the three-inch plank. She hit Jeb's pry bar instead and nearly knocked him over when it sprang loose from beneath the sled.

Kyle's mouth twitched.

Amelia bit her lip when she saw his shoulders shaking. He was really enjoying this! "Mama, why don't you manage the horses and I'll do that."

Her mother's chin lifted and she took a firmer grip on the wooden handle. "I can do it," she said, staring straight into Jeb's eyes. She wound up again and swung with more force, but missed everything altogether.

"I'm straining my gizzard down here," Shorty called from the middle of the sled. "Pretend it's me you're swinging at."

Her mother laughed then adjusted her grip on the handled. The crew was still snorting when she hauled back and put her petite body behind her swing. The maul hit the plank with a crack that jolted the men and shoved the slab back under the sled. Cheers filled the mill as they tossed aside their pry bars and finished dragging the crate into the building.

Her mother followed along, asking a million questions as they settled the mill in its final resting place. The light in her mother's eyes, and the warmth in her own heart, made Amelia realize that she and her mother belonged here with this ragged, boisterous bunch of men. And she belonged with Kyle.

When her mother headed to the mess hall to cook their lunch, Amelia went to the office where she'd left the kittens.

They hated being penned in their crate and their loud mewls of protest let her know about it. She closed the office door behind her then set them free, but within minutes they were crawling in and out of the desk drawer she'd set on the floor.

Amelia heard the scratch of paper moving across the floor and peeked behind her to see what the kittens were doing.

Cinnamon swiped at the paper and Ginger pounced on it. Hoping it wasn't anything important, Amelia wrestled it from beneath her little monsters and put it on the desk.

It was a letter from The Law Office in Philadelphia. As Amelia began to read, she remembered that it was the name of Richard's old law business. A man named Samuel Klein had sent the letter to her father, asking to talk to him about some gaming counters Richard Cameron intended to redeem from him.

Amelia sank back in the desk chair and stared at the note wondering if she'd just found important information on her father's financial decline. Who was Samuel Klein and why was Richard involved? Amelia reached inside her shirt pocket and retrieved the counters she'd found in her father's drawer several weeks ago. She looked at the inscription with sudden understanding. It wasn't a *D* at the end—it was an *O. TLO...* the initials for The Law Office. Dread snaked through her stomach.

After she took the kittens to the mess hall for her mother to watch, Amelia went to the bank. Richard glanced up in surprise when she entered his office. He sat behind a massive mahogany desk, rolling a pen between his fingers. "By the expression on your face I assume this isn't a social call."

She closed the door behind her. "I'd like to know where the money went that my father deposited the day he died?"

Richard's expression flattened and it seemed to Amelia that he was struggling to look nonchalant. "What are you talking about?"

"Kyle said he heard that Papa made a large deposit right before he died, but there wasn't any money in his account when I paid off our mortgage. That was barely a week later. What happened to the money?"

Richard stood and faced her. "Kyle must have misunderstood. There is no money in his account."

Though Richard didn't look away from her hard stare, something flickered in his eyes that confirmed Amelia's cause for suspicion. Still, a direct accusation would yield nothing from Richard, so she shifted her questions.

"Who is Samuel Klein?"

Richard's eyes widened and he gawked at her for a full two seconds before masking his shock. "He's an old friend of mine. What makes you ask?"

"Did you go to school with him?"

"I, ah... well, yes, that's where we met." His eyes narrowed as he studied her face. "How do you know Sam?"

"He sent my father this note requesting a meeting about some gaming counters you were trying to redeem. Why was Papa sending you money?"

His color turned ashen and Amelia knew whatever he was about to tell her would be awful. "Have you shown that letter to anyone else?"

"No. Why?"

He reached out and plucked it from her hand. "If this is found, Amelia, it will destroy your father."

Her heart dropped to her stomach. "Why? What did he do?"

"You don't want to know. Just forget you ever saw it." He ripped the letter into small pieces then crossed the office to drop it into the trash basket. "It's over now."

"Richard, I need to understand what was going on with him. If you don't want to give me an explanation then I'm going to write to Mr. Klein about it. I'll ask your uncles to investigate my father's bank accounts, as well."

"Don't be an idiot!" he said, whirling to face her, his expression so livid it turned her skin to ice. "I'm serious when I tell you this could ruin your father's reputation!"

"Then tell me what this is about. Please," she whispered, too panicked to force the words out any louder. "I have to know what he did."

He opened his mouth as if to argue then his shoulders sagged. "The money was for Catherine."

Amelia frowned, confusion spiraling through her mind. "Why would Papa give her money?"

Richard's expression filled with sympathy. "Why do you think, Amelia?"

His insinuation was too obvious to misinterpret, but if Amelia lived two hundred years she would never believe her father would cheat on her mother. He'd adored her mother. Gambling was one thing. An affair would have been the last possible vice she could ever have imagined her father being involved in. Especially with a sweet woman like Catherine Cameron.

"Papa was a friend of your father's. Maybe he felt inclined to help Catherine when she was widowed."

"Maybe," he said, but Amelia knew he didn't believe it. "He took over Catherine's support when my dad died. That's all I know for sure."

She swallowed the lump in her throat. She didn't want to believe it. But maybe that's why her mother had been upset the day they made streusel. Maybe she knew the truth. Maybe Amelia's father really had been having an affair.

Amelia fumbled to open the door. She had to get out of Richard's office. She couldn't bear to hear another heartbreaking word about her father.

"It's locked, Amelia."

She reached up to twist the latch, but Richard's hand stopped her. She whirled to face him, surprised that he'd crossed the room so quietly.

"I rigged it to lock when I shut the door. It's the only way to protect my privacy." He gave the knob a quiet turn to unlock it, but he caught her arm and stopped her from bolting out the door. "If you rush out of here looking as if someone just died, you're going to cause a tidal wave of gossip. If anyone finds out about this, your father's reputation will suffer as severely as Catherine's." He sighed as if his shoulders carried an unbearable weight. "People make mistakes, Amelia. Most of us regret it. Your father was a good man and I'm sure he never meant to hurt anyone." He gave her wrist a light squeeze. "Don't try to understand this. Just protect his privacy and let him rest in peace."

The realization that she may not have really known her father crushed Amelia. All those years she'd adored him, had considered him a pillar of integrity and honor, but if Richard was telling the truth about Catherine then her father had been a gambling, two-timing liar.

Chapter Thirty

Kyle glanced up when Amelia pulled into the lumberyard after lunch. She drew the carriage to a stop beside him and he could tell by her expression that she was upset.

"Are you too busy to take a walk?" she asked.

"Why?"

"I need to talk to you." Her nostrils flared and emotion filled her eyes. "Please. Can we go now?"

"Of course." After flagging Jake to take care of Amelia's carriage, Kyle helped her out and gestured for her to lead the way.

She took him back to the gorge where they'd dug her boat out of the sand and enjoyed one of the happiest days of their marriage. They sat on a fallen tree, its trunk stretched across the rocky bank with its limbs sprawled in the water. For several minutes they sat in silence, listening to the birds and the gurgle of the creek.

"What's bothering you?" Kyle asked, his gut in knots wondering what had caused Amelia distress.

She glanced up. "I don't want to spoil the day by talking about Richard and my father, but you're right about keeping secrets. They'll only cause problems for us later on."

The warm feeling Kyle had been carrying around with him since he and Amelia had made love started to turn cold. "What happened?"

She raised her knees and hooked her arms around her shins. "I know where Papa's money went."

Kyle met her eyes, but didn't say anything.

Amelia stared at the burbling water flowing down the creek as she told him about the letter and her trip to the bank. "I asked Richard why Papa was giving him money, and he said it was for Catherine."

"Why?"

"I asked the same question. Richard said Papa was having an affair with Catherine and had been supporting her since Richard's father died."

"Richard told you that?"

Amelia nodded, her expression beginning to reflect her struggle to control her emotions. "For the first time in my life, I'm ashamed of my father."

"Amelia, this doesn't make any sense."

"Yes it does. It fits the timing of Papa's money loss. He stopped making bank deposits in his business account five years ago. Alfred Cameron died five years ago. Fifteen months after that Papa's business account was empty and there weren't any more deposits made. Mortgage papers started appearing about two years ago."

Pure amazement filled Kyle as he gawked at his wife. "How did you discover all of this?"

"I've been looking through his files like you told me to do."

Kyle shook his head, amazed. "I've been having discreet conversations with the local mill owners and anyone else your father did business with, including James Hale, hoping to uncover what he'd been involved in, and all this time you've been gathering clues. Why didn't you tell me any of this?

Amelia shrugged. "None of it made sense until I found that letter today. I honestly thought Papa had gambled away his money." She sighed and her shoulders sagged. "I wish that had been the case. I don't want to believe Papa cheated on my mother, but there's no other explanation."

"Yes there is. I'd wager everything I own on your father's integrity."

"Why else would he have given Richard or Catherine money?"

"I don't know. Maybe he'd had a business arrangement with Alfred and felt obligated to continue it after the man died. He was friends with Alfred. Maybe he felt a need to take care of Alfred's widow. It could be any of a thousand reasons." He hooked an arm around Amelia's waist. "I'll go see Richard tonight and find out what's going on."

Amelia straightened up and gripped his arm. "I know he's your friend, Kyle, but I... I think there's something Richard isn't telling me."

"That's why I'm going to see him."

She held Kyle's gaze. "I'd rather tell Duke about this and let him see what he can find out about Richard's connection to Samuel Klein."

Kyle's heart kicked, but he couldn't disagree with Amelia. Too many things didn't make sense.

She drew a shaky breath. "I'm sorry if this hurts you, but I have to know what was really going on with Papa."

Kyle combed his hair back with his fingers, feeling as though he were betraying his friendship with Richard, but like Amelia, he had to know the truth. "I'm sure there's a sensible explanation for this," he said, but he couldn't guess what it might be.

"I hope so." The wistfulness in her voice shredded Kyle's conscience. Her eyes misted and she looked away. "You know, I finally understand what you went through the night Papa died. This is the first time I've ever doubted my father and it's an awful feeling. I can understand how you might have felt betrayed, Kyle, because I do, too. I'm so sorry I made you feel worse about what happened that night with Papa. The only thing you were guilty of is being human."

If only that were the truth. Kyle felt nauseous knowing Amelia would never forgive him for what he was about to tell her, but he couldn't allow her to doubt her father's integrity when he knew the truth. Tom Drake was an honest, loyal man who loved his wife and daughter, a man who had earned Kyle's respect and friendship. Kyle couldn't let Tom's memory be tarnished because of a cruel accusation that he could correct. Nor could he allow Amelia to be crushed by her own heartache over a man she loved. She deserved to remember her father with respect and love. And Kyle needed to honor his friend.

He lifted her chin, forcing her to look at him. "Don't you ever believe that your father cheated on your mother. I made the mistake of doubting him once, and I'll always regret it."

She raised her lashes, her eyes filled with heartache. "I want to believe Papa's innocent. I truly do," she whispered, her voice thick with pain, "but there's so much evidence."

"He wasn't having an affair with Catherine. I'm certain of it." Kyle knew he was the only man Catherine had been intimate with because she hadn't been looking for love. She had needed a friend. She had shared her body and her heartache only with Kyle.

"How do you know this?"

Kyle's gut churned and he felt nauseous, but he forced the words from his dry mouth. "Because I was having an affair with her."

The life seemed to drain from Amelia's eyes as she stared at him.

"I didn't want to tell you like this, Amelia, but it is the only way I can assure you of your father's innocence."

Amelia slid off the tree trunk, unable to believe her ears.

Kyle reached for her arm, but she stepped away from him. "I can explain this, Amelia. It was a casual thing between Catherine and I."

"Casual?" The flat of her palm struck him across the face.

He stood up, his eyes bright with insult.

Amelia didn't care if he throttled her. Her entire body quaked with outrage. "There is nothing casual about an intimate relationship, Kyle! Anything intimate outside of marriage is a life-destroying event for a woman."

Kyle stood in stony silence, increasing her anger.

"How could you ask Catherine to our wedding, or let me invite her into my home? You took your lover into our bedroom!" A tear-filled sob burst from her throat. "How could you be so callous?"

"She's not my lover, Amelia. Our affair ended when you and I decided to marry."

Unable to bear hearing the details, Amelia turned her back. Pain cut through her chest, but she couldn't condemn Kyle for something she herself was guilty of. She'd been intimate with Richard, too, and though it was in the distant past, it was no different than Kyle's more recent affair with Catherine. It just felt different. Much different.

"I'm sorry." He sighed. "I won't ask you to forgive me. I know I've hurt you too many times for that."

She turned to face him, knowing Kyle really didn't understand what it was going to take for them to make their marriage work.

"I have to find a way to forgive you, Kyle. We both have to learn to trust and to forgive each other because someday we'll have children who will learn how to live by our example. They'll need us to understand and forgive their mistakes instead of punishing them." She met his eyes, begging him to help her save their marriage. "How are we going to teach them to trust and forgive if we aren't capable of it ourselves?"

Chapter Thirty-one

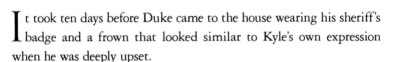

It took ten days before Duke came to the house wearing his sheriff's badge and a frown that looked similar to Kyle's own expression when he was deeply upset.

Amelia sat on the parlor floor playing with the kittens in her wounded quiet way she'd been doing every evening since Kyle had told her about Catherine. They still worked together and Amelia performed all but one function of a dutiful wife, but there was a wall of hurt-filled silence surrounding her that he knew he couldn't breach.

Kyle turned back to his brother. "I can tell by your expression it isn't good news, Duke, so don't sugarcoat what you've got to say."

"All right. Richard wasn't a lawyer. He didn't even graduate from college."

Amelia's face blanched and she glanced at Kyle as if asking whether he knew about it, which of course he didn't.

"He worked in a shipyard for two years."

Kyle stared at his brother as if he were speaking in a foreign language.

"The man I sent to investigate Richard visited Samuel Klein at a place called The Law Office. Richard and Sam were partners in that business."

"That was Richard's law firm," Kyle said.

Duke shook his head. "It was a gaming house. Sam claimed he met Richard at a shipping yard where they had worked loading cargo on ships. They started a gambling business in a small room in the back of a friend's shop. Over a period of a year they managed to save enough money to open their own business."

"This can't be right," Kyle said. "Richard wrote to Catherine announcing the opening of his own law office. There has to be a mistake."

"There's no mistake, Kyle. According to Sam, Richard handled the financial end of their business and he supposedly embezzled a good portion of their money before Sam got suspicious and started digging through their books. Sam knew the law wouldn't help him get his money back, so he confronted Richard and made him sign over his share of the business." Duke's expression softened and he looked at Amelia, his eyes filled with compassion. "Sam also learned that Richard was blackmailing your father and that's why Sam sent the letter to your dad. He wanted to help Tom."

Amelia sat frozen on the floor, her expression filled with disbelief and heartache.

"He said your father had delivered a payment to Richard every few weeks," Duke continued, "but during his last visit, Sam eavesdropped and heard Richard threatening to tell the authorities about Albert Cameron if your father didn't keep paying the counters."

Amelia glanced at Kyle, but he shrugged, unable to fathom the connection. "Your father banked with Albert Cameron, didn't he?"

"Yes. Papa and Albert were friends. What could they have been involved in that would get them in trouble with the authorities?"

"I don't know." Kyle pinched the bridge of his nose and closed his eyes, trying to sift through the confusing information, but none of it made sense. To even consider that a smart man like Richard was involved in blackmail was sickening.

"I didn't want to believe it either, Kyle, but I trust the man who gathered this information," Duke said. "He wouldn't give me facts unless he'd verified them."

Kyle lowered his hand and sighed. "I'm going to talk to Richard."

"So am I," Amelia said, getting to her feet.

⸺◁─▷⸺

Amelia, Kyle, and Duke followed Catherine into the parlor where Richard was reclining in a chair with a wine glass in his hand.

A smile lit his face when he saw Kyle, but when the shine of Duke's badge caught his eye, he lunged to his feet in one smooth motion. "Is the Pemberton closed this evening?" he asked, but his cocky grin faltered when Duke and Kyle exchanged an uncomfortable glance.

"May I offer anyone a glass of wine?" Catherine asked.

Amelia noticed Catherine's hand shaking as she reached for the wine bottle. Amelia dug her fingernails into her own trembling palm, hoping the pain would distract her from the searing pain in her heart.

Kyle waived off the wine and spoke to Richard. "You might prefer that we meet in private."

"Why? What's wrong?" Richard asked.

"I have a friend who went to visit Samuel Klein," Duke said.

Richard's face paled.

Duke shifted his stance, but kept his gaze locked on Richard. "Would you like to finish this conversation after the ladies leave the room?"

"Of course not," Richard said, as if he had no cause for concern and no idea why they were standing in his parlor worrying Catherine. "I've already told Amelia that Sam was a friend of mine."

"You also told her that Catherine had been having an affair with her father," Kyle said in his straightforward manner.

The wine bottle shattered on the floor and Catherine gaped at Richard. "That's not true!"

"Of course it isn't true," Richard said smoothly, clasping Catherine's arm and moving her away from the broken glass. He faced Kyle, his eyes brimming with anger. "I never told Amelia that lie."

Amelia gasped. "You told me that Papa was supporting Catherine, and when I asked why, you insinuated very clearly that they were having an intimate affair."

Catherine's shocked expression turned to outrage. "To my knowledge your father never contributed any financial assistance to my household. I barely knew the man."

Amelia ignored Catherine's denial, sensing Richard was using those precious seconds to formulate excuses and possible ways to manipulate the situation to his advantage. "You were blackmailing my father for your own gain, weren't you, Richard? I want the truth or I'm walking down the street to your uncle's house and telling him everything Duke has uncovered about you. I suspect that will make him rethink making you a partner at the bank."

"Go ahead," Richard said. "I'm sure your confession will make him rethink his opinion of your reputation as well."

"Speaking of reputations, Richard, why did you claim to be a lawyer when you were nothing more than a dockhand in a shipyard?" she asked, shifting the focus back to Richard.

Catherine swung an incredulous look at her stepson. "Is that true?"

Instead of exhibiting the shock or shame Amelia had expected Richard became livid, scorching them all with his fiery gaze. "I worked as a dock hand because Tom Drake killed my father!"

Amelia's breath whooshed out and she grabbed the back of the sofa. Silence filled the room and they stared at Richard as if he'd just drawn a gun on them.

"What are you talking about?" Kyle demanded.

"Five years ago your wife cried on her father's shoulder about my bad behavior, and when I refused to marry her, Tom attacked me. My father tried to pull him off, but Tom shoved him and caused his fall from the second-story floor that we'd been laying." Richard glared at Amelia. "That fall killed my father."

Kyle glanced at Amelia then back to Richard. "Why was Tom trying to force you to marry Amelia?"

Richard snorted. "Why do you think?"

Kyle staggered back a step as if Richard had slugged him in the gut. He looked at Amelia, his eyes begging her to deny the accusation.

"How could I tell you?" she asked quietly, her heart breaking over the devastation in his eyes.

"The same way I told you about Catherine," he said, his voice filled with pain.

Catherine gasped and shook her head as if telling Kyle his confession was a dreadful mistake.

Richard simply laughed. "How honorable of you to tell Amelia about the two of you."

Kyle turned on Richard. "What would you know about honor? You came to our wedding. You ate at my own table! How could you do that after ruining so many lives?"

"The same way you could sit beside me night after night pretending to be my friend, while sleeping with Catherine."

"That was a different situation, and you know it!"

"How?" Richard asked, throwing his hands up.

Amelia wanted Kyle to explain the difference as well, but he just glared at Richard. "You're the man Tom begged me to keep away from his daughter. You were at Tom's mill the night of the storm, weren't you? You'd gone there to force Tom to make another payment." Kyle shook his head as if everything was suddenly becoming clear to him. "No wonder Tom was so upset when I asked for my money."

"You bet I made him pay. And I would have foreclosed on his mill if you hadn't bought it."

"Why?" Kyle asked. "You were destroying that man."

"What did he do to us?" Richard gestured to Catherine. "My father is dead. His money is tied up in the banking business he shared with his brothers and they still control his money. If I would have left Catherine's welfare up to my closefisted uncles, she would have starved. I needed money to finish school."

"Then why didn't you?" Kyle asked. "Why didn't you graduate and become a lawyer?"

"Because I hated it. I hated school and I hated law."

"So the money you extorted from Tom was wasted."

"I built a great business with that money," Richard said, defending himself.

"You call swindling money from people a great business?"

"I never cheated our clients. My business was as successful as yours is, Kyle."

Kyle shook his head. "What happened to you? All this time you've let me believe you were my friend, that you were a big-shot lawyer from Philadelphia when you were nothing but a scheming, blackmailing gambler."

Richard's eyes flashed. "How dare you judge me!"

Amelia backed toward the door, unable to listen any longer to the pain and suffering she'd caused in so many lives. "This is my fault," she blurted. "I made a bad decision that caused this whole mess. I'm so sorry."

"This isn't your fault." Catherine's voice was quiet but filled with conviction. "Richard's bad behavior started when I married Alfred."

"Catherine, don't." Richard caught her arm, but she yanked away and turned back to Amelia and Kyle.

"I was in love with a man named Simon," Catherine said. "We were going to marry after the war ended, but Simon never came home. I was becoming a financial burden to my father, so I married Alfred believing he would take care of me. When Richard came home from his first year at college to find his father and I married, he was furious. I didn't realize until later it was because he cared for me."

Amelia had thought she couldn't feel worse, but Catherine's words cut straight through her. The entire time Richard had been seducing her, he'd wanted Catherine. Everything he'd ever told her had been a lie. He'd used her. And he'd tried to do it again.

She looked at Catherine, wanting to hate the woman, but she felt only heartache and sadness. They had both been used.

"I had no idea Richard was blackmailing your father," Catherine said. "I thought he was a successful lawyer who could afford to support me." She cast a scathing glance at Richard. "Until now I didn't know he was a liar and a cheat."

Richard cupped Catherine's shoulders and turned her to face him. "For five years, everything I've worked for has been with your comfort and happiness in mind. All I've ever wanted is to be with you."

"How naive do you think I am?" she said. "Five years ago you were courting Amelia."

"What else could I do?" Richard gripped Catherine's hands with his own. "I came home to tell you that I loved you, but I found you sharing my father's bed! I spent the summer with Amelia so I would stay away from you. Amelia meant nothing to me."

Kyle grabbed Richard by the front of his shirt and slammed him against the wall. "You insensitive bastard! You have no idea the pain you've caused Amelia. She gave you her heart and you used her."

"Well, what did you do to Catherine? Where's the difference?" Richard asked.

"I cared about her. I asked her to marry me. That's the difference."

Catherine nodded, confirming Kyle's statement. "I told him, no," she said in his defense.

Everything inside Amelia collapsed, all her hopes, her dreams, her belief in Kyle. He'd told her their affair had been casual. Now he'd admitted that he'd cared for Catherine enough to marry her. He'd wanted to marry Evelyn because he'd loved her. He'd *had* to marry Amelia.

Richard yanked Kyle around to face a gilt-edged mirror that ran from floor to ceiling. "Different faces, Kyle. Same man."

"Not even close, Richard. I haven't lied and blackmailed my way through life."

"No, you've just plowed over anyone who got in your way. You took advantage of Catherine and pretended she didn't mind being your whore."

Kyle slammed his fist into Richard's jaw.

As Duke leapt forward to pull them apart, Amelia fled outside, unwilling to listen any longer, unable to be in the same room with her husband and his lover, or witness the destruction she'd caused in so many lives.

◦═◦◦ ◦◦═◦

Kyle and Richard stood with chests heaving, glaring at each other.

"Don't you have any remorse, Richard? Didn't it bother you even a little that you were blackmailing a good man into an early death?" Kyle asked, his fists clenched at his sides.

"Don't judge me." Richard shoved his hair out his eyes. "Everything has always come easy for you, Kyle. Ever since we were boys you've led the way. Just once, I wanted to be better at something than you, so I went to law school to try to do that." Richard backhanded his bloody lip. "I hated it. I couldn't make grade my first year, and after my father died, there seemed little point in trying. I couldn't come back here and admit I'd failed, so I worked the dock while I tried to figure out what to do." He sighed and looked at Duke. "That's where I met Sam. We became friends and gambled at night with each other and some of the other dock hands. After a while, there were so many men sitting in that Sam and I had full pockets on a regular basis. That's when I realized how much money we could make in a gaming business."

"Then why did you keep blackmailing Tom?" Kyle asked, his anger being replaced by pity and disgust.

"I wanted to own my own ship," Richard said, his expression defensive. "I wanted to start my own trading company."

"I understand the allure of owning a trading vessel," Kyle said. "What I will never understand is your lying and scheming to get it. Tom Drake was a good man. He didn't deserve this."

Duke stepped forward, handcuffs jangling in his hand. "Blackmail is illegal, Richard. Let's take a walk to my office and talk about your future."

Richard's shoulders sagged. He turned to Catherine. "I did all of this for you."

"I never once encouraged you or your misplaced affection, Richard. Everything you've done was criminal and self-serving," she said. "If you want my respect you'll have to earn it by repairing the damage you've caused."

"You can start by apologizing to my wife," Kyle said. He turned to Duke and waived off the handcuffs. "If we charge Richard with blackmail people are going to dig until they learn the truth about all of this. The only way to protect Catherine and Amelia is to keep this quiet, Duke."

After a brief pause, Duke nodded his agreement. "What do you suggest?"

Surprise crossed Richard's face and he looked at Kyle. "You're not pressing charges?"

Kyle shook his head, sickened to his core by Richard's character. "As of this moment you have the opportunity to become the man your father raised you to be. If you don't return the money you stole from Tom, I will find you and make you wish Duke had hauled your sorry ass off to jail. That's a promise, Richard."

With that, Kyle made his apology to Catherine, and then headed home to his heartbroken wife.

⟨⟩

Amelia rushed to the lumberyard and saw Jeb and her mother sitting outside the bunkhouse talking.

Unable to greet them through her tears, she hurried into the office and swept her father's jacket off the file cabinet. She buried her face in the old, worn flannel, desperate for the comfort of her father's arms, but settling for an armful of fabric with the faded smell of soap and hair tonic and all the wonderful scents of the outdoors she'd always associated with her father.

Seconds later, her mother and Jeb entered the office with stricken expressions. "What's happened?" her mother asked, rushing to the desk where Amelia sat sobbing.

"I just wanted to make Papa proud, Mama, and all I did was let him down." Between her tears, Amelia confessed everything: her lost virginity, her father's blackmail, and Kyle's affair with Catherine. She talked about her father's collapse and how she'd blamed Kyle when it was really Richard who had upset her father so badly. Finally, she buried her face in her hands and confessed that she loved Kyle so much it was tearing her in half, but she could never go back to him because she'd forced him to marry her when he cared for another woman.

Jeb quietly stepped outside, but her mother sat on the edge of the desk and stroked Amelia's back as if she were still a little girl. "If Kyle wanted Catherine, he would have married her," she said.

"He asked her, Mama! Catherine declined."

"Then she didn't love him. Honey, we all have a past. Kyle and Catherine were probably friends because they didn't have any reason not to be."

"They were far more than friends."

"Well, as long as it's in their past it shouldn't threaten your marriage to Kyle." Her mother tipped her head to look into Amelia's wet face. "How do you think Kyle is feeling right now after learning about Richard?"

The quietly spoken question caught Amelia off guard and she sat back in the chair. Kyle's heart probably felt as raw as hers did. He'd lost a man he thought was his friend. He was surely feeling betrayed and hurt that Richard's friendship wasn't sincere, and that Amelia hadn't told him about her relationship with Richard.

At the thought of Kyle's heartache tears streamed from Amelia's eyes. She gave up trying to wipe them away. "I didn't know one mistake could ruin so many lives."

Her mother reached into her sleeve and pulled out a handkerchief as she'd done a thousand times or more while Amelia was growing up. "It was Richard's manipulation that ruined lives, honey, not your mistake. Giving yourself to a boy you love because you believe you'll marry him shouldn't destroy the lives of several people. Not that I'm endorsing intimacy before marriage, but I was close with your father before we married and it turned out fine."

Amelia gripped the handkerchief and her father's jacket in her damp fingers. "I should never have told Papa about Richard. If he hadn't known, he wouldn't have tried to make Richard marry me and Richard wouldn't have blackmailed him. Then none of this would have happened."

"Honey, a father is supposed to protect his daughter. I would have far less respect for your father if he hadn't gone after Richard. As deeply as I sympathize with you right now, it's a relief knowing your father spent his time at the lumberyard because of financial concerns. I wondered at times if there might be another woman. My heart aches considerably less knowing the truth."

"I wish I could say the same." Amelia wiped her face and blew her nose. "What am I going to do, Mama?"

Her mother sighed and patted Amelia's shoulder. "Go home and talk to your husband."

"He won't talk, Mama. He never does."

Chapter Thirty-two

K yle entered the depot warehouse where Marcus, his youngest crew member, was sitting in dim lantern light to read a book. "Why are you sitting beside this hot monstrosity?" Kyle asked, glaring at the huge black stove. He would die in this heat, but he couldn't stay home and witness the devastation in Amelia's eyes. She wasn't ready to talk, and he had no words to soothe her heartache.

Marcus glanced up in surprise and lowered his book to his lap. "There's a hole in the ash pan. Doesn't look too big, but I've been keeping an eye on it. I'll fix it tomorrow." Marcus looked at his watch. "You're about seven hours early, aren't you?"

"It's your lucky evening."

Marcus grinned. "It will be if my wife can get the baby to bed early enough."

Kyle forced himself to smile, but he felt like knocking Marcus's pretty teeth out of his head. The kid had been married a year and hadn't stopped grinning since his wedding day. Kyle jerked his chin toward the door. "Get out of here."

Marcus slapped his book closed and jumped to his feet. "Thanks, boss!"

"Don't tell me about it in the morning or I'll kill you."

The door cut off Marcus's laughter.

Despite the heat inside, the sudden quiet suited Kyle's dark mood. The hum of the stove and smell of drying wood was more inviting than the loud tavern he'd considered escaping to.

It was definitely preferable to seeing Amelia in pain, or remembering the gut-wrenching shock he'd felt when he discovered that Richard was the man Amelia had loved.

Richard hadn't even appreciated what Amelia had sacrificed for him. Kyle paced the warehouse, wondering if he'd ever really known Richard. Maybe when they were boys, before Kyle's father died, but after that, he and Richard had merely passed in and out of each other's lives. Kyle definitely didn't know the cad who'd confessed to blackmailing Tom.

Remembering the devastated expression on Amelia's face when Richard said he'd used her as a diversion from Catherine, made Kyle want to break Richard's ribs and blacken his eyes.

How could Richard have been so cruel?

Kyle sighed knowing his own words and actions had inflicted the most pain on Amelia. He should have found a way to tell her that he'd proposed to Catherine, and explain why he'd done it.

Why must he always struggle for words? All he'd wanted was to explain how sorry he was, how deeply he regretted hurting her. Why was that so difficult for him?

Frustrated, he kicked the black belly of the stove. Thunder rolled through the building and soot spilled from the pipe. Wood tumbled inside the stove and a loud pop shook the cast-iron box.

Cursing, he bent over to look underneath the stove to see if any glowing coals had slipped out. The wood floor was clear, but he was still too tense to sit down so he paced the width of the warehouse until his shin and shoulders ached. After an hour, he was exhausted, sick to his stomach, and falling asleep on his feet. With a hard sigh, he grabbed the chair, dragged it toward the back of the warehouse, and sat down.

All he could think about was Amelia's beautiful face wet with tears. Kyle scrubbed his palms over his forehead, wishing he could forget the heartbroken look in her eyes, but it kept circling in his mind. Just like the thought of her lying with Richard.

Kyle slouched in his chair and propped his feet on a stack of beams. He understood now that Amelia hadn't told him about Richard because she hadn't wanted to risk breaking their friendship. She hadn't intended to deceive him. Amelia was too sincere for deceit. She'd endured Richard's presence in their home to please Kyle.

Everything she did was for someone else. Kyle closed his eyes and leaned his head back, remembering the way she'd sat on the floor with Cinnamon and Ginger the night he brought them home for her. They'd made her laugh through her pain, and Kyle had watched her draw comfort from those two rambunctious fur balls, knowing it should have been his own arms that consoled her.

As thoughts and regrets tumbled through his mind, his breathing slowed and he drifted in memories, hearing the splash of the falls, feeling Amelia's soft skin against his as they made love. As if he were right there behind the falls, Kyle watched the way her hair swung around her shoulders as she lunged forward and fell on top of him. But as the night deepened, her image grew elusive and slipped from his grasp, and finally, he lost her altogether in the blackness.

The thunder of pounding feet and panicked shouts jolted him from sleep. Kyle bolted up in his chair. Smoke billowed around him and his throat felt clogged with burning smoke that stole his ability to breathe.

"Kyle! Where are you?" Boyd yelled from the front of the building.

"Back—" Kyle choked and staggered to his feet. A hard cough wrenched his chest and gut and doubled him over until tears streamed down his face. He dragged an arm across his eyes and peered through the smoke, but couldn't see more than three feet in front of him. The building was on fire. The stove! He'd kicked the stove like an idiot! And he'd never checked the stove pipe.

"Kyle! Answer me!"

He crouched to his knees and gulped a breath, but his hoarse squawk couldn't be heard more than a few feet away. The loud crackling of burning wood filled the air then a heavy shudder shook the building.

"It's coming down! Get out!" Boyd shouted.

"Give me your ax. I'm going around back."

That was Duke's voice. Kyle buried his face in his shirt and crawled toward the door. The heat drove him back before he'd gone three feet. Suddenly, he understood very clearly that he was trapped and he was going to die.

The building had no back door and no windows to escape through. Though the plank walls were old, he doubted he could kick through the wood, but it was his only hope of getting out alive.

On hands and knees, he felt his way along the wall toward the back of the building where the smoke wasn't as dense. Trying to gauge the condition of the wood through watery eyes was impossible. Kyle pushed against the slats with his elbow until he felt a board spring. Knowing his time would run out before he could locate a weaker spot, he stopped searching and lay on his back. He kicked the plank with both feet. Pain ripped through his tender shin, but he kept hammering the springy piece of pine. The board bowed beneath his fierce blows, but it wouldn't crack.

"Come on!" Kyle coughed and kicked harder as a spray of hot cinders burned his skin. The wall splintered several feet above him.

He heard the distant shout of Amelia's voice calling to him and he knew he didn't want to die. He needed to apologize to her, to explain what she meant to him.

He raised his numb feet for another blow, but the tip of an ax smashed through the planks.

"Duke!" Kyle called through his raspy throat then realized that Duke would never hear him above the roaring fire and shouting men.

The only way to let them know they were hacking the wall in the right place was to signal by moving the boards, so Kyle used his remaining strength to kick the planks.

More wood splintered as another ax gouged the building then several hands yanked planks free and pried the nails from the frame with metal pry bars. Kyle watched it all through a haze of smoke, his only conscious thought being to keep his feet moving and keep himself from igniting. He was barely conscious when Duke stopped swinging his ax and Boyd and Radford dragged him through the hole in the wall.

He gulped in cool air and coughed until he gagged. His nose ran and his eyes streamed, but he was free of the fire that was eating his building and burning up his profits.

"Kyle!" Amelia collapsed beside him. She reached out to touch him, but hesitated as if she might hurt him. "Are you all right. Are you hurt?" Tears streaked down her face and her mouth pursed.

He lifted his head and looked at her through streaming eyes. Soot was smeared across her face and one side of her gown was badly singed. Behind her, both mill crews were rushing across the yard at the depot, beating out hot sparks that settled on his pallets of lumber, keeping his mill building safe while trying to contain the fire to his warehouse, which would become a total loss.

Amelia touched his chest. "Can you talk? Do you know what happened?"

Caught in a hazy web of pain, Kyle backhanded his eyes and dragged his sleeve beneath his nose. He tried to sit up, but gasped in pain and fell back in the grass. Fire burned through his shoulders and both palms as if he'd been branded. His head ached and his legs and feet throbbed.

Amelia doused her palms in a bucket of water that Boyd had set beside them when checking on Kyle before he ran back to battle the flames. She gently pressed the cool liquid to Kyle's face. Her own was covered in tears. "Please be all right. Please don't close your eyes, Kyle."

"How—" He coughed, gagged, and inhaled the damp air into his raw throat. "How can you... even care?" he asked, panting hard, feeling as he were going to throw up.

Her brow furrowed and she touched his hot, tight face. "How can I... Oh, Kyle, how can you ask that?"

Even through his muddled senses, Kyle could see the raw pain in her eyes, but before he could croak out an apology, he turned his head and threw up in the damp grass. He struggled to fill his lungs with fresh air while his two crews put out the fire. His thoughts tangled and he couldn't keep track of the time or what was happening around him. Someone laid wool horse blankets over him, someone else fed him gallons of water then the glowing sky slowly turned black.

Chapter Thirty-three

Kyle woke to silence in his own bed with Evelyn frowning down at him. He coughed then grimaced at the pain in his raw throat. It made his eyes water and his nose run and thoroughly pissed him off. "How bad is it?"

"You lost the warehouse and your inventory. Radford says your insurance will cover most of the loss. You're lucky you're alive. If Duke had come by any later..." She compressed her lips and her eyes misted. "How could you have sat beside that stove and let a fire start?"

"What was Duke doing here in the middle of the night?"

She shook her head. "He said he stopped by your house because he was worried about you, and that's when he smelled smoke coming from the depot. He sent Amelia for help. I know it's none of my business, but why were you at the mill? Duke said Marcus was supposed to be working that night."

He couldn't answer, so he asked, "Where is Amelia?"

"She's sleeping in the guestroom. I sent your mother home for a while and told Amelia I would have Radford bodily put her to bed if she didn't get some rest. Your mom and Amelia sat with you for almost twenty-four hours, and neither of them wanted to leave you. I promised I would wake Amelia as soon as you opened your eyes."

"Don't." Kyle caught Evelyn's wrist then gasped at the pain in his fingers.

"You have burns the size of a cigar tip speckled across your hands and back," she said. "Before you ask, the doctor says it will be two weeks before you'll be able to do any work."

Kyle looked at his hands and felt the urge to steeple them in prayer and give thanks for his life, for Amelia, and for having another chance to tell her that he loved her.

He raised his gaze to Evelyn. "Why did you choose Radford over me?"

Her eyes widened in surprise and she seemed at a loss for words.

He barreled ahead, knowing he had nothing left to lose. "I want to understand why. Didn't it bother Radford that you were promised to me while you were kissing him?"

Hurt flashed across Evelyn's face.

Kyle cursed himself for offending her. He coughed and winced from his burning throat. "I'm sorry, Ev. I didn't mean that the way it came out." He gingerly patted the bed. "Sit a minute."

He eased over and she sat beside him. "Is this still eating at you?" she asked, her expression full of sympathy.

"No. I know you and Radford belong together and I'm content with our friendship. I just want to know what I'm lacking that Radford has."

"You weren't lacking anything."

"Well, obviously I was," he said, looking pointedly at her wedding band.

"I married your brother because I love him. Not because I didn't love you. I guess you and I were convenient for each other. Radford and I needed each other. That was the main difference," she said. "You wanted a wife. Radford needed a woman who could help him heal. You loved the girl who'd been your friend, but Radford loved the woman you couldn't see. I didn't choose Radford. My heart made that decision."

"I need to change, Ev," Kyle said, not attempting to camouflage his desperation. If he hadn't already lost Amelia, he was close to it, and it scared him enough to face the truth about himself, however painful it would be. "Amelia deserves better than I'm giving her."

Evelyn's eyebrows lifted. "You *have* changed, Kyle." At his skeptical look, she smiled. "I could tell the day of the picnic. You've found your sense of humor again, and I'm sure your feelings for Amelia are the cause. You just have to stop expecting everything to be perfect."

"I don't."

"Yes you do. You wanted me to be perfect for you and the life you had planned for us, but I wasn't. When you realized I had flaws, you tried to ignore them. Radford saw my faults and loved me *because* of them."

"You aren't flawed."

"Yes I am!" she said with an exasperated laugh. "And so are you. We all have flaws. That's my point. You only see what you want to see. It's like looking at Lake Erie and only seeing the pretty rippling surface. There is an entire world down there of ugly predators, beautiful plants, life and death. If you're only looking at the surface of life, Kyle, that's all you'll ever see."

"Well, how do you notice all that other stuff if you're too busy?" he asked with mounting frustration.

"You stop what you're doing and stick your head in the water."

"What?"

Evelyn smiled. "Let me try this another way. I didn't fall in love with Radford because he was perfect. Radford's character is a result of everything he's experienced in growing up with three brothers, surviving a horrible war, and falling in love with his brother's fiancée. It doesn't mean he's proud of his past, but he's the man he is today because of each one of those experiences. So are you, Kyle. You control things now because you had to when your father died. Your heart talks to you, but your brain speaks the words because you want to control what comes out. Stop trying to control everything and just pay attention to what's important." Evelyn shrugged. "That's all I can tell you. I'm a pregnant woman, not a wise woman."

Kyle touched her hand. "I think I'm finally beginning to understand what happened with us," he said, knowing he needed to talk this openly with Amelia, but fearing his ability to do so.

"Good. Then settle whatever is between you and Amelia and find a way to be happy. You both deserve it." She bent down and kissed his cheek. "Now shut up and get some rest."

Kyle leaned his head back on the pillow as Radford entered the bedroom with Rebecca perched on his shoulders, her dirty little hands strapped across his forehead. Wild curls shot in umpteen directions and spiraled halfway down her back. Her small feet were tucked in Radford's hands to keep her from falling as she bounced on his neck.

"Giddy up, horse!" she demanded.

Radford whinnied and galloped to Kyle's side.

A laugh burst from Kyle's raw throat and he coughed until his eyes watered, but the pain was worth watching his brother act like an idiot. They had come such a long way from the anger that had nearly destroyed their family less than a year ago. He'd thought he would never be able to forgive Radford and Evelyn. Now he knew this was how it should be.

⊷⊷ ⊷⊶

"You look awful," Boyd said, entering Kyle's bedroom without his usual long-legged swagger, his expression weary and filled with concern.

"So do you." Kyle propped himself up in bed, wincing in pain as he visually inspected his brother to make sure he wasn't injured in any way. Black rings of fatigue circled Boyd's eyes and his clothes were gray with ash dust from the fire that was still smoldering almost thirty hours after igniting. "Did you kill it yet?" Kyle asked, referring to the fire.

Boyd shook his head. "There're some ties and beams that are smoldering, but we're still hauling water from the gorge to make sure it stays contained. We should snuff it out by this evening."

"Then go home and sleep. You're too exhausted to do any more."

"Duke and Radford are at the depot now. They'll take care of things for a few hours. When I get back, the three of us will figure out how to clean up the mess."

"Ask them to come here so we can all discuss it."

"Forget it."

"I can't manage the walk today."

Boyd gawked at him. "I wasn't suggesting you come to the depot, you idiot! Forget about the mill. It'll be there when you get your arrogant ass out of bed."

"Arrogant?"

"Yes!" Boyd yanked off his hat and threw it on the nightstand. "Who cares about the mill! You almost died last night, you ambitious idiot! Two more minutes in that building and you would have been..." Boyd's nostrils flared and he thrust his hands in front of Kyle, his fingers and palms a mass of cuts and burns. "I was tearing that building apart with my bare hands, Kyle, and I couldn't get to you. Every second all I could think about was you breathing smoke. Rafters were slamming into the floor and I kept wondering where you were. I died every time I heard a crash. Not hearing your voice was even worse," he whispered. His eyes flooded and he turned his back.

Seeing Boyd break down was Kyle's undoing. He tried to swallow his emotion, but it rose up hard, gripping his chest until he couldn't breathe. His brothers could have died trying to rescue him.

"I never realized how much you wanted to be a lawyer, Kyle, because you gave it up so easily to take over the mill when Dad died." Boyd lifted his shoulder, grabbed his filthy shirtsleeve and wiped his face. "Until last night, I'd never considered how much you've sacrificed for us." Moisture and soot streaked Boyd's face, but he seemed oblivious to the bare emotion he was showing. "I'm sorry I've never thanked you for that."

Kyle looked away from the devastation in Boyd's eyes. "I don't even know if I would have liked being a lawyer. It doesn't matter now. I'm happy running the depot." He glanced at his brother. "I'm serious, Boyd. I'm content here."

Boyd studied him for several seconds before giving a light nod of acknowledgment. "Duke's going to come see you later, but I've asked the rest of the crew to give you a couple of days to heal before they start tromping through your bedroom."

"I'll be out of this room tomorrow," Kyle said, already feeling caged and restless.

"I'm too exhausted to kick your stubborn ass," Boyd said, sitting down on the nightstand with a sigh, "but don't even think about coming back to work until Doc Finlay approves it." Boyd's expression brooked no argument. "I'll take care of things until you're back on your feet. You should be grateful to be alive, Kyle. Get some rest. Spend some time with Amelia. This was as hard on her as it was on us."

Kyle sank back into the softness of the pillows, but even the slight movement made the burns on his skin sting. His leg still throbbed and his back and head ached. "You know, I've always thought I had to look after you and Duke," Kyle said, his throat hoarse from emotion. "But I never realized that I depended on both of you, too." He met Boyd's eyes. "I didn't run the depot alone, Boyd. You and Duke were always here to help me."

Boyd braced his palms on his knees. "All I've ever done is irritate you."

"I won't disagree with that."

Boyd grinned and stretched his legs out in front of him. "Sorry."

"You've also made me laugh, Boyd. Without you to push me and prod me back into living, our responsibilities would have buried me."

They sat in silence for a minute. Finally, Boyd tugged his filthy cap over his head and stood. "I'm tired, Kyle. If you don't need anything, I'll come see you tomorrow."

"You'd better. I want to know what's going on at the mills."

"Yeah, yeah." Boyd tried to grin, but his eyes were weary, his face stained and smudged from the emotional war he'd just endured. "If Amelia gives me a good report on your cooperation, I'll give you a report on the mills."

Kyle nodded, silently wishing his brother success in whatever he decided to do with his life. "When I'm healthy enough to come back to work, I'll mortgage my house to get you the money for the tavern."

Boyd's brows lowered. "No, you won't."

"The lumberyard is doing better, and now that I know what was happening to Tom's money, I'm confident I can rebuild his mill. I'm not going to stand in your way anymore."

"You never were, Kyle. I had enough money in my own account to buy the tavern from Pat. He's been running it for me for two months now."

"What?" Kyle gaped at his brother. "Then why were you talking about getting a loan from Richard?"

"Because I thought we might need the money to keep the mills running. I would have mortgaged the tavern back to the bank to get the loan."

Kyle stared in stunned disbelief. "Why didn't you tell me you'd bought the tavern?"

"Because you needed me to be here."

Chapter Thirty-four

It was past midnight when Kyle felt four tiny paws on his stomach. He lifted his head off the pillow and stared down at Cinnamon. "How did you get up here?"

She ducked away from his accusing gaze and crawled up his chest, nuzzling his chin until he laughed and swept his sore palm over her soft fur.

"I see you've been taking wheedling lessons from Rebecca and Amelia."

He scooped Cinnamon into the crook of his arm and sat up, glad for the company. For the fourth consecutive night he'd slept alone while Amelia stayed in the guest room in consideration of his discomfort.

Since the fire, his mother had been staying with them, and Kyle and Amelia hadn't had a moment of privacy. She'd waved away any attempts to talk, telling him they would have plenty of time to do so after he healed.

Between Amelia and his mother, Kyle hadn't been left alone during the day or evening unless he was in the bathroom. Tonight, he'd finally convinced his mother to go home by telling her that he was feeling strong and was barely suffering any pain. Of course, he'd been stretching his recovery a bit, but he really did feel better, and her concern was suffocating him. So she'd hugged Amelia goodbye and promised to come back and help her can preserves in the morning.

Kyle left his bed and wandered through the dark house with Cinnamon tucked in the crook of his arm. The night silence mocked him. The monotonous sound of peepers mingled with his own tense breathing. He stumbled over the rocking chair leg as he'd done almost every night since Amelia had moved it. He clutched Cinnamon and kept himself from falling, but instead of cursing, Kyle felt like howling out his heartache.

From the moment he'd gone to her father's lumberyard, he had begun systematically killing Amelia's ability to laugh. He hadn't meant to hurt her any more than he'd meant to cause Tom's collapse, but his own self-serving actions were at the root of her heartache.

She said they had to learn to forgive each other, but Kyle wondered how she would ever manage to forgive him after all the heartache he'd brought to her life.

He wandered into the kitchen. The bathtub still sat beside the stove where she'd left it because she'd taken her bath late and was too tired to bother draining it. Her washcloth hung over the edge of the tub. Kyle ached to hear the sound of her laughter, of her pouring water over her head and shoulders while she bathed.

He stuck his fingertips in the cool water. Evelyn had told him to look beneath the surface of life, but all Kyle could see as he stood alone in his kitchen with a purring fur ball in his arm was Amelia's smiling face glistening with water, her laughter filling the room as she smacked him with her wet towels. She'd been vibrant that day, filled with wild exuberance from the minute they put her little rowboat in the creek until he'd poured her into bed because she'd drunk too much wine at his mother's birthday party. She loved adventure. She was passionate and exciting, and he wanted that spirited woman back in his life.

He turned toward the guest bedroom, vowing he would find a way to apologize and express the depth of his feelings.

Amelia opened her eyes to see Kyle standing beside her bed with Cinnamon in his arms. She'd always thought of Kyle as strong and invincible, but seeing him hurting and vulnerable broke her heart.

As long as she lived, she would never forget the horrendous roaring sound of the flames as they engulfed the warehouse, or the taste of fear in her mouth knowing Kyle was trapped inside. He'd been so panicked when they pulled him from the building, his eyes so wild, that Amelia knew a few minutes longer and he would have died alone, confused and frightened. The thought made her throat ache, but it was also a feeling of self-pity that caused her eyes to mist as she sat up in bed. She loved him so desperately that for one reckless moment, she considered throwing away her last shred of pride and begging Kyle to love her.

Instead, she tipped her chin and tried to see his eyes in the moonlight and night shadows. "Are you all right?" she asked, wondering if he was suffering discomfort from the burns, or if Cinnamon had disturbed him.

"No," he said, his voice hoarse. His presence overwhelmed the tiny room as he gazed down at her. "I'm filled with remorse and regret and a chest full of feelings I don't know how to express. I'm going to try, though. No matter how badly this comes out, Amée, I need to tell you what I feel."

Pain filled his expression as he gazed down at her. "I don't care how it comes out, Kyle. All I'm asking is that you be honest with me."

"I promise," he said, sitting on the bed beside her. He looked down as Ginger jumped onto the mattress to curl up beside Cinnamon who had been sleeping with Amelia. His eyes met hers. "I don't know where to begin."

"Do you love Catherine?" she asked, needing to know, and sensing Kyle needed a hard shove to get him talking.

"She's a friend in my past who gave me a place to go when I needed one. That's all."

"Are you saying you don't love her?"

"It depends on what you call love, Amée. Catherine is a good woman who needed my friendship. I felt protective of her and I cared about her. If that's love then yes, I love her." He stroked the kittens, but looked at Amelia. "If friendship is another form of love then I love Evelyn, too. I care about my brothers and my mother, and I adore Rebecca, and even our demon twins. That's love, isn't it?"

"Of course, Kyle. That's not what I'm asking."

"I know." He gave her a tender smile. "There are many shades of love, but only one that is filled with passion, that can make a heart soar or send it crashing onto the rocks. Until I married you, I didn't know that kind of love existed. I didn't know I'd be willing to lay down my pride and bare my soul to show you how much I care. But I will, Amée. When I look at you, I see a woman who loves me, someone I want to spend the rest of my life with. I love every flaw that makes you unique and every expression that crosses your face."

Her eyes welled up. "I love you, too," she whispered.

"I know you do. And I love the girl who dresses in my old shirt and those britches that drive me to distraction. I love the sassy lady who kicked me in the shin, and the passionate woman who makes love to me all night."

His beautiful confession of love left her speechless.

"You know what I see when I look in your eyes?" he asked, caressing her bare arms with his thumbs. "I see strength and tenderness. Resilience and intelligence. I see a child who likes to play and a little girl who misses her father. I see a woman who needs a baby of her own and a daughter who will always need her mother. I see my own longing for companionship, passion, and love reflected in your eyes."

To her shock, Kyle knelt beside the bed on one knee and clasped her hand between his own. "My days are empty and meaningless without you. I never had the opportunity to ask you to marry me, Amée, but I can still ask you to be the love of my life."

To see her proud, arrogant husband on his knees, spilling every emotion in his heart, made her eyes flood.

"I don't care about the past—yours or mine," he said. "What matters is our future." Sincerity filled his eyes as he stood. "Your past is what made you become the woman you are today. I don't care about your relationship with Richard, except that he hurt you."

"You really don't?"

"No. All I want is to make you happy."

Amelia wiped the tears from her face. "I don't believe you're really saying these things."

"I should have told you this long ago." He gave her a brief, sweet kiss. "I want to start over. I want to do things right and treat you the way you deserve to be treated. I want to make you laugh again."

"We can't start over, Kyle. We need to remember what we've learned and use it to make our future stronger. We need to keep going right from this moment forward."

"However you want to do it, Amée. I'll go forward, or start over, or take whatever path you wish to walk as long as we're together." He brushed the backs of his fingers across her wet cheek. "Is there room for two in this bed?"

She shook her head. "No."

Pain filled his eyes as he lowered his hand. "You need time yet. I understand."

"No you don't." Amelia slipped out of bed. With care for his burns, she gently took his hand. "I want us to move forward, together, in our own bed." She lifted her face and kissed him. "Take me to our room."

The tension in his body seemed to drain away. "Really?" he asked.

She answered with a nod and a smile.

They walked together through their parlor, down the hall, and into their bedroom. Inside, Kyle cupped her jaw and gazed down at her.

Amelia prepared for the touch of his lips, but he didn't kiss her.

"I have one last confession to make," he said.

She clapped her palm over his mouth. "Don't you dare tell me anything that's going to break my heart."

He nodded and she uncovered his smiling lips. "I think we should get a couple more kittens."

"What?"

"We could get the rest of Missy's litter if you want."

A breathless laugh escaped her and she shook her head, barely able to believe her ears. "Are you serious?"

"No," he said, "I just wanted to hear you laugh."

He hooked his arms around her waist then lowered his mouth to hers in a kiss so hot and deep, Amelia thought their bodies would melt together.

She kissed his cheek and neck. "Are your hands and back too sore to make love with me?" she whispered, brushing her lips over his earlobe.

Quiet laughter resonated in his chest. "Not if I stay off my back, and don't use my hands."

She gasped and laughed in the same breath. "Well, how do you propose to participate then?"

A mischievous grin spread across his gorgeous face. "You'll see. Close the door so the girls don't surprise us. I don't want kitty paws swiping at me while I'm trying to make up to you."

Amelia laughed and pushed the door shut. "They would more likely be swiping at me for stealing your attention."

"I suppose the demons have grown on me."

"Bosh. You've loved them from the minute you saw them."

Kyle shrugged, his grin fading into an expression of intense longing and passion, reflecting the powerful emotions bursting in Amelia's own heart.

"Take off your gown, Mrs. Grayson."

"My pleasure," she whispered, welcoming her husband's arms, his tender kiss, his promise for a future filled with love and laughter and dreams come true.

⇥ THE END ⇤

Dear Reader,

Thank you for taking the time to read *The Longing*. The Grayson family has taken up permanent residence in my mind and they are all clamoring for their stories to be shared. Boyd's book *Lips That Touch Mine* is next in the series, and he's got his hands full with his feisty neighbor, a gorgeous widow, who is trying to shut down his noisy tavern. If you would like to spend more time with the Grayson family, receive a notice when the next book is coming out, or learn more about the books in this series, please visit www.wendylindstrom.com and sign up for New Book Alert!

I sincerely hope you enjoyed *The Longing* and consider it a 5-star keeper that brought you many enjoyable hours of reading. If so, and you would be willing to share your enthusiasm with other readers, I'd be very grateful. Telling your friends about my books and posting online reviews is extremely helpful and instrumental in elevating this series. It not only helps other readers find my books more easily but enables me to publish books more frequently. I have many wonderful stories to share with you, so please continue to spread the word.

Even with many layers of editing, mistakes can slip through. If you encounter typos or errors in this book, please send them to me at www.wendylindstrom.com (use Contact link).

Thanks again for your enthusiastic support. I'm wishing you many blissful hours of reading.

Peace and warmest wishes,
Wendy

About the Author

Wendy Lindstrom is a RITA Award-winning author of "beautifully poignant, wonderfully emotional" historical romances. *Romantic Times* has dubbed her "one of romance's finest writers," and readers rave about her enthralling characters and the riveting emotional power of her work. For more information about Wendy Lindstrom's other books, excerpts, and sneak previews, please visit www.wendylindstrom.com.

Please remember to sign up for New Book Alert! And post your online review!

CPSIA information can be obtained at www.ICGtesting.com
Printed in the USA
LVOW08s1713130614

389977LV00001B/117/P

9 781939 263087

[15]